ALDEK'S BESTIARY

ROMUALD ROMAN

Introduction
James Whipple Miller

Illustrations
George Heck

CHESTNUT
HILL
PRESS

Literature Art Music

Chestnut Hill Press
Philadelphia
2022

Literature Art Music
ISBN (hardbound): 979-8-9857500-0-3
ISBN (paperback): 979-8-9857500-1-0

In memory of Roxy the boxer,
loved by three generations of our family.

1995—2009

Until one has loved an animal,
part of one's soul remains unawakened.

—Anatole France

Some animals are cunning and evil disposed, as the fox; others, as the dog, are fierce, friendly, and fawning. Some are gentle and easily tamed, as the elephant; some are susceptible of shame, and watchful, as the goose. Some are jealous and fond of ornament, as the peacock.

—Aristotle

TABLE OF CONTENTS

He who makes a beast of himself
gets rid of the pain of being a man.

—Samuel Johnson

AUTHOR'S FOREWORD

As a youth, I climbed steep, rocky mountains, participated in street demonstrations, and attempted to read Immanuel Kant. I boasted that thirty years of intensive life were preferable to a long life of tedium. I was vocal, but aimless. I was also quite unhappy.

Five decades have passed. My youth is gone. I no longer climb, hike, and ski to absorb an overabundance of youthful exuberance. Now I amble along the creek in a local state park. I chat with passersby and their dogs. They recognize me as "the walking Pole with Nordic poles."

I care deeply about American political life, but … with moderation. Never could I burn the flag, throw stones, or destroy statues. No, those are passions of youth. My brain—no longer willing to follow Kant's rambling, incoherent-to-me logic—rebels. No, philosophy should be a balm for the wounds of life, not cause anxiety. This morning I listened to a Roman sage during my walk. Destructive passion, he tells me, must be moderated with reason. Accept mortality; face death with equanimity. Be willing to practice poverty; use wealth properly, he says, and he speaks of the importance of friendship, the need to care for others, and the need to accept adversity without resentment.

Such thoughts are indeed balm for my soul. They harmonize with the breeze in majestic trees towering above the walkway and with the faint gurgle of the creek below. When I hear a bird's song, I turn my iPhone off and listen. When a dog I am acquainted with approaches me to say hello, even a senator will have to wait his turn.

And no longer do I try to convince anybody of my truths and opinions. I doubt they ever had value. In fact, I no longer have strong opinions at all. No more arguing! I'd rather give people entertainment by telling a story—a story that brings a smile or a moment of reflection, or both.

That's my role in life. Let me serve others by giving a brief respite from routine thoughts. I lack the material wealth to build a hospital or library, but if my animal stories make you relax and chuckle instead of worrying about problems, then I will have succeeded far beyond Jeff Bezos, for he has only his billions, but I have made a new friend.

Why do I write light, entertaining stories? I'm now a happy man.

How did this happen? Is my second motherland, the United States, a better mother to me than my first motherland? Or maybe, with age, I now accept life as it is instead of trying to change things or "make things better."

Whatever the reason, I understand now what I am and where I am: a small bubble of consciousness floating haphazardly around the material realm. What a relief! Instead of fighting to prove I am somebody, I enjoy every hour of who I truly am.

This work—in truth, 'twas but idle play—I dedicate to my wife, my children, and all the beasts in our hearts.

EDITOR'S INTRODUCTION

Aldek's Bestiary is a collection of short fiction centered on human connections with animals. This is the first appearance of Romuald Roman's fiction in English. Known to his friends as "Aldek," this unique writer has published two novels and four collections of stories in Polish.[1]

Troubadours once engaged listeners night after night with continual plot twists in long, passionate romances. We have centuries of fairy tales filled with vivid imagery told to children for their moral education. Along these lines, Romuald Roman tells his classic stories. But these tales touch on deeper truths about our psyches and our species.

Barack Obama holds that literature and art are good at "reminding us of our own folly … and shortsightedness. What books and art and stories can also do is remind you of the joys and hope and beauty that we share."[2] How did Barack Obama know exactly how to describe *Aldek's Bestiary*?

Each of these twenty-one stories features an animal in a Polish family's life. Six occur in Poland. To understand Polish life under Communist rule, the Solidarity movement, and post-Solidarity crackdown—in a most enjoyable manner—read the Poland Stories.

---

1   Novels: *Ośrodek Zero: Tajemnica Doliny Syrokiej Wody* (*The Zero Resort: A Mystery of the Syroka Woda Valley*, Warsaw, 2014) and *Powrot* (*Return*, Warsaw, 2019). Short stories: "Przystanek Idaho" ("Idaho Station", Warsaw, 2000); "Kierunek: Filadelfia!" ("Direction: Philadelphia!" Warsaw, 2005); "Zakopiański Dom Wariatów" ("Zakopane Madhouse," Warsaw, 2015); and "Amerykański Dom Wariatów" ("American Madhouse," Warsaw, 2017).

2   Michiko Kakutani, *NY Times* Book Review, "Barack Obama Opens Up about Writing *A Promised Land,"* 12/09/20.

"Oskar Weasel" and "Bureck the Heartless Cat" are both situated in the narrator's childhood in Zakopane, a spa town at the foot of the Tatra Mountains. "Chamois Leoś" and "Otto the Sparrow Hawk" are also situated in Zakopane, headquarters of Tatra National Park.

Among the Roxy Stories, "Such a Good Dog!" stands out with a broad sweep from 1940s Poland to present-day Philadelphia. Recent Polish history comes alive, as do complicated dynamics of a family spanning two cultures and three generations. It's all delivered with humor and grace.

Marta of the Marta Stories is the wife, mother, and boss of the family, the narrator's "she who must be obeyed." Mikimoto oysters, frigate birds, and an African gray parrot represent the animal kingdom here—all in humorous tales of marital relations.

The Philadelphia Stories relate a generational chasm between parents who emigrated from Poland in their mid-thirties and children who've grown up American. Two cultures in one family make for a rich stew of conflict, misunderstanding, and affection.

People need simple stories that touch the heart. That's what attracted me to these charming yet profound narratives. You can learn much about storytelling from *Aldek's Bestiary*—how to lie, how to tell the truth, how to have a friendly conversation, how to weave the absurd into reality, and much more. However, the greatest reward of reading these compelling tales is to meet their humorous, perceptive, animal-loving, animal-hating narrator Aldek, one the most likable characters of modern fiction. In this book, you can get to know him, too. I think you will find he's a great friend.

WISE THOUGHTS ON BEASTS

What are human beings? Are we beasts? I won't answer this question. You must decide for yourself. History's great sages may help you form your opinion. You can peruse this sampling of thoughts on humans and beasts as a warm-up before you read on, or come back to these pages later for inspiration. May the stories that follow stir your emotions and awaken your imagination!

Humankind differs from the animals only by a little, and most people throw that away.

—Confucius

Man ... is a tame or civilized animal;
with proper instruction and a fortunate nature,
then of all animals he becomes
the most divine and most civilized;
but if he be insufficiently or ill educated
he is the most savage of earthly creatures.

—Plato

I fear animals regard man as a creature of their own kind which has in a highly dangerous fashion lost its healthy animal reason—as the mad animal, as the laughing animal, as the weeping animal, as the unhappy animal.

—Nietzsche

Wild animals run from the dangers they actually see, and once they have escaped them worry no more. We however are tormented alike by what is past and what is to come. A number of our blessings do us harm, for memory brings back the agony of fear while foresight brings it on prematurely. No one confines his unhappiness to the present.

—Seneca

Man is the only animal whose desires increase as they are fed; the only animal that is never satisfied.

—Laozi

How does man know, by the strength of his understanding, the secret and internal motions of animals? From what comparison betwixt them and us does he conclude the stupidity he attributes to them? When I play with my cat, who knows whether I do not make her more sport than she makes me?

—Montaigne

Man is by nature a social animal.

—Aristotle

When a man has pity on all living creatures, then only is he noble.

—Buddha

POLAND STORIES

I saw, deep in the eyes of the animals,
the human soul look out upon me.

—Thoreau

PAW, A ZAKOPANE DOG

August of 1984 was a warm month in Zakopane. In its second half, there was no inkling that summer was ending. The sky was an intense blue. Thin mountain air cleansed the lungs of city dust and dirt, filling the heart with the will to live.

Among the yellowing ash trees planted by Tomek's father along Tetmajera Street, above the tops of the firs in Scherer's Woods, where eight-year-old Tomek had shot at crows long ago with his slingshot before Mrs. Sokołowska caught him at it, you could see the bluish, wavy line of Giewont and Czerwony Wierch peaks. The afternoon mountains lost their morning intensity of color and sharpness. Warm summer air blurred the edges of gullies. The Church of Mother of God looked like a watercolor painting.

Mother did not sense the August heat. She stood at the gate in a brown woolen dress and a homemade sweater, wrapped in an old black shawl. She had to continually brush back her wind-swept hair. She had cried all night, and her face seemed older and more tired.

She looked at her grown son, her grandchild, and her daughter-in-law for the last time, as they were about to leave Poland, and she was staying. She knew that any conversation now, any word, would cause a new stream of tears. She was silent.

Next to Mother sat the five-year-old dog, Paw. She was small, black and white, quivering with excitement at the sight of people getting ready to depart. Her doggie instinct told Paw that this time she would not be going along. She wagged her tail every so often, watching every move made by Tomek and Marta, wrestling their baggage into a Fiat 600.

They tried to make fast work of it to shorten the interval for good-byes. The car, which normally could barely fit two adults and a child, now had to take a whole family and bits from an accumulation of thirty years of living: four pictures of Mother, nineteen books, fifteen records, clothing for every season, documents, family mementos—and provisions for the journey.

On this day, grown-up Tomek did not cry. He felt the sight of his mother and the empty house being etched into his memory and to last for the rest of his life: not a photograph that, over time, would lose its sharpness and color but an image carved, as by chisel on granite, into every brain cell, making permanent every sharpened contour: Mother's face as she stood by the fence, his daughter Kasia swallowing tears, his wife Marta's trance-like movements. *"Pack, stuff, don't cry … pack, stuff, don't cry," he kept thinking. "Nothing this sad will ever happen to me again. Let's get it over with."*

Farewell, then, Mother. A last kiss, the slam of a car door, and … on the way. Behind us, Mother and the dog stay at the gate. Thirty-five years of life left behind with them.

Farewell, my Zakopane. Farewell, Poland. You were a cruel stepmother to me.

It took me fifteen years to write these words about leaving my mother. Because it was supposed to be fiction, I changed my name from Aldek to Tomek. Now yet another fifteen years have passed. For a long time it was too painful to return to that time—a mother, a home, a dog. Within a few years, nothing remained. Before looking back, I had to wait until memories of faces, voices, and smells became foggy and unreal. Time—the great doctor. Time, the healer of nostalgia and bitterness.

Finally, I can now recall those pieces of my life without pain. Even more, I smile at those memories as if they were from somebody else's life or on TV.

I sort through random memories as if they were a cache of old photos never sorted into an album, photos neglected in a shoebox. For decades, silent and still, such a shoebox might wait until an unknown somebody tosses all it contains into the trash.

But I still exist, and each salvaged photo moves my thoughts to times when blood was vigorous in my veins, when my brain was sharp and my heart inspired. Difficult times, but times when I had energy, hope, and young dreams.

Now, when I reread those words I wrote about one of the saddest moments of my life, I remember my mother's tears. I see this trembling dog Paw sitting at her feet.

My mind moves to a different memory, a story about a different Paw. Not Paw the sad dog abandoned by family leaving home without her, but a young and vigorous Paw—the smartest thief on Tetmajera Street. Paw, who loved her mistress so much that she tried to feed her. Who somehow knew her human family did not have enough food on the table.

What year was it? 1984.

In 1984 the local Communist authorities in Zakopane, Poland, concluded the easiest way to get rid of my family (You ask why they wanted to get rid of us? Because we owned a big house they coveted.) would be to modernize our house into a high-quality hotel and give us a choice of staying during the seven years of construction without electricity, water, and heat, or … go away.

The "invitation" to go away included the issuance of passports for the entire family, which would allow us to emigrate to the West. They thought we would leave Poland and leave our home for them. Nobody expected that we would attempt to survive in this place, suffering severe mountain winters in a shell of a building. It would be almost suicidal for my sick mother, and unthinkable for my pregnant wife. But my mom, in her late sixties, refused to go away.

"I would rather die in my own house than in some shelter for refugees abroad," she declared. The government had announced martial law. Martial law allows Communist officials to create order quickly without following the law. Instead, they created new laws. General Jaruzelski, the Communist dictator, decided all the laws and rules of everyday life.

"So what?" my mother thought. She was from that generation of Poles who survived five years of Nazi occupation. She'd seen soldiers, even a tank, in front of our house and had not fled. What threat were these Polish Communists compared to a Nazi tank? It only refreshed her memories of times when she was young and brave. Why not be brave again now, when she has nothing to lose? Nothing but to die of cold.

I, on the other hand, reluctantly agreed with my wife that we must abandon our homeland—abandon the beautiful Tatra Mountains, our friends, our jobs—and start a new life in a new country. Where? Maybe Austria? Or Australia? Canada? The U.S.? Somewhere that lies and injustice are not concealed by governmental slogans.

I was young, Marta even younger. We could emigrate and move from country to country, seeking an opportunity to settle down. But my mother was too old and fragile. I hadn't even tried to convince her to go with us. It was her decision; she was left alone with Paw.

A few days before we left, I noticed that the dog took responsibility to care for my mother. Paw must have sensed we were leaving, catching the sadness in our voices and seeing all the packing and preparation.

A few days before our departure, when Marta and I were sitting in Mother's room talking about our unknown future, Paw entered from the veranda door. She used to come and go, walk on the street and visit dogs or people whenever she wanted. Always silent, shy, and polite, never barking or showing aggression, like a friendly shadow. Good dog.

At this particular moment, however, Paw was walking with difficulty. She was carrying in her mouth a one-pound piece of fresh steak. For a small dog, it was a heavy load, and Paw walked in a strange way, holding her head upright to keep balance. Once inside the room, Paw left the steak on the floor in front of my mother, proudly wagging her tail in expectation of thanks from her mistress. Mother was so surprised and, for a while, had no idea what to do.

"Oh, Paw! Paw! You have stolen something again! From whom? And what I am going to do with it?"

Paw moved her tail faster and mischievously smiled at Mother.

Yes, dogs smile. Not all dogs. For some—golden retrievers, for example—it is natural. For others, especially mistreated dogs, it is almost impossible. But people who love dogs immediately notice a dog's smile. And our Paw definitely could smile.

Looking at her mischievous smile, I had an idea of what to do with this beautiful steak.

I looked at Mother. Likely she had the same idea I had.

Then I looked at Marta. She wasn't smiling. Her face was frozen— In fear? In anger?—staring at the dog, our dog, who stole somebody's steak and brought it home. In broad daylight. Probably all the neighbors were witnesses to the crime. Now, these neighbors would think we trained Paw to be a thief, to steal steaks from poor, hungry people. They would get sick and die. It would be our responsibility.

Marta's mind wandered this long tunnel of gloomy thoughts, but I never entered it. I saw a light at the tunnel's end, but not the tunnel itself, and I am sure my mother thought the same. I salivated, imagining how we'd prepare the meat. Chop it into small pieces to sear in butter; coarsely dice a yellow onion and two potatoes; throw it all into a pot with a cup of heavy cream, add more butter for flavor, and add flour to thicken. Pop the pot into the oven for three or four hours. Tonight, we would feast!

Marta knew me well. She reacted immediately.

"You do not dare to think … " she whispered to me in a firm tone that made me ashamed of my intentions.

"Of course not. How could you suspect me to. … But now that you mention it … "

Seeing her glare, I changed course. "No, no, of course not. I do not think. I am looking at this steak, I am only looking at this steak, but I do not think at all."

"He doesn't think. Nobody's thinking." My mother came to my defense.

Marta picked the steak up from the floor and plonked it onto the kitchen table. With gusto, she cut it into small pieces. Then she gave this huge pile of red meat to the dog.

Surprised, Paw politely looked at Mama.

"And nothing for you, my beloved mistress?" asked the dog's eyes.

"Eat, Paw, eat. It's all for you," responded my mother, as if she never had other ideas about dispatching the steak.

We watched our obedient dog eat, and eat, then take a break, exhausted by eating, then eat again, then take a longer break, and continue. Paw was like a python, methodically swallowing a horse.

You could see her belly stretch and grow round, but Paw could not stop eating because never in her dog's life had she had such a wonderful meal. And she ate it *all*. When it was over, exhausted Paw could not move. She rested next to the empty bowl. She was too heavy to walk.

And all evidence of the crime had vanished.

"This will be a great lesson for her," said Marta. "We did not scold her for stealing, but she will suffer terrible stomach pains, and she will remember never to steal again."

"Maybe," I said, doubting the efficacy of this method to train dogs, envious that my dog had a steak for lunch, and I'll have to have Oscypek cheese sandwiches and tea. The thought of the smoky tang of the sheep's milk cheese against my palate helped me forget how the steak might have tasted.

"I would like to know who she stole the steak from," I whispered, more to myself than to Mother and Marta. But I was overheard.

"Don't tell me that you want her to steal another steak from the same place!" Marta exclaimed.

"Of course not! How dare you think this terrible thing!"

"I know you. I know what to expect," she whispered as if to herself. She knew me well.

This friendly exchange of opinion about my character was interrupted by a knock on the door. Our neighbor, doctor Ala Tatar, appeared. Ala was a young cardiologist, living nearby in a nice villa, where she owned a small apartment on the first floor. We'd known each other since we were children. Ala treated my mother like her second mother and visited often. Whenever something bad happened to her, she shared the sorrows of her busy, lonely life with my mother.

This was such a day. Ala was in tears.

"I sacrifice my entire life for other people. I work double shifts, I stay at the hospital at night when patients need me, and after several exhausting days, finally, I had a weekend I dreamed about, and …"—Tears stopped her speech for a moment. "And I planned that, instead of those terrible hospital sandwiches I would make for myself a tasty steak, and"— more tears—"when I was just about to start grilling it in the garden, somebody—during those few seconds I needed to get the salt and pepper from the kitchen—stole my steak! People are terrible! Oh, how terrible they are!"

With complete conviction, Mother reaffirmed this dim view of humankind. "Yes, Ala. People are monsters. Stealing a young doctor's food is a sin!" Then, after the slightest pause, she changed the subject. "We have sandwiches with Oscypek cheese for lunch. Would you like some?"

Ala agreed. She ate her sandwich, chewing slowly, eyes closed for long moments. Was she pondering the depravity of the human race or, perhaps, savoring the simple flavors of bread and cheese, as she was giving thanks to God for this bounty? Maybe she thought it was good to suffer loss, to appreciate even more what you have not lost. In any case, the poor young doctor would never experience the savory juiciness of her purloined steak.

Paw pretended she didn't know Ala or understand human language, but she suffered. She felt shame.

Between slow bites of her sandwich, with her physician's experienced eye, Ala stared hard at Paw's ballooning stomach.

"Is Paw pregnant?" she asked.

Mama's cheeks turned red. Never before had I seen her react with such embarrassment. Could the lovely doctor's X-ray eyes see the stolen steak in Paw's stomach? Was this the moment to confess our sins?

Paw burped. She burped again. Then she put his head down and fell asleep. Ala looked fondly at her. "I guess she just has gas. Feed her watery rice for a couple of days. That will cure her indigestion."

Mama's face relaxed.

"Thank you, Ala. You are so kind to help our poor Paw."

Whatever special nests we make—leaves and moss like the marmots and the birds, or tents or piled stone—we all dwell in a house of one room—the world with the firmament for its roof—and sail the celestial spaces without leaving any track.

—John Muir

MARMOT FAT

During the first years of my American life, every week I received letters from my mother in Poland. They were thick letters because Mama, an artist, included lots of drawings showing her life in an empty house and, later, in a house during construction. People tried to help the old, lonely woman. Workers informed her when they were going to shut off the water or disconnect the electricity. They carried buckets of water to the kitchen and ran long electric cords to friendly neighbors, allowing her to heat the one room she slept in and boil water for cooking and baths. But, my mother wrote, a small electric heater was not sufficient to keep warm. On the other hand, a more powerful heater would blow fuses. So she spent a lot of time in bed covered with all available comforters and blankets. Paw was always in bed with her, knowing her mistress needed her body warmth. In the middle of winter, Paw brought to Mama her new friend Mishuh, a small mutt so ugly that a rat looked handsome in comparison. But Mishuh had good character and immediately started sharing responsibility with Paw to bring warmth to my mother's bed. Paw warmed Mama's belly, and Mishuh warmed her feet.

I looked at Mama's drawings and was thankful her four-legged friends tried their best to replace her lost family.

What could I do to help her?

Our first seven years in the U.S. were the most difficult. Marta and I were both working and studying at the same time. We had little money and big dreams about a house, a car, and a better place to live. Great plans and tiny income. Nevertheless, in each letter I sent to Mama—and I tried to send one every week—I inserted some money, one dollar, sometimes five or even ten dollars, inside each envelope. Twenty dollars a month—and Mama sometimes received more—would make a significant difference in her life. I was only praying that people working at the post office did not open my letters and steal the money. But they did not. I knew because Mama informed me about the contents of each letter she received from me.

"At least she is not hungry," I thought. "At least she has money for medications, and to pay the electric bill." I tried to convince myself that I was fulfilling my duties.

And Mama, with her inner strength, was still alive. From spring to late fall she could paint, but in winter—not. A few times in the winter the electric heater stopped working at night—maybe it was the fuse, or maybe by mistake somebody disconnected the electric cord providing power from Mama's neighbors—and water froze in a bucket.

"In times like this, my dogs save my life. Last night, Paw licked my face when he noticed that I was uncovered and cold," was a description beneath one of Mama's drawings.

Seven years. They were building this hotel for seven years, and my mother survived this terrible time with the help of her two canine companions, Paw and Mishuh.

Probably convinced by my mother's determination, in the end the Communist authorities allowed her to stay in the new hotel. She was provided her own apartment with a kitchen and bathroom, a painting studio, and a nice bedroom. So, in some way, she won!

*   *   *

Our American life started in Boise, Idaho. We met such wonderful, friendly people that I wrote a book about them and their beautiful state. We lived in Boise for seven months. Only seven months, you ask? Why not stay in this beautiful place?

The main reason was that Marta discovered an uncle in Pennsylvania. He was a monk in the Order of Saint Paul. They had established an impressive sanctuary of Our Lady thirty miles from Philadelphia in Doylestown. This uncle wrote us several letters and convinced us to move to Philadelphia.

"Don't stay in the wilderness of Idaho. It's the end of the world. It's like Siberia. Come to Philadelphia, where you will have many opportunities to work, make money, follow the "American dream." As a priest, I meet hundreds of Polish immigrants, and—believe me—most of them are not as smart and educated as you are. And you know what? They graduated from universities, opened their own businesses, and bought beautiful houses. Here where I live, everything is easy. American universities are not very difficult. Once you have an American diploma, it is easy to find good work. As far as I know, working here is not hard because people are friendly. And last but not least, you will have me around. And I—your family—will assist you as much as I can."

Wouldn't you listen to such a promising invitation? Who wouldn't? In my mind I envisioned a beloved priest with lots of money and a lot of influential friends—like in Poland, where priests are community leaders. Like in books. What he said was persuasive, especially because all the jobs I had had in Idaho were temporary and for minimum wage. So, after reading the third letter from Marta's uncle, we bought a 1971 Ford Granada (only slightly leaking oil), packed all our belongings, and drove to Philadelphia.

* * *

We met Uncle Daniel in his sanctuary. He was a round-faced man, wearing the white robes of the Saint Pauline order. Nothing special about him. Although rather short, he was not obese, nor was he thin. Shy, mostly silent. When he did speak, he spoke slowly, showing no emotion—a far cry from his enthusiastic letters. He had already spent twenty years in the U.S., but his English was not fluent. Maybe this was because he was taking care of the Polish cemetery in Doylestown, and his work was limited to officiating funerals and comforting relatives of deceased Poles.

Daniel was an only child growing up in Poland during the Second World War. Chaos and destruction surrounded him during his early years. His father, in the Polish army, went away to war and never returned. He saw sights no seven-year-old should see. Then the war ended. The Russians installed the Communist regime. Polish society succumbed to it. Where could he go to find a peaceful life? Where could he indulge his passion for books and music? At fifteen, he had already seen enough of the cruel world of war, materialism, and politics.

In those days, Catholic churches in Poland were islands of rationality, education, tradition, and deeply moving music. The Vatican gave funding to Solidarity, the great workers' movement of the 1980s. If the Nazis and the Communists were on the negative side of the register, creating huge problems for ordinary citizens, then the Church and Solidarity were on the positive side. Providing rays of hope, these institutions stood up for ordinary people.

"What choice did I have?" said Daniel, when we asked him to tell us how he came to be a monk in America. "I could become a clerk or accountant under the Communist regime, spending my life being careful to obey the Party rules. Or I could live like St. Paul the Hermit in contemplation and peace—far from the horrible restrictions of our society—with laws only of humility and love. In the same circumstances, you yourself might have been drawn to the monastic life."

I have to admit; I never aspired to be a monk. My upbringing in the highlands of the Tatra Mountains instilled in me a need for the independence and exploration I experienced almost every day of my youth as I rambled up fir-filled mountains, along barren ridges, or down dark ravines with deer, wolves, and mountain rustics carrying antique rifles. Each day was a new adventure.

So I could never live as Uncle Daniel did under the protection of his monastery. And as it turned out, we soon found that he had no clue about real life. His main source of knowledge about America was the observation of people who visited the church and discussions with fellow monks during meals. His superiors took care of all his needs, including food, clothing, and entertainment. Yes, the monks had a TV room and a library in the monastery. During their free time they could walk through the rural areas surrounding the church grounds. Daniel's only family for many years were other monks. Nine of them lived in the monastery. They knew everything about each other. So long was he separated from his few relations in Poland that, when he was informed of our existence, he must have suddenly realized, from somewhere deep in his subconscious, that he longed for real family.

The moment we met, he was moved so much that he was close to crying. But he controlled his emotions enough to explain a complicated relationship between my wife's great-grandfather and Daniel's part of the family. He told me he was happy to support us financially. Although he had taken a vow of poverty, he saved his monthly allowances received from his superiors. In the past, he spent this money on sweets, books, and other unnecessary items. But from the moment he was informed that he had his own family in the U.S., he saved his entire allowance for us. Saying this, he handed me an envelope. I pretended I did not need any money, but he insisted I must take his savings. Finally, I opened the envelope and found inside the sum of $360.

Uncle Daniel proudly looked at me.

"Now you will have seed money, to start your life in Philadelphia. And don't worry, you will also have an entire house to live in, and you do not have to pay rent. One Ukrainian lady, hearing you were coming, told me you could stay in her property in the area of Kensington."

*   *   *

This is how our Philadelphia life started: in an abandoned house in the most crime-infested part of the city. Daniel eventually understood that immigrant life is more complicated than monastery life. But he was generous of spirit and action-oriented. He felt responsible for us and did everything he could to help us. He even broke monastery rules and visited us almost every day. Surprisingly, he always had something for us: a piece of sausage, a huge jar of orange jam, two pillows, four plates, an electric kettle—always something. I suspect he "borrowed" these items from the monastery kitchen. I will never know for sure.

He was more and more enthusiastic every day:

"You repaired the oven? Fantastic! I told you, for somebody as talented as you are, it was possible! And what about the toilet? You still have to flush it with buckets? It's not easy, I imagine. Do you have tools to repair it? No? All right, maybe I can help."

The next day he came with old tools, pieces of pipe and even a soldering kit. I don't understand how it happened, but I—with no skills, just with a desire not to disappoint Daniel—worked and worked until the toilet was running. I even replaced leaking pipes!

If I had known how difficult and expensive graduate school would turn out to be, I would never have enrolled in Drexel University. But Daniel persuaded me that graduate school was valuable, and going to university in the evening is just relaxation after work.

The true attraction of graduate school I discovered at a Święconka Easter gathering at the Polish cultural center. I was chatting about graduate school with some Polish students when one of them told me that once you are in graduate school, you can borrow money from the bank. When I was considering attending Drexel, the admissions officer enthusiastically filled me in on how to manage the finances—loans, financial aid—and how the university student jobs office could help me find good work, even before I completed my degree. Between the loans, scholarships, and work opportunities, as a grad student I could live like a king—especially compared to a student's life in Poland.

As for Daniel, there was much about America and Philadelphia he simply didn't know. We listened to him, trusting he had a deep knowledge of the Polish immigrant community, but in reality he hadn't a clue. Daniel did not know a single Pole who came to Philadelphia and, instead of looking for a job, started university courses. The Poles Daniel knew were blue-collar workers who gradually became owners of contracting companies or professionals who came to the U.S. as well-known physicians or engineers.

But Daniel did not know about the reality of juggling children, jobs, and school. He enthusiastically supported my entering the university. We trusted him. Wouldn't you trust a priest—rather, a monk—who had spent twenty years in America and met a thousand Polish immigrants? That's exactly what I did. And thinking everything would be easy, I translated my Polish diplomas, paid for a notary seal, and sent documents for evaluation. Based on this, Drexel enrolled me in graduate school. Then I borrowed money from the bank to pay for the first semester.

At the university, I asked my professors to help me find a job. One of them recommended me for a technician position. When I told Daniel about my progress, he radiated happiness:

"Didn't I tell you? It's so easy!"

If I told him I wanted to build a rocket and fly to Mars, he would say:

"Great idea! I am sure you can do it!"

Daniel witnessed how I graduated from the university and passed my board exams, and he encouraged Marta to follow me.

"You are smarter than your husband, aren't you?" he said.

"I think I am." Marta never hesitated to confirm the obvious.

"Now is your turn to go to college."

Within seven years, Uncle Daniel, who never went to an American school, cajoled Marta and me into becoming American professionals. We found good jobs, bought a house in the suburbs, and achieved our American dream.

By the time my family achieved in the U.S. a social status similar to the one we had had in our abandoned motherland, Poland had changed from a Communist, Russian-occupied country to an independent democratic republic. Poland became a country governed by law and justice.

I, who had been kicked out of Poland, could now visit my homeland. When I think about my decision to leave Poland and all of the changes that took place within seven years of my departure, I see that God often mocks human plans. My entire life, everybody around me thought Communism would freeze Eastern Europe for fifty to a hundred years. Maybe more, because it sickened people's morals and weakened their courage so much that they became craven cowards whose only pursuit was gaming the system. Then the bright sun of Solidarity rose! Founded in 1980 at the Lenin Shipyard in Gdańsk, the union's membership reached 10 million in just one year, representing one-third of the country's working-age population. Lech Wałęsa was awarded the Nobel Peace Prize in 1983. Alas, this was too much for the Communist government. The ray of sunshine disappeared in two years as the Party disempowered Solidarity and returned Poland to a Communist gloom. Forever.

I lost hope. It didn't matter that the government forced me to leave Poland so they could seize our home. I had already left.

Thirty million fellow Poles lost hope. The rest of the population was happy to be confined inside a socialist playpen.

But amazingly, at the time I was establishing my new life in the U.S., Communism was defeated everywhere in Europe: in Poland, in Germany, in the Czech and Slovak Republics, even in CCCP, which changed its name back to Russia. The Polish embassy in Washington, D.C., issued me a new passport, dropping the word "Socialistic." We were now simply the "Republic of Poland."

As soon as I could, I flew to Warsaw. Within a few hours I took a night train to Zakopane. In the morning, on Tetmajera Street, I admired the newly renovated hotel that used to be my home. They allowed my mother to keep her small apartment in the hotel as long as I did not try to move back to the country.

The emotions were powerful when I opened the door and entered the house I had left seven years before. I found the door to our apartment and found my Mama. She was much older, fragile, and attended by two dogs: Paw, who recognized me immediately, and shy Mishuh. He did not like other people to pet him—only Mama.

She was crying. When she could finally talk, she proudly showed me her new apartment. She pointed at new paintings on the walls.

"Now it is warm the entire year. I can paint all day long."

"Do you have enough money for paint, and frames, and canvas?"

"Oh, yes! People order portraits from time to time, and they pay me. I have enough money."

"Sure?"

"I wouldn't lie to you."

I met doctor Ala again. She took care of my Mama during the hotel construction and renovation.

"You must understand," Ala explained, "those years incredibly weakened your mother's health. She might look healthy to you, but her body is exhausted from the cold winters and insufficient nutrition. It's only the excitement of seeing you that gives her energy. Within a few days she will collapse into bed. The worst part is that, even though she has high blood pressure, she doesn't want to take medication. She won't tell you this, but she wanted to save your house by surviving in it. She did it. The house is yours. Since she has achieved her goal—she thinks—she doesn't have to live any longer."

"Jesus! What can I do?" I was devastated, hearing this.

"Nothing," Ala said. "There is no going back. You must return to America, and continue your life with your family. You have been through too much and achieved too much over there to return to Poland. And even if life in Poland is more and more 'normal,' it's far from the proven stability of American life. Think about the future of your children."

* * *

She was right. I returned to America.

Six months later, Mama died of a stroke. It was at night, while she was asleep, so probably she did not suffer. Just a moment of pain, and everything was over. It happened at Christmastime, three months after I started a new job for the federal government. Because of this, I had only three days of vacation and had to apply for administrative leave to go to Poland and bury my mother. I begged my bosses to give me at least a week. They gave me only two days. I could not understand the cruelty of their bureaucratic behavior.

I flew from Philadelphia to Frankfurt and Frankfurt to Warsaw. From Warsaw I took a train to Cracow, and from Cracow I took a taxi to Zakopane.

Mama's body was already in the morgue. But both dogs, Paw and Mishuh, refused to leave her bed. Mama's friends visited the dogs twice a day to take them outside, but they spent only five minutes in the yard and then immediately returned to the room to resume their vigil for Mama. They lay in the same places they had during the long, cold winters: Paw at the head of the bed, Mishuh where Mama kept her cold feet. Seeing me, the dogs did not raise their heads, did not wag their tails. It wasn't me they were waiting for. Evidently their lives made no sense without Mama.

I had the weekend and three goals: organize my mother's funeral, find a shelter for the dogs, and return home on time. If I failed, I would lose my new job.

Thinking about these goals, I scanned the room. On the night table, there was a box containing all of my letters to Mama since my departure. I opened the box. The money I had sent was still folded inside each letter. All of it. She had not spent a single dollar.

Crying, I took the dogs for a walk. They reluctantly left the bed and wanted to immediately come back inside. I left them on the bed and walked downtown to the morgue to see Mama. They did not allow dogs in the morgue. I have no idea why.

* * *

I arranged the funeral and invited her friends and neighbors.

After the funeral, I asked people to take whatever mementos they wanted from Mama's apartment. They took pictures, and books, and even small pieces of furniture, but nobody answered my pleas to take the dogs. The entire time this procession of strangers walked around them, the dogs did not move from her bed.

Once the neighbors dispersed, I ordered a huge dumpster and paid workers to put everything from Mama's apartment inside, including the bed, including all the letters, documents, and photos. From the box with my correspondence I took the cash and trashed the letters. The dogs stayed on the floor, scared, trembling. I asked the workers if they knew anybody who would take care of Mama's dogs for money and keep them until they died. They promised to inquire among their neighbors. I had no other chance to save the dogs. There was no SPCA in Zakopane. Should I take them to the vet and euthanize them? I couldn't. How could I do such a thing to creatures who, in my absence, provided the warmth of their bodies and the comfort of companionship to my mother? How could I sentence to death her only friends from the times when she cooked canned pasta on a hot plate and ate it in bed because it was too cold to sit at the table? These cherished dogs, who had never left her. But my thoughts did not bring me to consider how unpredictable Fate mocks us all—even innocent dogs. In retrospect, I should have taken Paw and Mishuh to a vet, stayed with them till the last breath, and buried them in the backyard of the home where they had spent their lives.

But at that time, I had no idea.

$*$ $*$ $*$

The next morning, a guy with a strong rural accent called me and said that he could keep the dogs for money. The address was—I still remember—Jan Kaleciak, Kotelnica 3, 37-501 Zakopane.

Not very far. I called a taxi and drove to this place. He was a dirty, middle-aged local man living in a shabby house. Probably a drunk, I thought.

"Do you have a dog?" I asked.

"No, sir. I never wanted one, but since you will pay me, I can take care of your dogs. You see, my house is partially fenced. I will build a fence around this side, and the other side, and they will stay safe and enjoy life. A much better life than they had with your mother."

"How are you going to feed them?" I continued my interrogation.

"They will eat what I eat—eggs and bacon, meat, vegetables, kasha. I eat a lot of meat. Dogs like meat."

"How much?"

"Two dogs for ten years—such small dogs live a long time with all that good food that would cost me a lot of money. I'll say … a thousand dollars."

"You must be kidding. For that, you could take care of a child."

"So find somebody else."

"OK," I said. I started walking to the taxi I had waiting for me.

"Stop, stop! How much you can pay me?"

And the bargaining continued until I paid him all the cash I had with me. All the money from the envelopes on my mother's night table: $765.

My American savings did not help my mother, but at least it saved her dogs. It was an incredible sum of money, enough in Poland to buy a good used car, like a Fiat 650. I thought about it. I came to the conclusion that this high price was an assurance that this man would construct a yard for the dogs, so they would enjoy running free in the field, barking at the moon, chasing rabbits, and eating good food. He spoke with a highlander's accent. Highlanders are men of honor; they are proud to keep their word. I had no time. More than anything, I wanted to believe I had arranged everything for the best.

Mama used to say "disasters come in pairs." Two months after my return to the U.S., Father Daniel was taken to the hospital. The diagnosis was prostate cancer. He was optimistic and did not take his cancer seriously.

"It's simple surgery," he told me when I visited him. "The doctors at Doylestown Hospital are as good as the ones in Philadelphia and New York. In a few months, we'll laugh at this. Tell me about your new job. How much do they pay you? So much! Is it possible? Bravo! Didn't I tell you that you would prosper in Philadelphia? And please, stop asking me about my health. In a few weeks, I'll be fine."

But even after four months, Daniel's health did not improve. Radiation did not help. Chemo made him fragile and lethargic. Staying in the hospital deprived him of physical and mental strength. When I visited him, I noticed him gradually losing hope. But one day, with new energy in his voice, he said something that completely surprised me.

"It seems that the doctors have done their best, but the cancer has moved to my lungs," he said, "and I must die. But—you might have heard about this: I was told by one of my fellow monks that the only medicine that can cure my lung cancer is the fat of a marmot from the Tatra Mountains. I know it's difficult to get this cure because poachers killed most of the marmots. But you worked for this national park for six years, in a managerial position, right? You know people over there— who is who, you know. What do you think? Could you find a poacher to save me? Maybe God created one marmot to save me from cancer?"

He removed a gold chain with a medallion of Our Lady of Częstochowa, his only precious possession, and gave it to me.

"Could this pay for the marmot fat?"

Can you imagine my thoughts? My list of ethical rules to guide me to a proper response? The sense that I faced a "lose-lose" situation? For six years prior to my immigration to the U.S., I worked for the National Park of the Tatras.

An enthusiastic environmentalist educated in forestry, preserving the ecology of those unique mountains was my passion. When I thought about my life in Poland, I could list plenty of mistakes, failures, sins even. But there was one part of me—my fanatical love of the Tatras's natural ecosystem—that nobody would mess with. My destiny had been to protect this tiny chain of mountains and its unique animals and plants. Love of the Tatras was my religion, and if I sinned as a Catholic, I never sinned against the natural world.

And now my dying priest relative was saying, "Maybe God created one marmot to save me from cancer?"

I knew there were approximately 300 marmots that had their homes at the border of the upper meadowland with bare rocks above. Their existence was threatened by eagles, ravens, foxes, and—worst of all— poachers. Marmots whistle to warn each other of approaching danger, signaling them to escape into the cracks between rocks and into their underground tunnels. But what is useful against natural enemies reveals their location to humans. Unscrupulous hunters locate and exploit their shelters much more efficiently than natural predators would. Greedy poachers charged hundreds of dollars to hospital patients desperately looking for their last hope: marmot fat.

Sick people have always believed in "miraculous" remedies. The marmot fat myth started in the mid-nineteenth century, when Zakopane became a mecca for people suffering from tuberculosis. The highlanders told them that Tatra marmot fat would cure their TB, just like Tatra bear fat heals arthritis or sunburn. Even if doctors told them that marmot fat folk medicine wouldn't restore their lungs, they would still pay a fortune for the yellowish suet.

At the end of the nineteenth century, when marmot fat became the rage, there were thousands of marmots and a few families of bears. When I lived in Zakopane, there were hundreds of marmots and no bears. But people suffering from terminal disease still believed in mountain panaceas. They did not want to die; they longed for a cure. When tuberculosis was cured—by antibiotics, not by marmot fat— patients diagnosed with lung cancer continued the cruel and unethical tradition of paying poachers to kill endangered species. False hope resulted in a marmot killing spree. Even though the National Park of Tatras had trained mountain rangers to protect marmots from poachers, the rewards of "pseudo-medication" had been so high that highlanders risked imprisonment to hunt marmots. Money spoke more loudly than fear. For the poachers, love of nature did not exist, because their lives had been entirely integrated with nature. Highlander habits and customs follow the seasons, the fauna, and the flora of the Tatras. Every year, mountain meadows had grown more silent as fewer and fewer marmots whistled to each other.

Oh, how I wanted to save these animals!

I had written in the local press about the evils of killing them. I had participated in meetings with villagers to convince them that poaching would be punished. All of my friends knew me as a passionate environmentalist. And now I was looking at the pale face of a priest— my friend, my family—who whispered, "Could you find a poacher to save me?"

Is an animal, even the rarest one, more important than a human being?

Could I allow a man who was so good to me and my family to die without hope?

Could I tell him, "No. I refuse. False medication won't help you"?

Maybe his hope would cure him. Why I am so certain that marmot fat doesn't help? Saying no would deprive him of his last hope, his last strength to fight for his life.

* * *

I promised to buy a flask of marmot fat from a poacher.

But how could I, a former employee of Tatra National Park, find a poacher? Somebody ready to kill a marmot for me. For money.

I made some calls to Poland asking different people for help. One by one they refused. Some expressed surprise, others openly condemned my change of character, but most gave a simple, "Sorry, don't know anyone" and quickly changed the subject. I called anyone who might even barely remember me—everyone I knew. I had no honor and felt no shame. This was for Daniel, the kind man who had guided our early days in the U.S. Finally I found a young woman, a janitor in a local high school, who said she understood my motives and promised to search among her neighbors. After a week, I called her again. (At that time, calling the U.S. from Poland cost so much that I couldn't ask anybody to return my calls.) She told me that she found a man who could sell me a pound of marmot fat for $200.

I said yes.

One of my friends arranged the payment, and during my next call, I was told that a poacher had started his hunt.

I radiated pride and goodwill when I announced to Daniel that he would have his special medication.

I was not ashamed. I did not care that one marmot was forcibly removed from his hole, nor that the poacher bashed his head with an ax. This marmot would die to save Daniel's life. It would be quick and painless. Thinking about it, I started to believe that the smelly animal fat actually would save a noble human being. That's the strength of belief. And strong beliefs can erase memories. You may remember being burned by a hot stove as a child. But if you believe, you can walk over hot coals. Did I mention that strong belief can also erase critical thinking? Walk on hot coals? Please explain your logic!

In two weeks I received an express package from Zakopane, Poland. The sender was somebody I did not know. The poacher, perhaps? Inside a double-ply plastic box was something described as "homemade scrapple." Marmot fat!

Daniel started his new treatment immediately. His belief that the cure would work made him feel better every day. The upcoming MRI would confirm his hopes.

But it didn't.

Instead, it confirmed that the cancer was growing. It entered his bones. All hope for a successful outcome was lost.

When the doctor informed Daniel about the progress of his disease, at first he did not believe it.

"But I feel much better, Doc," he protested.

"I am glad to hear it," the doctor said, knowing that "feeling better" was an illusion.

After the doctor left his room, Daniel's emotions moved deeper, moment by moment, into despair. The pain was growing. Increased doses of morphine allowed Daniel to sleep almost all the time. Marta and I forgot about marmot fat. There was no reason to think about it anymore.

Three weeks after he received the fat, Daniel died.

Not many belongings remained by his bed: a book of prayers, an old rosary, a family photo of Daniel with his parents and two older sisters, a photo of my family, a pair of slippers. And … a plastic box with half-eaten marmot fat. In the uncovered box I saw a note written in such a way that one could read it only after unpacking the inner plastic container. It was written in Polish, with big, childish letters.

"You overpaid for this fat. If you want more, contact me directly, and I will sell it to you for fifty dollars. My address:

Jan Kaleciak, Kotelnica 3, 37-501 Zakopane"

The same man!

I had left my dogs at his place!

What kind of man was he? Now I evaluated his behavior differently. He was untidy, for sure. But was he a dog killer? What about Paw and Mishuh? What was their fate? Is it possible? Jesus, did he kill them? For fat?

No, that's crazy. Of course that couldn't be true. He was probably only a poacher, a marmot hunter. I told myself I should stop thinking about this. I would never know the truth, and I was not brave enough to visit Poland to check whether Mama's dogs were still alive. I immigrated to America to have my ordinary, normal life. No dwelling in the past.

Hamlet: *Do you see yonder cloud that's almost in shape*
           of a camel?
Polonius: *By th' mass, and 'tis like a camel, indeed.*
Hamlet: *Methinks it is like a weasel.*
Polonius: *It is backed like a weasel.*
Hamlet: *Or like a whale.*
Polonius: *Very like a whale.*

—William Shakespeare

OSKAR WEASEL

"I remember him as if it were yesterday, as he came plodding to the inn door, his sea-chest following behind him in a hand-barrow—a tall, strong, heavy, nut-brown man, his tarry pigtail falling over the shoulder of his soiled blue coat, his hands ragged and scarred with black, broken nails, the sabre cut on his cheek, a dirty, livid white ... "

No use. I couldn't concentrate. I had a great book to read, *Treasure Island* by Robert Louis Stevenson. Walking with Mama that afternoon, I had promised myself I'd read till midnight. But that evening I couldn't read. The memory of loud "Reeeeeee! Reeeeeee!" ringing in my ears as a tiny animal fought for its life disturbed me. His high-pitched scream was stronger than my imagination of a one-legged pirate or of a skeleton showing the direction to hidden treasure. A big, ugly mutt, sharp, white teeth slobbering over black jowls as he moved in for the kill—that image pushed barrels of golden coins right out of my mind.

The word "barrel" triggered a new direction in my thinking. Barrel—barrel in the cowshed—inside the barrel, a weakened, hungry, thirsty weasel. The tiny animal awaited the third round of a fight to the death with Reks, the merciless dog. This round would be the last one. A two-pound weasel is no match for a forty-pound dog, especially if the weasel has starved for forty-eight hours.

* * *

Mama and I stayed in a villager's tiny house, two kilometers from the center of Krynica. Our hosts were simple people. Their tiny field was too small to feed them. The husband also worked repairing roads and doing construction, while his wife rented one room to poor vacationers who could not afford to stay in a hotel. We paid for the bigger room. Their entire family—father, mother, and their two boys, a couple of years younger than me—crowded—I don't know how—into a room much smaller than ours. Their room was not only tiny, but it bordered a cowshed where two cows, a horse, and a she-goat smelled in the summer like, like, you-know-what. If you think you are poor, look around. There are many less fortunate.

The hosts introduced me to their two boys. The older was Olek, a heavy youth with a pock-marked face and bully's stance. The smaller, Bolek, was slightly younger than me. His farm overalls had only one strap, his hands were grubby, and his sneer was a close imitation of Olek's. The boys showed me their animals: first the goat, which was old and aggressive, and when I approached her, she charged at me. Thank God, I had enough time to climb the apple tree. It saved me from the mean goat but not from the mean laughter of the brothers. Meeting the goat was a part of the game with a city boy.

The horse, Karyh, was exhausted. He did not even try to look at me. His only goal was to rest. Both cows, Krasula and Malina, were timid and lazy. They allowed me to pet their big heads. They chewed their food with the same rhythm as their breathing.

In the evening, after strolling in the park, we stayed at this family's home. Our room was dirty and reeked with farm animal odors. There was no bathroom—only a basin and a jar with water from the well. A toilet was outside, but it smelled terrible. Mama taught me how to clean the seat before use. They had no toilet paper, only old newspapers.

I hated this place! I was feeling uneasy with those boys around, and I was angry at my mother.

* * *

How did we get to this dirty little farm? A few months before the end of the school year, Aunt Janina—my Papa's wealthy sister who had no children and paid for my language and music lessons—said:

"Your English is so poor that I doubt you have any tutoring. Who is this person I pay to teach you English? I would like to meet her."

"No, Aunt, please no. I would be ashamed."

Of course, I would be ashamed. I did not want the friendly Mrs. Jane, who "taught" me English, to be fired by my demanding aunt. Mrs. Jane's teaching method was to pull together a large group of students and let them have fun, reading and memorizing short, funny dialogues in English. No grammar, no homework, no grades. Just fun. I loved it! The only problem was that Mrs. Jane's English was rudimentary, and her students did not want to wear out their young brains by memorizing English words.

"I am going to convince your mother that it would be best for you to spend your whole vacation in London," my aunt told me. "My old friend Mrs. Zosia Skąpska has grandchildren who do not speak Polish. If you play with them for two months, you will speak English much better than you do with your current teacher. Let me talk to your mother."

And she tried.

My aunt told my mother that sending Aldi—she called me "Aldi"—to England would be difficult and costly.

"Yes, a lot of money!" my aunt said. "But that is not all. Obtaining a passport to the West is the main obstacle, even for a child. We live in a Communist state during the Cold War. England is allied against us. Vacation in London would be almost like sending Aldi to the moon. But I, as his aunt and godmother, will move heaven and earth, ask favors of all my friends, and even pay bribes to authorities to achieve this goal. I will send Aldi abroad and open his eyes to the world."

Because she loved me, my aunt couldn't allow me to grow like an uncultivated weed in a provincial town and be poorly educated. "Aldi needs a different perspective and a valuable tool: the English language."

Throughout her entire life, my mother never made independent decisions. Like a snow pea plant, she required a supporting stick. Mom's stick was her mother, my grandma.

It had been already nine years since my mom followed her mother's direction and obediently left my father to live in poverty. No wonder my mom immediately consulted her dictator about my aunt's proposal.

"No way," protested Grandma. "We are not going to send this little boy to England. Imagine what could happen to him during the long trip. He would fly there? Oh my God, that's even worse, to allow a child to fly! What kind of person would do something like that? And London—such a huge city. So much crime. He could be kidnapped. He could be murdered in London! We would never see him again."

Thus Grandma convinced my mom to say no.

My aunt was terribly peeved.

I did not spend vacation in London with upper-class, English-speaking children.

To make up for it, Grandma spent our meager savings to send me and Mama on a ten-day vacation to Krynica. This tiny resort, only seventy kilometers from where we lived in Zakopane, was well-known for mineral springs that healed old people with digestive or rheumatic problems. Anyone could stroll on the resort grounds, listen to the resort band, and drink free water from several "healing springs." Around the grounds, there were sanatoriums and hotels for people with money, over a hundred private villas renting rooms for people with a bit less money, and—much farther away—tiny farmhouses where villagers rented rooms to the poor.

Mom rented the cheapest room from these highlanders living outside the resort. It took us half an hour to walk to the resort. Then, while strolling along colorful flower beds, we could sip free, smelly water and melt into a crowd of people rich in money and poor in health.

I hated this place.

*   *   *

Fortunately, their parents instructed Olek and Bolek to play with me. We paid them money. They were ordered to be nice. They reluctantly agreed and tolerated my company. As a part of their duties, that evening they showed me their kingdom.

Not everything was bad.

They said I could sleep in the hay in the barn. I lay down for a few minutes, and the aroma of dried grass was pleasant. I was almost asleep when an invisible insect or spider bit me. But at least I tried. I also tried to pet the older cow and their vicious dog Reks.

In the nearby stream, the boys told me, people could catch trout with their bare hands. Hard to believe, I thought. Around the stream, in the dense brush, lived wild animals, they said. They saw a fox a few times. The other day they saw a weasel.

I had never seen a weasel, not even in pictures.

My new friends filled me in. "They're itty-bitty, maybe a kilo," offered Bolek.

Olek interrupted his brother. "S'posed to catch birds and fish, but they'll eat up our hens, and the eggs and rabbits, if they can. Bite your finger off if you try to grab 'em! Only good weasel's a dead weasel." This last sentence was said with the gravity of a papal decree.

And—just imagine—during my stay, they caught a weasel.

It was our fourth day in Krynica. We arrived home after strolling around the resort. The older brother screamed my name:

"Aldek! Aldek! Hurry up!"

He wanted to show me something in the cowshed. I left my mother without asking for permission and ran out to the wooden structure. At first, I couldn't see anything in the dark. I stopped at the door and looked around. Gradually, I saw what was going on.

In a narrow space between the cow barrier and the wooden wall, the younger brother and their dog Reks had cornered a tiny animal.

A weasel.

Bigger than a squirrel, more like a small cat, his brown fur shiny, a white patch on his throat.

* * *

I've always liked to name animals that fascinated me. A one-legged pigeon visiting our window was "Kulas," our highlander neighbor's horse was "Kopytko," a mouse who lived in our kitchen and avoided Grandma's traps was "Munia." But what would be a good name for a weasel? He must have a special name because weasels were rare animals. They like to hide during the day, then slink around to steal eggs at night. So I'd never seen one before. Maybe I should give him a strong and proud name, something like Hector, but everybody calls his dog "Hector"; I needed a name that didn't relate to known characters—a rare, unique name. Then it popped into my head. Oskar! I'd never heard of any dog named Oskar. In fact, I didn't know any humans named Oskar, either. I probably heard that name when, lights out, my mother surreptitiously tuned our Soviet-made Pioneer radio to the 10 p.m. Radio Free Europe "Music from Vienna" program. Yes, a name not common in Poland, with a foreign ring to it. I immediately gave him that name. All this ran through my mind in seconds as I gaped at the battle emerging in front of me.

Hyper-alert, Oskar looked at Reks. His tiny black eyes followed every move. Reks was ten times bigger. Oskar knew where danger lay. Not the humans. The dog.

I had no time to wonder how it happened that the weasel allowed himself to be captured. The scene before me took my full attention.

Reks's huge head was as big as the entire weasel. He growled. He salivated. He bared white fangs enormously bigger than Oskar's pin-like weasel teeth.

Cautious, Reks waited. He sensed his tiny adversary was aiming at his eyes. He had killed many cats and squirrels. They always went for the eyes.

After a few minutes of mutual evaluation, Reks tried slowly, carefully to approach the weasel. The wild animal waited until the dog's huge, black eyes were close enough to reach with a single leap. Yes, Oskar would go for the nearest eye, the left eye, and attack the dog's most vulnerable place. The weasel jumped. Jumped and missed, because the dog was smarter. He made a dodge to the right.

Now the dog knew how far and how high the weasel could jump. Another tense moment ...

Like Japanese samurai, in complete silence, both animals concentrated on tiny shifts of their positions. Then, in a fraction of a second, the weasel feigned an attack, and the dog leapt back.

This pattern repeated several times. The dog was too careful to risk losing an eye; the weasel dared not leap great jumps, uncertain of connecting with his target. From time to time Oskar uttered a strange sound, something like a ticking machine or maybe like a scared bird. Loud and high-pitched:

Tchik! Tchik! Tchik!

The two brothers tried to encourage their dog to fight. They patted his back and spoke to him with soft, low voices:

"Take him, Reks! You are a good dog! You are a brave dog! Go for it!"

But Reks knew his adversary, nervously wagged his tail in response to his masters' encouragement, and hesitated.

Finally, Olek, the older brother, made a decision:

"You, City Boy! See that barrel in the corner?"

"Yes ... ?" I was hesitant, unsure of his intentions.

"Open the lid and tell me what's inside."

I stepped over to open the lid of a small wooden barrel.

"Empty."

"Good," muttered the bigger boy.

"Now you, Bolek." He looked at his brother. "Bring me a blanket! There's one somewhere near Karyh." Karyh was their old, overworked horse. Last night the boys had dried his sweaty body with the same blanket.

Bolek brought the blanket. Olek shook it, then threw the heavy canvas, like a fisherman's net, over the weasel. Reks led the race to immobilize Oskar under the blanket, but Olek kicked the dog aside and took the blanket with the weasel inside. He put it in the barrel and replaced the lid.

"Enough for today," Olek announced. "That weasel's too strong. He's ready to fight today. He could hurt Reks and escape. And we need fun. Fun, not a disaster! You agree, City Boy?"

I did not say a word.

What could I say?

What should I say?

I mumbled 'goodbye' and turned toward our room.

* * *

"I will not be part of this sadistic game," I decided once we had left the barn and I was on my own again. "I won't be a spectator of this killing. Oh, no! I'd rather walk around the terrible resort until dark than be like one of those boys in the barn. I don't want to see it. Let them do their killing without me. I am a different person than those two. Even if they wait for me to show me how their trained dog kills wild animals, I won't go with them. I will read in my room, and I won't join them to witness the murder!"

And can you believe this decision did not help me?

For I soon realized avoiding participation in their evildoing didn't clear my conscience.

Why didn't I share this story with my mother? I should have. She'd have been devastated by the boys' outrageous cruelty. She'd realize how stupid she was to take me to Krynica instead of allowing me to travel to London. She would have regretted putting me in a position to be taught cruelty by village boys.

But she had already cried enough, and I was feeling some compassion toward her. The real culprit who caused all of this was Grandma. Mama was merely *her* mother's instrument.

The next day was another boring day. My mother had pre-paid our hosts for nine nights, and if we left for Zakopane earlier, they wouldn't return overpaid money. Therefore, we had to survive a few more days in this place.

It was raining, and both of us had already had enough of walking through the roses and drinking water from Saint Joseph's spring that supposedly cures ulcers. But we had to do it. There was no alternative. We drank so much of that water that we had to stay close to the public toilets all day. Even worse, we found that overdoses of Saint Joseph's water caused digestive problems.

When we returned to the farm, the boys' entertainment resumed.

Oskar jumped halfheartedly, not as eagerly as yesterday. When Reks slowly approached the prisoner, the little warrior found a new way to scare the dog. He started a high-pitched screaming. Loudly.

The dog, alarmed, leapt back. Meanwhile, the boys did not stop encouraging the dog to attack. But the mutt remembered the sharp, tiny teeth and waited for his moment.

I had had enough watching and left the scene. When walking back to our room, I noticed that Olek had also gotten bored and, again, had caught the tired weasel in the blanket and thrown it into the barrel.

Why did I feel so awful? What could I do? Fight with two boys much stronger than I am? Tell my mom? Oh, please that would be useless! Useless and stupid! Maybe tell the boys' parents? Also stupid! Peasants kill wild creatures. They consider them nothing but pests. Wild animals eat their hens and sheep, destroy their crops, and deprive them of food. What was this weasel doing in the cowshed? He had probably tried to kill their chickens and eat their eggs.

No use thinking about it. There was nothing I could do. I should force myself to read my book and pretend nothing was happening.

But I could not read my *Treasure Island.*

I closed my eyes, but I couldn't sleep.

There was a voice in my head: warning "Tchik! Tchik! Tchik!" And then long, fearful cries, full of "Reeeeee ! Reeeeee!"

And I couldn't keep doing nothing.

I rose from my bed. My mother immediately asked:

"What are you doing?"

"I have to go to the bathroom."

"Do you have to? It's dark outside. Maybe I can walk with you."

"No, thanks. I have a flashlight."

We had a flashlight for walking to the outhouse. I turned it on in the room and walked into the dark yard. Once I closed the door, I turned the flashlight back off and cautiously looked around. Reks was chained in front of the house. Good! He started barking, but when I whispered, "Reks! Reks! Good dog!" he recognized me. Maybe the dog knew he should tolerate the presence of his owners' paying guests?

I walked quietly toward the cowshed and slowly opened the door. Easy! No lock! Inside, I turned on my flashlight again and entered.

The horse noticed me, moved his head toward me, rustled in his stall, but did not utter a sound. In the middle of the night, animals are sleepy, too.

I approach the barrel to remove the lid.

The weasel had chewed through the fabric and lay atop the canvas. He stared up at me with piercing eyes.

How to save Oskar?

Sometimes it is best to gather your thoughts before acting. This was such a time. I thought carefully: "Hm … To reach for Oskar with my hand isn't an option. The animal would surely bite me. I need a tool."

Yes, a tool. I looked around and found a wooden rake leaning against the wall. "Such a long handle! That's exactly what I need."

I carried the rake to the barrel, slowly inserted the handle of the rake, thinking, "The weasel will climb it, jump to the ground, and scamper out the door into the bushes." Ah, the best-laid plans of mice and men ...

The tiny prisoner did use the rake handle to escape from the barrel. Unfortunately, my plan had a defect: I still held the handle when Oskar ran to the top with alarming speed. For an instant I was paralyzed with surprise. I had no time to remove my hand. Oskar's entire soul had but one goal: escape! My hand lay between him and his freedom. It had to be dealt with. Instinctively, without slowing his upward speed, his sharp teeth raked deeply into the upper part of my hand. With a fierce hiss of pain, I stifled the urge to scream. I knew I couldn't wake anyone.

Oskar achieved his goal. He vanished into the night.

The entire episode, from extending the handle into the barrel to Oskar's scampering escape, took no longer than a second or two. The flow of blood almost made me faint. This was a significant injury. Silently, I took three slow, deep breaths, then released a few silent sobs. If the hosts caught me, I'd be in deep trouble.

I ran away from the scene of my trauma. Directly to my room.

My mother was awake. Instantly, she noticed my bleeding hand. Completely terrified, she could only whisper:

"Oh, my God! Oh, my God!"

"It's OK," I said. "Don't worry. I only need some disinfectant." Of course, we did not have any.

"Should we go to the hospital?" my mother asked her twelve-year-old son, weak from loss of blood.

Hospital? What hospital? How to get to a hospital in the middle of the night? Fortunately, I was a voracious reader of books about exotic travel—hunting lions on the Serengeti, battling anacondas on the Amazon, and punching white sharks in the nose in the open sea. So I knew injured adventurers did not hesitate to use their precious liquor in such situations.

"Let's go to Krynica," I replied. "We can cleanse the wound with whiskey."

As silently as we could, we crept away from the farm and walked toward town.

We soon spotted a tiny bar, loud with drunken locals. Mama and I entered. At first, the boisterous highlanders didn't notice us. Mama showed my injured hand to the barkeeper and he immediately recognized the problem. With a loud guffaw, he said, "I guess you won't never feed them squirrels again, will ya?"

"Ya little idiot, never feed the squirrels!" burst out a drunk highlander, seated at the bar next to where we stood. He sipped from his grimy glass as he gestured a toast to my hand, then turned to the crowd at large: "To city folk! May you always entertain us with your stupidity!" He reached out and took my hand, as if to inspect it. Suddenly, he poured the half shot of vodka remaining in his glass over the wound. This time I did not stifle my scream. "Eeeeeeee! Eeeeeeee!" I must have sounded just like Oskar in his moment of terror.

The highlander chuckled. Looking past me straight into my mother's eyes, he offered, "Don't bother to pay me. Stay with us, and drink up. You'll find we like city folk!"

My mom. Was that the reason he was such a friendly guy? He liked my mother?

"You are kind, but we must go," she excused herself. We escaped back into the night.

Nobody was chasing us!

Thank you, God!

Silently, without our hosts ever knowing, we reentered their house on tiptoe. Reks did not even bark.

*   *   *

I couldn't sleep the entire night, not only because of pain, but mostly because I knew that Olek and Bolek wouldn't forgive me for what I did. Early in the morning, I could hear them talking to each other. I expected that they would try to beat me up when I walked to the outhouse. As long as I could, I tried to stay in the room, but I had to pee.

I asked my mom.

"Can you walk with me to the toilet and wait for me?"

She did not understand why, but she protected me both going and coming back. The boys watched me, making signs that they would cut my throat.

We would see ...

I knew I took a risk to save a weasel's life. But I wasn't going to be stupid just to prove I wasn't afraid of fighting. Of course I was! Why fight for nothing? To fight, knowing you would be beaten? Better smart than brave! Especially when dealing with reckless punks stronger than you.

My mom had no idea how I was injured, who did it, or why. She accepted my wound without asking, as she meekly accepted all the blows of fate. If somebody wanted to define "strong woman," here's my suggestion: "opposite of my mother in every aspect."

"We must go to Zakopane now," I commanded. "If not, those boys will break my arms and legs."

"Jesus! Why?"

"Because they hate me!"

"Jesus! Why?" My mom was so scared she could only repeat herself.

I raised my voice. "C'mon! Let's pack up and get away from here." And we did.

Within an hour we were sitting on the bus to Zakopane, and two hours later we arrived at home.

* * *

That's the story of how, instead of London, I visited Krynica.

In London I would … my God! I cannot imagine what I would see and experience in the capital of England. I'd enrich my knowledge, improve my English, and be a special kid in my neighborhood.

But Krynica? Krynica changed me from a sissy city boy into a different person. After my experience with those rough rustics, I knew I could act like a man, not a swaggering bully but a man of reason. I understood that unwarranted bravery is meaningless and dangerous. But bravery exercised out of compassion for others is thoughtful bravery—my kind of bravery.

At that time, my papa's mother was still alive. (This is my *other* grandmother, not the one who caused this entire debacle.) Quite elderly, Granny lived in her past, repeatedly telling me the same stories about *fin-de-siècle* Kraków—all pretty ladies in flowered hats and handsome barons inviting them to dance the quadrille. Ancient Granny loved to talk about ancestry, family names, and coats of arms.

"What's a coat of arms?" I asked. It sounded like an unusual item of apparel. "Do the arms have hands at the ends? Are there dozens of arms hanging down from a single jacket?"

"Now, you stop being silly! A coat of arms," she explained to me, "is a symbol that shows you belong to the class of knights, you follow the rules of chivalry, you believe in virtue, and you spread goodness in the world."

"Really? Then I have my coat of arms!"

"You? How could you—a small boy—have a coat of arms?"

I showed her my right hand with a still-fresh wound left by Oskar. If saving him was not a chivalrous act, what meaning does "chivalry" have? Grandma looked at the wound. It was quite a gash. I told her of my Krynica adventure.

"Yes, Aldek, you acted like a chivalrous knight. You certainly have earned your coat of arms."

The heart is a strange beast, not ruled by logic.

—Maria V. Snyder

BURECK THE HEARTLESS CAT

The destruction of Poland by Communist rulers, combined with the destruction of my family by my mother's mother, darkened every day into a gloomy, hopeless fog. Even my boyhood days.

I was five, maybe six years old. I remember how poor we were. I remember, after each meal, how I felt I would gladly eat a bit more, and definitely something better, something tastier, like scrambled eggs or a piece of juicy ham.

My father lived in the same house, but he and Mama no longer shared a common room. She stayed with me and her mother in one room. He had his own room, and Granny, his mother, had another one.

Granny owned the house. It was left to her by her father. For her, this three-story stone house represented history, family values, indeed the essence of Polish culture.

Papa's room was full of beautiful furniture, books, paintings, and collections of old china and silver. In my explorations while he was at work, I discovered bottles of wine hidden between books and cans of ham in desk drawers. On the Chippendale desk was a portable electric stove and an old balance syphon coffee maker. Oh, this coffee maker! When I watched it, first there was the smell of burning fuel, then the sound of steam traveling along metal pipes, and then a new aroma, the aroma of coffee. And finally … bam! The balance changes, and coffee drip-drops into the cup! What a miracle!

He never offered me a taste of his coffee.

Not once.

*   *   *

There were other treasures. A Pelikan pen with a white star on the top. An empty Romeo and Juliet cigar box. Several pocket watches, two of them gold. Pipes made of exotic wood. Examining these treasures, I'd sit in his comfortable, soft armchair. And everywhere, the smell of his cigarettes … and aromas of the food he cooked at his desk, shared with no one.

Papa did not care what I ate, or maybe he only pretended he didn't care. In their Cold War—the Adult Cold War—I was only a pawn. No, not a pawn. Rather, a bishop running from one corner of the chessboard to the other. They used me as a messenger: "Tell your father this," or "Ask your mother why." I did not like those missions.

This Cold War started when Grandma forcibly moved in with our family.

So you can keep them straight, "Granny" was Papa's mother. She owned the house. "Grandma" was Mama's mother. At times, she was a red-eyed demon.

I was there when Mama, her voice trembling and tears in her eyes, revealed to my Papa that Grandma planned to visit us—in fact, to stay with us to help run our household. My Papa exploded:

"No, no, and no! I'm not going to live with my mother-in-law. No way! It's your choice. Your husband or your mother. This vicious woman has already destroyed your sister's family, and now she wants to destroy ours? Never!"

But my mother—my fearful, delicate mother who never opposed her husband—straightened her spine and shouted:

"I am not going to abandon my mother at this moment when she has no place to go. She will stay with me!"

"In my home? Against my will?"

"Yes! I have no choice."

That was our family's *King Lear*. Shakespeare in his tragedy used kings, knights, and armies. In ours, there were feuding mothers-in-law, a stocking machine, one child, and a cat. A Shakespearian tragedy? Well, nobody died and no nations fell, but it was definitely a tragedy. Did Lear, heart-torn on the heath, suffer more than I? Did he, reluctantly and fearfully, have to carry messages of spite across the battle lines of a fractured family?

Fractured or not, we lived together within one flat like sardines in a can, awash in oil of … what? No, not olive oil, more like crankcase oil. An oil of hatred that enabled family members to ignore, pretend not to hear, slip past, avoid, and otherwise move around each other without colliding.

Papa hated his mother-in-law, Grandma, while at the same time Granny, his own mother, infuriated him every day with her arch superiority.

Grandma fanatically despised both Papa and Granny. She hated their entire family—yes, she even hated the ancestors they were so proud of. Grandma had a mission, her true north. It was to protect my mom from "that pompous villain and his witch-mother."

Believe me, I got it from all sides. "I love you, my poor child, but remember, some inhabitants of this house are evil creatures." Maybe not those exact words, but I can tell you, I got this same message from Papa, Grandma, Granny, and the aunts and uncles who aligned with one side or the other. Every adult took me aside to coach me except Mama. Always meek, she was considered by Granny, Papa, and their entire family to be a half-brained "artist." The rest of the family worked, both actively and passively, on my childish understanding of the world, instructing me whom should I avoid, dislike, and hold in contempt.

I was five or six years old.

And, from time to time, I was hungry.

Hungry children are easily persuaded.

* * *

As a penalty for choosing Grandma instead of following his command, Papa deprived Mama of money for food. He knew she had no savings and no other income. The only income my mother and her mother had was a tiny state retirement that Grandma received once a month. It was not enough. Definitely not enough! My father knew this, and he hoped hunger would break his wife's and his mother-in-law's will to oppose him. It didn't. It only made them more determined and resourceful.

My mother did not know much, but she studied art and had learned how to paint portraits before she had married. Desperate for food money, she visited neighbors and offered to paint their portraits for a small amount of money. It didn't take long for her to discover that it was not a good time to hawk portraits. Who would buy a portrait under Communism? The wealthy burghers who had supported our great *fin-de-siècle* artists, Jacek Malczewski and Józef Chełmoński? Sorry! Burghers no longer existed. Any the Nazis failed to exterminate were taken care of by the Communists. How about our new ill-educated rulers and apparatchiks? Nope! Even if they weren't cultural morons, it would be against their doctrine: Destroy all traces of capitalist times; erase all old ways of living.

A portrait was a best-forgotten relic of capitalist society. Even doctors and lawyers, who at times wanted to have a portrait for their office or living room, feared openly sinning against the new postwar anti-bourgeois rules. A portrait would show they were different from the rest of society. That would be dangerous and unpatriotic. Under Communism, everybody was equal.

In any case, Mama was no Jacek Malczewski. She switched from portraits to paintings of flowers. Still she did not sell anything, not because Communists disliked flowers but because her flowers were poorly painted. Mama's flowers were ugly, graceless plants, hardly distinguishable from weeds. They didn't sell.

Next, she tried to sell landscapes, but alas! They were no better than her flowers. Poor Mama, she painted our three-dimensional world as a flat surface. This method of painting worked well for prehistoric caves, on the walls of Egyptian tombs, and even in early medieval works. But ever since linear perspective was devised early in the fifteenth century by Filippo Brunelleschi, painters have depicted objects positioned in three-dimensional space. Needless to say, Mama's flat mountains didn't catch on.

Not knowing any other direction to take, my mother tried to perfect her style of painting. She continued spending our food money on tubes of oil paint. Nothing changed. Neither her ill-shaped landscapes nor her rough-daubed roses found any admirers.

At this grave moment, Grandma had a revolutionary idea: No more dreams of selling art—just simple work for money. Grandma was told by a lady in the grocery store that in the mountain town where we lived, authorities were allowing a pseudo-artistic co-op to open. It was called Co-op Zakopane, and their first project was to produce cotton stockings with snowflake embroidery.

These stockings were described as "artistic and based on highlander folklore." Potential buyers did not know those fancy stockings were made of cheap, plain cotton from a supplier in Cracow, mass-produced on embroidery machines by Zakopane co-op members like my mother. This was OK because the entire system of Communism was based on lies. No reason not to call these stockings "handmade" in a country where leaders were openly telling us that Russian occupation was not an occupation but "friendly assistance."

Following the norm of cheating and lying, the Co-op Zakopane shop displayed photos of old peasant women embroidering stockings in front of "traditional" log houses, the Tatra Mountains in the background. The stockings were grayish white with dark brown embroidery of geometric, starlike snowflakes. When a woman—young or old, doesn't matter—puts these stockings on, her legs immediately looked weird and heavy. And there was absolutely no way to find a piece of clothing to match these stockings. They looked best completely hidden inside a drawer. But those details were not important to Co-op Zakopane. The system rewarded production, not sales.

The co-op opening created an opportunity for people like my mother who had unique skills. Based on her papers from the Academy of Fine Arts in Cracow, she was given an opportunity to be a co-op worker and could rent a special machine from her employer. My mother rented the machine. Then, she attended an obligatory, one-hour course on how to use this noisy devil to make snowflake stockings. Unfortunately, because the co-op instructor was only obliged to teach future employees for one hour and was not obliged to check their progress, at the end of the instruction, her skills were not much better than when she started.

A large, rotating circle of hooks and needles, the monster—no doubt created by Dr. Frankenstein himself—moved several threads around a plain stocking spread in the middle. Yes, that's right: She rented complicated machinery to engage in a hopeless task producing something useless and ugly. When Mama was making stockings, even with full attention, the threads tangled periodically. She would have to correct the pattern, start again, work for a few minutes, cry awhile once she noticed that the pattern was wrong again, remove the part of the pattern she had already made, correct positions of hooks and needles, and start again. Oh, gods! Ye who watched Sisyphus rolling his boulder up a hill in Hades and did not cry, cry now for my poor mother making artistic stockings for Co-op Zakopane!

To make it even worse, Mama did not work alone. Her mother usually observed the progress and checked that her daughter's work was proper and efficient.

"If only my eyes were young and good," she was saying, "I would show you how to make these stockings. But you know I can't. But I still see how sloppy a worker you are. Focus! Try your best! Correct this thread! Not that—this one, don't you see?"

Mama trembled and often cried. But with the silent determination of a woman with a hungry child, she worked and worked for hours.

You might think having your own mother as your quality inspector would not be the worst thing that could happen to you. Wrong! Grandma had no mercy. Every minute, she wanted to prove that her youngest daughter—who was not able to find a decent husband—was clumsy and lazy and could not perform simple work. "Have you no skills? Can't you pay attention? You have no dedication!" Grandma's assault was relentless. Alas, instead of efficiency came tears, mistakes, and broken threads.

* * *

A second disaster befell Mama in the form of a cat, Bureck. A nondescript gray creature, he walked in one day without asking. Like Grandma, he soon was living with us. Bureck means "gray cat" in Polish. His previous owner was our neighbor, a highlander who gave him this name. I guess he never thought of naming him Horace or Socrates.

Plain "Bureck" was good enough for a mouse-catcher. He was a lazy mouser, though, so our highlander neighbor did not care when the cat moved out of his home and into ours. Observing him, I thought Atlas would be more apt a name because he was unusually big and he preferred to stay immobile. But I'll stick to the truth, so Bureck it is—an ugly name for an ugly cat.

Once inside our home, the place Bureck chose to watch life go by was on top of the stocking machine table.

My God, this creature was probably related to Zeus's eagle who gorged himself on Prometheus's fresh liver. The cat became Mama's eternal torment and Grandma's beloved assistant. Bureck loved the sound of the stocking machine. It lulled him to sleep. Bureck's purring then would accompany the staccato clicks of moving needles and the rumble of turning spindles, creating a complicated post-modern musical performance. Mama played solo on the Co-op Clickinspindle, while Bureck made low, continuous, vibratory sounds like a string symphony.

The feline's happy sounds were barely noticeable as long as mother worked without breaking threads. But they would crescendo to a Wagnerian *fortissimo* if she stopped working. Silence made the cat mad.

And once angry, he did not hesitate to punish my mother by breaking the thread. He knew very well that tangling or, even worse, breaking the thread was the worst thing that could happen to her.

She looked at the vicious cat, reproached him, and asked him why he thwarted her work. Maybe I exaggerate, but I think at this very moment Bureck was quite proud. He knew that my mother the machine operator would be soon reprimanded by her mother, the know-it-all. He knew he had a partner in crime, and he loved to maltreat his victim.

Alarmed by Bureck, Grandma appeared. She looked at her frightened daughter with disdain and hissed:

"Start working! Now! Even the cat can't stand your laziness. How did you screw up again? Don't you know that we need money? If you are only tangling the thread, nobody will pay you for your work. You cannot be so selfish. What are you telling me? What? Your eyes? Your eyes are young. Look at my eyes. See? See my glasses? So, work, and do not complain!"

And my poor, trembling mother desperately tried to make the machine work again and fix her errors. No matter how tired she was, she continued this torture.

* * *

A month passed.

The entire load of decorated stockings was ready. Mama took the completed product to the headquarters of the Co-op Zakopane. Prior to being paid, she had to visit the quality control section. She had a feeling that something terrible might happen. And she was right. The meticulous inspectors found that six pairs of the stockings were good, and eighty pairs were not good. So they counted how much they had to pay my mother for six pairs of stockings, and how much she had to pay them for the wasted eighty pairs of stockings, and how much for renting the stocking machine. My mother not only did not make any money, but she owed them a lot. They understood her sorrow and created a financial plan for how much she should pay them every month during the upcoming year. She said "yes." She could not protest.

They had to be compensated. But she was devastated.

Well, now this sad story needs a good ending. Like, for instance, that when mother returned home, Bureck had disappeared. Or that my Grandma had disappeared. Or that we had a wealthy relative, and he died, and my mother inherited a fortune.

But nothing like this happened. The cat lived with us for two more years. No inheritance. No miracle.

But …

One day, in desperation, or in an explosion of boldness, my usually shy mother approached the manager of a popular cafeteria and proposed to decorate the walls with her paintings of pretty women's faces. Surprisingly, the woman manager did not ask for a bribe—which we wouldn't have been able to pay. She looked into my mother's eyes and said yes.

Mother decorated the cafeteria with her paintings. They looked like portraits, but they were painted from Mama's imagination. She called them "fantasies." Each fantasy portrait had big, big eyes and a sad smile. Men fall in love with such women.

Judge Piotr Dumanski, who visited the cafeteria with his wife Marianna, noticed my mother's paintings. He spotted a picture of a woman who, in his opinion, resembled his wife.

"Look at this painting," he said. "This woman looks exactly like you." ("Only prettier," he thought.)

"Only not as pretty as you," he added.

"Really?" asked the wife shyly.

"Are these paintings for sale?"

They were for sale. Oh, yes! They were for sale!

The judge ordered a portrait of his wife. And he was happy because he paid less than expected, and his wife was happy because she did not have to waste weeks in an artist's studio sitting for a portrait to please her husband. But the happiest person in the world was my mother.

She had a feeling that her method of "face-matching" worked. How simple it was: Paint a pretty face first, and then sell it to a woman who recognized herself in the painting. What an innovative and profitable approach!

Soon, Judge Dumanski's friends began a new trend of decorating their villas with my mother's portraits.

There were more and more clients.

Our life changed like a Hollywood movie. For breakfast, Mama started serving scrambled eggs or a piece of juicy ham. We had money for everything—especially for paint, canvas, and picture frames, because Grandma had done the math. She now wanted her daughter to increase production and paint hundreds of portraits, as quickly as possible.

* * *

And Bureck, our cat?

Well, not so good. Grandma wanted to increase the production of paintings. And knowing how persuasive Bureck could be, she trained him to force my mother to work without breaks.

Mama tried to defend herself. Her imagination was not able to create a vision of a new face every week. But Grandma demanded a portrait not once a week but every two days—or even every day. Grandma had a feeling that if Bureck was sufficiently aggressive, Mama would paint like a robot. Maybe she was right, but Bureck refused to cooperate. Angry Grandma switched from a soft voice and special tidbits—even ham—to smacking the cat with a kitchen rag or even a broom.

Bureck became nervous and absent-minded.

One day when coming home from bird-hunting, Bureck met his end under the wheels of a crudely designed Żuk pickup truck with a high load box, a high center of gravity, and too small a track width. Żuks were notoriously difficult to drive, let alone to drive while noticing cats crossing the road. I don't know if the driver was aware of anything—maybe only the sound of driving over something not very hard. In his defense, I have to say that he was transporting containers of slops from local hotel kitchens. Even if he recognized our Burek, I know he did not want to risk overturning that malodorous load. Still, the driver ably demonstrated that, in addition to keeping Polish commerce on the move, a Żuk can also provide a graceful solution to a family dilemma!

I did not cry.

Surprisingly, Mama's tears flowed. Strange creatures, women—or is it only women artists? Or could she have been, perhaps, weeping tears of joy?

Look carefully at the chamois:
upright, alert, at cliff-edge,
he shows the peace of being fearless.

—Highlander saying

CHAMOIS LEOŚ

After graduating from college and then arming myself with a master's degree in ecology, I started working for Tatra National Park. The Tatra Mountains, part of the Carpathian mountain chain, form an eighty-kilometer natural divide between Slovakia, to the south, and Poland, to the north. Slovak and Polish national parks protect both sides of this international preserve. The most notable mammals there are three protected species: the Tatra chamois, the Tatra marmot, and the Tatra lynx. This unique environment is also home to many other species, including snow voles, brown bears, wolves, red deer, roe deer, wild boar, and eagles. The Tatras are like a miniature of the Alps but "more spectacular," locals would say. The mountain town where I spent my youth, Zakopane, nestles at the foot of the rugged Tatra peaks.

I knew these foothills—the endless variety of life of their ridges and valleys. The ideals of Rachel Carson's *Silent Spring* were etched deeply in my heart. John Muir was my great hero; I'd often quote him. "When we try to pick out anything by itself, we find it hitched to everything else in the universe" became my favorite quote when I was older. But as a youth I recited, "The mountains are calling and I must go" almost every summer morning when I set off for my next peak-and-valley adventure. I loved the Tatras, and I would gladly have worked for nothing to save their natural beauty.

Park headquarters were located in an old building "provisionally" constructed in the late 1940s as a temporary office. By the time I arrived in the 1970s, years after what its life expectancy should have been, the building was decrepit and riddled with dry rot. "We'll wait for its natural collapse and save the demolition cost," the bureaucrats must have thought in between sharpening their pencils and adjusting their green eyeshades.

From this near-ruin of a headquarters emanated the sticky stench of rotting wood, clouds of dust and dirt, and occasionally, the unsettlingly loud crack of a beam adjusting its load. Light and ventilation clearly were not priorities when this "temporary" building was built decades before. The interior was dim; the smell of mold was everywhere. This distinctive smell stuck to your clothes and lingered on into the evening, even after you left work and returned home.

"It's only a building," I thought. "People who work here, people and their enthusiasm—that's what's important. Appearances don't matter."

When I reported to work, the fight for the director position was over. At the retirement of the old director, the reality of Communist bureaucracy took over. In this system, political loyalty was far more valuable than competence. The two deputy directors—Forestry Deputy Director Kłoda and Development Deputy Director Podstepny—bloodied themselves with guerrilla warfare against each other, spreading gossip and intrigue. Finally, tired of the dual denunciation spree, the District Committee of the Communist Party nominated an outsider to be the new director. The current staff remained in their former positions: two deputy directors who hated one another.

I had no idea about these people or why they had fought so viciously. An informed staff member made it clear: "They fight for power, to control the budget, for the payoffs from the semi-legal timber trade. And they fight to be lord of all the highlanders living in this mountain region."

This last comment was recognition that, in effect, the park director was in charge of the highlanders' livelihoods. Only he could determine if their logging was legal or if, perhaps, their tree felling extended into a "protected area."

The new director, Leon Mruk, took the position just two weeks before I came to work. "Love of the Mountains" didn't even make it onto the list of reasons that he had maneuvered himself into this job. "Advancement Opportunity" was, with near certainty, at the top of the list.

He did not know his deputies. He didn't know the mountains, nor did he understand the highlander dialect or the social problems created when private lands had been "nationalized" to create Tatra National Park. Locally, Leon Mruk had no friends and nobody he could trust. But he knew he could bully anyone and everyone. He had strong support from the Party District Committee. He was their man. He could do no wrong.

Deputy Director Podstepny was my immediate superior. He considered Mruk—rather than his own behavior—the cause of his misfortune. Although he was a Party member, Podstepny wasn't well connected, like Mruk. Podstepny was a disappointed party member and a sore loser to boot. He thought highly of himself, believed he deserved the director position, and blamed Mruk for his disappointment. Many years later, American president Donald Trump couldn't face a loss, right? *That* was Podstepny.

Interestingly, I liked Podstepny from our first handshake. Unlike Trump, he was slim, elegant, and full of ideas. He shared stories with me about his passions for nature photography and skiing. I quickly concluded Podstepny was to be the savior of the Tatra Mountains, whereas the party careerist, Mruk—a dumb, nasty egotist—might easily destroy rare habitats because of his appalling ignorance. During inevitable future fights, I would join Podstepny's side. His boss, that baby-faced apparatchik Mruk, would be my ideological enemy.

I was not fortunate enough to learn office politics at my mother's knee. An artist, she preferred painting to scheming. She neglected to admonish her naïve son, "No matter what, my boy, remember this: Follow Machiavelli's principles to the letter!" So I must admit that I was inexperienced and likely not a natural political talent.

As a teenager, however, I had once read *The Prince* with deep fascination. Mruk's Machiavellian strategy was obvious to me: "If you cannot be both, better to be feared than loved." Was I Machiavellian? No, but I could see that Mruk was.

* * *

My first years at Tatra National Park were wonderful. I led a carefree life. My boss, Podstepny, was in charge of park development, and as his only subordinate, I became his eyes and ears in the mountains. I was the king of fresh air. My job was to leave the office and "inspect" something: ski slopes on Kasprowy Wierch when fresh powder covered the summit, newly repaired rock trails through spectacular Zawrat Pass, or the Morskie Oko mountain chalet where they baked the best apple pie. I had lots to do. I never worried about a shortage of activity. I was a Polish John Muir. I loved the outdoors.

After a year of working alone, Deputy Podstepny, who wanted to make himself more important, hired two more university graduates: Voyteck and Les. Both were freshly baked foresters with master's degrees from renowned universities. Now Podstepny had three professional ecologists under him. He didn't become park director, but he certainly rose in status. Voyteck, Les, and I enjoyed one another's company. We knew we had but a slim chance of a promotion or a raise, but we had a lot of fun. It was like being continuously on vacation with my friends. I even started publishing stories and working toward my Ph.D.

Once while mountain-climbing high in the peaks, I encountered two French climbers. Pierre and Marie were friendly and well educated. They promised to arrange a stipend for me to climb the French Alps with them. Now I had a future to dream about—a future in France! Meanwhile, I felt quite virtuous saving the Tatras from trampling tourists, rock-chipping mountaineers, poaching highlanders, and scientists scaring "my" eagles.

My new coworkers helped me eagerly. We were the good guys. We were the bodyguards protecting Tatra National Park: Voyteck, Les, Aldek, and our boss, Podstepny! Together we mocked Director Mruk, who did not know the names of the mountain peaks, who was too out of shape to walk trails through the hills and forests.

"If I were a judge, I'd throw Mruk in jail on general principle, even if he committed no crime," I would tell my comrades. "Bloated, greedy bureaucrats should not be allowed to roam free!"

One day in the office we were drinking Polish "oolong tea," made of artificial dye and something smelly, definitely not tea leaves. We were pontificating about how long it would take for our teeth to turn brown.

With nothing better to do, we calculated how many cups we usually drank per day.

"Many cups."

"More than eight a day, I bet."

"Yes, but it's a harsh winter. We spend so many days in the office."

"Which is better: Do we dye our teeth brown, smoke cigarettes, and wait for spring, here in the midst of warmth and camaraderie, or would you rather go outside into a freezing blizzard?"

It was a cold winter. Tourists stayed in their hotels; we stayed in our office. More than a meter of snow had fallen in the Tatra valleys. No wonder our boss, Deputy Director Podstepny, had gone to Warsaw to the forestry ministry on business matters. Probably working hard to set a new trap for Mruk or leave a new denunciation to destroy Deputy Director Kłoda's career.

The telephone rang.

I was the leader of our section, the only one with a telephone on his desk. I picked it up.

"Hello, Department of Development," I announced proudly.

"Mr. Roman?" Director Mruk recognized my voice. "I need you immediately in my office."

"Something strange must have happened," I thought. "Why is he calling me?"

Without delay, I rushed to his office, a modern, well-lit, and airy addition to our crumbling building. In the Party, rank had its privilege.

The rotund man was sitting at his desk. In front of him on a chair was Deputy Kłoda, the man in charge of the Forestry Department. In the corner was Bachleda, a shy forest ranger from the Chochołowska Valley.

"Do you know how to shoot, Mr. Roman?" asked Director Mruk.

"Yes, sir!"

He looked at me unconvinced then continued. "Then take the GAZ SUV with a driver, go to the place that this forest ranger will show you"—he didn't remember Bachleda's name, of course, but the forester nodded vigorously—"and shoot the sick chamois that's stuck deep in the snow. When you get back, you will write me a report that the animal could not be saved, and you will leave it here on my desk. Now tell me, do you know which closet we keep the rifles in?"

I nodded. "Well then, open it with this." He handed me a key. "And finally, go to Mr. Kubrak, show him the gun, and tell him to give you ammunition. Five bullets, in case you miss. You understand everything?"

"Yes, sir!"

"That's good. Now get to work."

"Yes, sir!"

* * *

A choice made in the moment, a single impulse … At the time, you have no idea that you will pay for your choice for a lifetime, if not even into the next life. These moments live in memory for years and years. They suddenly seize your consciousness when you least expect it again and again. We re-experience every detail of a bad decision over and over.

Leaving Mruk's office, I didn't understand how a regrettable decision could poison the future with wasted yesterdays too painful to recall. No, those thoughts never occurred to me.

I don't believe I thought at all. Quite happy to take on the mission, I ran to our office to invite Les and Voyteck to accompany me. They also deserved some adventure. Excited, we rushed to the garages, where a designated driver already awaited us.

"To Chochołowska, Driver Marian!" I commanded.

"I know; Transportation Manager Lizuk already told me," he responded.

We're off to Chochołowska Valley. It would take two hours in a heavy snowfall.

* * *

The chamois was about a hundred meters from the road—a big, old male, larger than domesticated goats. The beast had only one broken horn and only one eye. His stocky body was covered with thick brown-black hair. He probably broke off the other horn and lost one of his eyes in battle for a female when he was healthy and much younger, many springs ago. Now approaching death, the old male lay on his side in deep snow without even the strength to lift his head. He'd given up, no more energy to fight for life, only desperation showed in his bloodshot, half-closed eye.

"You know what? Maybe instead of you, I could shoot him?" suggested an overzealous Voyteck.

"No way. Leon ordered *me* to kill the chamois." Among ourselves we called Director Mruk by his first name, "Leon." I went on to remind Voyteck I was the oldest, the first in the line for promotion, and thus first in line to kill the chamois. "Everything clear?"

"OK," agreed Voyteck reluctantly.

"Beautiful chamois," Les muttered under his breath. "Why is he so weak?"

"From the cold, from lack of food," I explained hesitantly.

"So maybe if we feed him, he'll recover?" Les wondered.

"And we wouldn't have to shoot him?" added Voyteck, continuing the thought.

We paused, undecided, yet feeling for the dying chamois. He was one of only 153 mountain chamois that, according to the most recent "Animal Census in Tatra National Park" report, live on the Polish side of the Tatra Mountains. If we shot him, only a 152 Tatra chamois would remain. An endangered species, if there ever was one! We stood silently, waiting for a sign from Providence. We hesitated. We knew that Director Leon Mruk ordered the animal to be killed. At the same time, our temptation to save it was strong. And each of us probably thought the same thing: How could we possibly kill this magnificent animal?

Providence spoke to us through the words of the only highlander among us, Driver Marian Chotarski: "You know how important the Tatra chamois is for Polish highlanders, the Górale? Listen to this song first, and then decide whether to kill the chamois." With that, in a raspy, singsong voice, with strong crescendos followed by whispering diminuendos, Chotarski sang a hauntingly beautiful song in mountain *gwara*, the local dialect. I understood most of the words he sang; the drama and emotion needed no translation. Later on, I spent the evening drinking beer with Chotarski and asked him to teach me the song. He sang it slowly and softly, pausing after each verse as I wrote down the words. Years later I translated it into English:

The Tatra Chamois

Look at me jump ahead
Over crevice, under ledge
Rump muscles in rotation
Shoulders strain in formation
"Rat-a-tat," hooves resound
Sparks ignite, granite pounds
Silent glide in Lichen Glade
Splash right through Rainbow Cascade

> Breathe with ease, make a rally
> On up the Strążyska Valley
> Hips a-rock, hips a-roll
> Climb the Northern Giewont Wall
> Sheep in meadow? I say "Bah!"
> Be like me—a Tatra chamois!

That afternoon, with the one-eyed beast almost motionless in the snow, we listened to our highland colleague, fascinated by the rustic beauty of the song and the twinkle in his eye as he leaned into occasional suggestive words: "rump muscles" … "shoulders strain" … "sparks ignite" … "hips a-rock, hips a-roll." How the highlanders enjoyed their music!

When the last words faded away, a moment of quiet …

It was Les who broke the silence. "How can this be? Here we are, three outspoken defendants of the Tatra Mountains. Can we kill an endangered animal so loved by the local people?"

"Yeah, I know. We don't allow mountaineers to climb in reserved areas, and we chase off aged mushroom-pickers. That's what we do. We don't slaughter helpless beasts!" Voyteck offered.

"How can we be ecology 'heroes,' stand here over a legally protected animal, and ask each other who will pull the trigger?" My indignation was complete.

Meanwhile, Chotarski said nothing. He kept his silence, waiting to see if we were done confirming our self-righteousness.

Finally, the highlander spoke up. "Well. What's your decision, guys? Are you taking this chamois somewhere to save it or … a bullet in the head?"

"And … what about Director Mruk?" I asked hesitantly.

"The fat man? We will carry the chamois to the garage and tell him we're going to take care of the animal," the driver responded.

"We?"

"Come on! I'm gonna help you, and other coworkers will help you. It's a beautiful chamois. We shouldn't allow it to die!"

So the four of us hefted the old chamois onto a blanket and into the rear of the SUV. Chotarski drove down to our park headquarters and parked next to the garages behind the administration building. Once more, each holding a corner of the old blanket, the four of us transported the chamois from the SUV to an empty garage. We laid the chamois on the floor in the empty, unheated space, leaving a bucket of water and hay in front of him. Chotarski informed the other drivers and the mechanics that a sick chamois was temporarily in the garage while in recovery. They wanted to help, so they brought a pile of snow and a few small fir trees to create more natural surroundings for the patient. When my colleagues returned to the office to make calls for volunteers to help us, I dragged myself to Director Mruk's office to report.

* * *

The old man pretended not to see me for a moment. Then he raised his head, gave me a piercing look with his watery eyes, and asked:

"Did you follow my orders?"

"Er … " I couldn't get my voice out.

"I ask, did you shoot the chamois, Mr. Roman?"

"No."

"And why is that? Did I not order you to shoot it?"

"Yes, sir. You ordered it. But … but when my coworkers and I saw that the animal could survive, we decided to try to save it."

"You and your coworkers? Who was there with you? Did I tell you to take anyone with you?"

"No, sir. But I only took my coworkers from Director Podstepny's department, Voyteck Wyszyński and and Les Porowski. I thought it'd be a learning experience."

"*Jasna cholera!* You three decide to disregard my official order and play Good Samaritan at the expense of the park? Was it your boss Podstepny who trained you so well against me? On what authority? Where did you get this idea from? How could you fumble the first opportunity I give you? I thought you had potential!"

I was silent. What could I say?

"I will tell you now," Mruk raised his voice "that I will not give you one penny for your negligence. Pay for the treatment of this chamois from your own salary. I will remember what you did. Insubordination and … stupidity. Get out!"

I returned to our office, devastated.

Once I was away from Leon, I found that our office was boiling with activity. It didn't matter that the stinky smoke of *Sport* cigarettes made a murky haze through which we saw silhouettes but couldn't make out features. The only telephone was working to the limit, connecting us to big cities in Poland. We wanted to find a suitable home for our chamois.

Les had called two zoos, in Cracow and in Warsaw, but both refused to save our patient because, as they said, a wild chamois could not be healed outside of its natural environment.

So we would be the first to do it!

Fortunately, Voyteck was more successful than Les: He talked to a local veterinarian who promised to visit us and examine the animal within an hour.

Lizuk Lidki, the supervisor of our park's drivers, promised he would turn a blind eye to the fact that his crew helped us shelter the chamois. Then he called his wife, a pharmacist, and she promised to "arrange" any medications prescribed by the vet.

I told my colleagues about my conversation with Leon, but my account of his rage didn't make an impression. Understandably so, since

I was the one exposed to the director's vengeance, not them. It was I who given the order and I who disobeyed it. Why should they be concerned? When I finished telling of my encounter in his office, Voyteck laughed and suggested:

"You know what? Since our chamois does not have a name yet, due to Director Leon Mruk's extremely friendly attitude toward the animal, let's call our new pet 'Leoś,' the diminutive of 'Leon.' What do you say?"

Everyone laughed. So in honor of the distinguished apparatchik and director of Tatra National Park, Leon Mruk, we named our patient "Leoś," our "little Leon."

At 5 p.m., when even the most hardworking managers went home, we moved Operation Save Leoś to the garage. We cleaned up the part of the room where old tools were kept, removing everything. We sprinkled the cement floor with snow, then added a few spruce branches; it was the driver's idea to make Leoś feel like he was at home in the Chochołowska Valley. We put hay next to the chamois's mouth so that he could eat lying down. We recreated a natural environment as best we could.

The garage was only slightly warmer than outside. The veterinarian, Dr. Wolski, arrived to see Leoś. We watched with great trepidation as the elderly gentleman examined the barely breathing animal. We awaited his opinion: Would the patient survive?

The doctor observed Leoś for twenty minutes then concluded, "I haven't found any visible injuries. It looks like you were right, and it's just age, the snowstorm, and starvation. This is an old animal; when conditions are harsh in the mountains, the old ones go first. We'll find out soon enough. For now, I'm going to give him intravenous glucose and vitamins, and in the morning we'll see if he feels better or not. And here's a prescription because it won't end with one intravenous drip. When I come tomorrow morning, I may prescribe more medications."

We were happy with Leoś's diagnosis.

"And how much we owe you, Dr. Wolski?"

"Gentlemen, why do you even ask? Of course—nothing. We all do it for Leoś, to save this magnificent beast!"

We thanked the doctor and the drivers (in the coming days they'd keep their promise to help). We left for dinner full of optimism. One issue was still open: How would our boss, Podstepny, react when he returned from Warsaw? We had two days until his return. Somehow, it would be OK.

Late, but with hearts aglow with our actions to save the chamois, I returned home. My wife Marta had prepared a delicious dinner. Usually she told me to eat first then tell her what happened later. This time, she was so impatient that she didn't protest when I ate and talked at the same time. I told her everything. Each word, each gesture, I repeated to her the entire list of Good Samaritan deeds we accomplished. When I finished, I proudly waited for her to applaud my achievements.

Marta listened up to the moment when we started our full-blown battle to save the chamois and proved to Director Mruk that we young John Muirs were able to oppose his soulless order.

Silence. But you know women, don't you? I believe sometimes they don't understand the depth of a husband's emotion nor the importance of his decisions—especially if it involves a long, complicated story. My story was long. It took half an hour to describe the basic events without even going into my emotions or the possible repercussions of my decision.

"Say something," I said, seeing her rise from her chair and move toward the sink to do the dishes.

"There is nothing I can say," she responded coldly.

And until the end of the evening, she did not say a word. Was she angry? Was she afraid we'd be in trouble? Did she think I should have followed orders and killed an innocent, protected Tatra chamois? It was a mystery to me. All my actions were on the side of saving a life. How could she find fault with that?

Fortunately, the next day, my friends and I were so busy that I forgot about Marta and her moods. In the early morning, the three of us met outside the garage. We eagerly opened the door and looked into the gloomy interior. Almost invisible in the dim light, Leoś stood in the farthest corner of the room. He stood! His one eye attentively watched us as we first moved toward him. He then bowed his head, as if to attack, and swayed menacingly, almost shaking with anger.

After several seconds, he spread his front legs apart, lowered himself, and ... urinated. Slowly, like a slow-motion video, he then collapsed to the floor. We closed the door and waited in the street for the vet, not wanting to scare the animal again. Doctor arrived soon and was pleased that Leoś was able to get up on his own.

"It's normal that his strength wears off after a few seconds," he said. "But now that we know he's recovering, we can give him more medications."

Together with Dr. Wolski, we entered the garage. Leoś was too weak to get up a second time, and the doctor injected him with antibiotics provided by Lizuk's wife. Then he taught us how to use a big rubber squeeze bottle to force a solution of food and vitamins into the animal's open mouth.

"You need four men to feed him," he said. "But, gentlemen, you must practice this activity now, while the animal lies weakened, so he does not break free. One of you hold his hind legs, the other his front legs, the third Leoś's head, and then, the fourth will squeeze the food right down into his throat. When you finish feeding, everyone must jump back on command, so that Leoś doesn't hurt you."

"Thank you, Doctor! But don't worry about us. It's a piece of cake. We can do it!"

We practiced—only once, but it went well.

The next morning when we opened the door, we found the same situation as before: Leoś waiting for us, his head bowed menacingly, his determined gaze shifting from one of us to the next.

Only this time, there was no cowardly peeing. Oh, no! As soon as we took a first step toward him, Leoś bounded on all four legs to attack. We barely escaped! Had he been stronger, he would have reached us in a single leap, and we wouldn't have escaped from this "raging bull" chamois. Thanks be to God, we survived!

But what to do now? No doctor could advise what to do; Leoś was a dangerous warrior. That was something medicine could not cure. We entered into heated discussion outside the garage door. In our excitement, we didn't notice that our boss, Podstepny, was present and listening. He had returned a day earlier than expected. Seeing him, we told him everything that had happened during his absence: Mruk's order to kill the animal and how we had collectively gone against the evil Leon.

His face brightened with understanding.

"And you named this chamois Leoś? Oh, that's great. I wonder now who will be the first to inform the old man that the chamois is named after him! You are brave! Bravo, boys! So now … do you have any idea what to do next?"

"Well, actually, no, because he jumps amazingly far. And with his single horn, he could nail a man to the door! He is dangerous."

"I understand. You should use a piece of plywood."

"So he'll stab his horn into it when he tries to gore us?" Les asked.

"Exactly!" Podstepny was a smart man.

Within a few minutes, a friendly car mechanic found us a large piece of six-ply plywood. Podstepny commanded, "Open the door." In front of us, we held our shield against Leoś's piercing horn.

* * *

Leoś expected us and was prepared to fight. We, too, were prepared.

We moved slowly toward him. He waited, glowering at us, waited a bit more, then tensed up, and suddenly: Attack!

He smashed into the plywood between Voyteck and Les. But the blunt tip of his horn failed to puncture the plywood. Leoś bounced back. Addled from the impact, he stood uncertainly. That's when we jumped him.

Les seized his front legs, Voyteck got his rear legs, and I grabbed his horn in one hand and the hair on the top of head in the other. Podstepny—our boss—put the tip of the bottle into Leoś's mouth and poured the glucose solution down his throat! The chamois snorted, then choked, but a big swallow of the medicine went down.

Patient care accomplished, escape became our top priority. Afraid Leoś might kick us, we edged backward toward the door. I made the high-pitched whistle I'd been practicing. It mimics an alarm signal that a chamois gives when danger nears. We are not dangerous, being park rangers, but Leoś had no way of knowing that. Ultimately, though, both sides being too tired to fight, we slowly backed away. He never attacked us. He watched but did not follow. I'd say he conceded victory in that clash.

Podstepny was proud of our teamwork and accomplishments.

"I wonder if Mruk watched from the window," he said. "If he did, he must be steamed now." Podstepny savored our moral resistance to needless killing, gleefully imagining how Mruk might have responded.

By the way, Podstepny was right: Mruk had a view of the garage door from his window, and he could easily have seen the melee with Leoś. Probably did.

We wanted to keep it secret that in one of the Tatra National Park buildings a few employees were tending a sick chamois they found in Chochołowska Valley. "Let's avoid sensationalism, people peeking in at the garage door, visits from the local press, or phone calls to park management," Podstepny said, even though publicity would have infuriated Mruk even more.

Mruk was already grinding his teeth just thinking about my disobedience; it would be hard to imagine his temperament if our good works were publicized. Even Podstepny was too cautious to exceed certain limits when annoying the old man. We decided to keep our mouths shut, even at home. If asked about Leoś, our response would be, "Baseless gossip!"

On his third visit, Dr. Wolski advised us that if Leoś was stronger the next day, we could start feeding him carrots, cabbage—any vegetables we could take from our wives' kitchens. Within hours, a pile of food sat in the corner of the garage. Everybody wanted to share food with Leoś.

Keep in mind, this was 1976, when the government had failed to curb the downward economic spiral. Even with billions in foreign loans, Poland had entered a period of severe food rationing. You couldn't find sugar in the stores, or meat, or cooking oil. Poland's agricultural products, as well as most of our manufactured goods, were shipped to Russia for foreign exchange. We Poles were left holding the bag, and the bag was empty.

Meanwhile, we continued to call zoos, inquiring if a successfully rehabilitated Leoś might live in their facilities until spring. They were reluctant. Here's what they told us: "First, your animal hasn't healed yet. And second, we have no space and no money for animals that don't attract visitors. Your old, sick goat is no panda. Now, a panda we'll take! That would bring fame and visitors to the zoo." Also I suspect they foresaw problems because if, God forbid, the chamois died, people would say, "What a shame that the national park saved the animal, only for the zoo to kill it."

We finally realized nobody wanted Leoś! It was hard to take in. From time to time, his "patron," Director Mruk, sent spies to our office: Kubrak, the spare parts manager; Trzebuniowa, the double-dealing accounting clerk; and Lizuk, the office manager, who was skilled at playing two sides simultaneously. They visited, one after another, offering a bottle of glucose, or a bowl of oat gruel, pretending to want to help, while reporting back to Mruk everything about our chamois. Thanks to this infiltration by the hostile camp, the old man knew our plans. No problem! Let him know everything! We'd been successful so far.

On the third day, we saw with our own eyes that Leoś was eating hay and vegetables in large quantities.

On the fourth day, his huge appetite surprised us. Then his appetite increased even more. Day after day, it was harder and harder to feed him. We began to allow people to see Leoś but only on the condition that they would provide food or money for his upkeep.

Our main problem now was how to manage everything until spring. Lizuk demanded that we return the part of the garage we were using to keep Leoś, so we started searching for a nearby empty stable or shed to keep our chamois. The few highlanders living in this area demonstrated their lack of altruism. They refused us. Routine feeding was no longer fun, either because Leoś had become more aggressive and stronger. It was not dangerous but more of an obligatory chore to take care of him. Our initial success in healing the wild animal made our lives complicated.

But not for long.

After thirteen days, as we did every morning, we went into the garage to clean up. We still used the piece of plywood as a shield when we brought a new batch of food. We were careful, ready to defend ourselves, but Leoś didn't attack. He appeared dejected and tired. We found a pool of red urine in the spot where he had spent the night. Blood!

We called Dr. Wolski at once. He listened carefully but refused to examine the animal.

"This is bad news," he said. "If Leoś has blood in his urine, it means he has a kidney infection. I'm not qualified to perform kidney surgery, especially on a chamois. Who is? Nobody. I'm sorry, gentlemen, but I can't help you."

The next day, Leoś died.

Dr. Wolski performed an autopsy and found the real cause of Leoś's struggle to survive had been that he had five bullets from small-caliber weapons in his kidneys. Was he shot by biathlon athletes? They are known to use chamois as a moving target while training to run and shoot in the Chochołowska Valley, we heard. After bringing Leoś to the garage and administering antibiotics, we helped him fight his first infection, but the bullets in his kidneys were still there. Leoś had to die. We extended his life by twelve days.

Sad.

Bloody sad.

None of us cried, after all this, because we were too ashamed. Everyone, however, even our boss Podstepny, was tight in the throat with regret. What bastards, those biathlonists! How could somebody be so brainless and so cruel? They kill animals for fun, and they call themselves atheletes?

After a few days, I ran into Director Mruk in the corridor. He stopped and regarded me sternly.

"Have you learned anything, Mr. Roman, or are you still stupid?"

I didn't answer; I was unsure of what he meant. Was it stupid to disobey him?

But a year or so later, when I was invited by my friends from Club Alpine Française to climb the French Alps, Director Mruk refused to let me go, with a clear and firm "no." When I needed his signature to work on my Ph.D., he again said "no." And when there was an opening in the office, and I applied for a promotion, he said "no" again. He was punishing me for disobedience. I had proven I was not loyal to him.

So what did I learn from the Leoś story? Beware of noble impulses? Choose your prospective patrons with an eye to Party politics? Calculate each step? I am not good at any of that.

What if … if I had shot Leoś, as ordered? Then I could have climbed the Alps in France and written a highly touted Ph.D. dissertation. Would I have one day replaced Mruk as the new park director? Would I have been embraced and protected by the Party?

A more important question is, would I have been happier than I am now?

Perhaps, but I don't think so. I quietly croon an Edith Piaf song to myself in celebration of my life of noble disobedience:

Non, rien de rien
Non, je ne regrette rien …

A sparhawk proud did hold in wicked jail
Music's sweet chorister, the Nightingale
To whom with sighs she said: "O set me free,
And in my song I'll praise no bird but thee."
The Hawk replied: "I will not lose my diet
To let a thousand such enjoy their quiet."

—"The Sparhawk," Alfred, Lord Tennyson

OTTO THE SPARROWHAWK

The sparrowhawk is not a nice bird. The few blue feathers on its head are almost invisible, and the rest of the body is gray and brown—camouflage colors for the hawk's quest to kill. The sparrowhawk is small, and it kills even smaller birds—mostly sparrows, doves, and songbirds, including, as Lord Tennyson noticed, nightingales. This killer prefers small birds to rodents or insects. Thus, sparrowhawks don't kill our enemies—mice, flies or mosquitos. They kill larks, thrushes, and hummingbirds—birds that lighten our days with songs and fun-to-watch activities.

The only "use" for sparrowhawks—and this was centuries ago—was falconry. In seventeenth-century England, reflecting their lowly status, priests hunted with sparrowhawks, not falcons. Even earlier, in the Middle Ages, small-sized sparrowhawks were the choice of ladies in pre-feminist recognition of the fairer sex's "fragility."

Medieval falconers' name for a male sparrowhawk was "musket," derived from the Latin word *musca*, meaning "a fly." A nasty fly, to be sure, able to enter people's homes to chase a cardinal and eager to prey on the warblers sitting at the bird feeders. This "fly" can rip a quail apart in seconds or even destroy a pigeon. Pigeons take longer to succumb, tortured by the sparrowhawk's cruelly curved beak for a minute or more before the spark of life disappears from their eyes.

No wonder that in 1976, the sparrowhawk was the only bird of prey that hunters were allowed to kill with a rifle. Shooting at other Tatra raptors—peregrine falcons, golden eagles, Eurasian pygmy owls, or common kestrels—was highly illegal with serious penalties.

But sparrowhawks? Open season. You could shoot 'em down at high noon right in front of park headquarters. No problem. Farmers blasted them with buckshot, young lads went after them with slingshots, and nobody felt sorry for the wren-eaters and warbler-killers.

But I did not follow that murderous trend. No. Instead, I saved the life of a sparrowhawk. In return, the sparrowhawk fed my family during a time of hunger.

* * *

1976. A disastrous year for Poland. Our agricultural production was shipped to Russia to make up for poor harvests there. We Poles call that political era "late Gierek" because it was the second half of Edward Gierek's leadership of the Party and nation. In 1970, he promised Poles a good life—in fact, a wonderful life. There was one condition:

In celebration of the wise leadership of the Party that created such a wonderful Communist society, we all had to join hands and, as one nation, with one spirit, work harder than ever before.

"Will you help me?" he asked on TV, radio, and the garish posters pasted on each storefront and every utility pole.

"We will! We will!" Gierek's fellow Poles passionately responded.

People worked harder. Gierek borrowed money from the East and West to build huge factories. His aim was to increase GDP by boosting steel and coal production. In anticipation of the new world evolving from his visionary imagination, he spent borrowed money to increase salaries. He filled stores with Western products, from Tabasco sauce to Levi's jeans, so Poles could have a taste of their new world even before creating it. Alas, the dream began to falter when bankers said, "Time to pay us back."

The Russians pointed out: "Your steel was produced with our ore, so pay us back." Lend more money to Gierek? No way. Everybody wanted their money back from him. From *him*? No! From us, the people! But we had already used our money to buy blue jeans. We'd burned our tongues with exotic (and expensive) Tabasco. Sorry, no dollars to return to Western bankers, no rubles for the Russians. In 1975, the economy collapsed, and God did not grant us a good harvest. Winters were cold, but Polish coal was shipped to the West and to the Soviet Union to repay foreign debt. So we froze that winter. By summer, severe hunger had started.

Oh, how it all changed in just five years! I still remember 1971 well. Many stores, most newly opened, thrived in my town that year. At Parfumerie de France you could buy French perfumes and Italian shampoos. Papeteria sold school supplies, including beautiful Chinese fountain pens and leather knapsacks made in Germany. Even Warzywa i Owoce now carried an array of fresh organic fruits and vegetables. Cured hams, smoked cold cuts, and French cheeses were found at Delikatesy. Each store had a unique, welcoming aroma—a cloud of exotic scents from the Parfumerie, the subtle aroma of fine leather, the slightly acrid smell of cured meat.

Did I mention that in 1971 Poles also discovered a delicious drink called Pepsi? Our beloved poet Agnieszka Osiecka won the national contest to invent their simple, catchy slogan for Poland: *"Pepsi, to jest to!"* or "Pepsi, this is it!" Since that time, to the Polish palate, Pepsi and stuffed cabbage *gołąbki* has tasted far better than champagne and caviar. Imported products were exciting and exotic. The Pepsi campaign was so successful that in the 1990s they created an English version for the U.S. market: "Pepsi! The cola is it!" They chose our Polish slogan because it was much catchier than the Hindi slogan they used in India. *"Yeh hai Youngistaan Meri Jaan!"*—"This is the young era, my dear!" Huh?

Ah, those were the days, my friend.

Within five years, that wonderful time was but a memory. Store shelves emptied. No sugar, no bread, no radios, no furniture, nothing. People with money who wanted to buy something—let's say, a stove— would find that stoves all across Poland had disappeared from stores. So they bought ... a refrigerator! They felt so lucky to spot it, the last refrigerator for sale in town, or maybe even in Poland.

But the lack of stoves or refrigerators was not the worst problem. The lack of food was life-threatening. The government issued coupons to ration sustenance to the population. The rations were not enough to feed us properly but enough to keep us alive as we gradually lost weight. There were coupons for sugar, meat, alcohol, cigarettes, even soap. On each coupon there were specified qualities and quantities.

Unfortunately, within a few weeks, there were far more coupons than products. People waited in lines day and night. Children helped parents. Retirees offered to stay in line for an hourly wage. People who desperately needed something spent money for "standers." Unemployment reached zero because anybody could find a job as a "night line-stander."

The entire population—except Party dignitaries—became accustomed to waiting in long lines and dreaming the store they were lined up in front of would receive a delivery the moment they reached the counter. Desperate potential shoppers would buy anything available, even a tired radish or limp carrot.

Anything, that is, but white vinegar. Poland's two white vinegar factories enthusiastically competed with one another, and suddenly there was enough white vinegar to supply the nation for a decade. Gradually hundreds of bottles of vinegar accumulated on the shelves because families already had bottles at home. Abundant vinegar—the one accomplishment of the Polish People's Republic's socialist economy.

During that time I was still working in Tatra National Park as an ecologist and park ranger. This was a transitional phase of my "career" in Poland. Two months earlier, I had raised the director's ire when I disobeyed his order to euthanize a rare Tatra chamois. Fortunately, it would be another couple of months before I screamed at him what I really thought about his plan to transform Tatra National Park into a hunting ground for Party apparatchiks. But that's another story. The point is that I still had a job I loved, and I was glad to hang on to my meager salary.

As you may recall, what I didn't like about the job was Director Mruk. I despised his ignorance about our precious national park as much as I despised the way he used his position to curry favor with the Party. He would invite big shots to visit and give them illegal venison—seized from poachers, cut into steaks, and chilled in boxes of ice—as a token of his appreciation. This gesture would occur after a brief tour and a gigantic meal at Casa Maria, the most expensive restaurant in

Zakopane, where they would leave a big table littered with drained wine bottles, empty beer steins, cigar butts, and greasy spills.

Yes, my job had its frustrations. On the other hand, it was easy. My fellow employees, like me, had no desire to go elsewhere. Why give up our leisurely existence? And Deputy Podstepny, our supervisor, had no time for us or for *his* work. He found another passion, unrelated to this story, so I won't burden you who it was. Suffice it to say that our supervisor left us unsupervised.

Director Mruk, however, observed and remembered every mistake, lapse, or stumble. He knew he had a group of rebels in his office. I was the ringleader. I was the one who disobeyed his direct order and refused to shoot that distressed chamois. But time had passed. As long we avoided rocking the boat, everything seemed back to normal. Mruk now had little time to monitor us. When he wasn't traveling to attend Party meetings, he was welcoming Party dignitaries to Zakopane. His focus was on his main responsibility: to secure the favor of Party higher-ups and advance his career by means of obsequious loyalty.

Months went by. One day, an alarming call rippled our peaceful existence at Tatra National Park Headquarters. I had left my office and was walking down the hall, proudly showing off my private roll of toilet paper on the way to conduct some business. So it was Les who answered the phone ringing on my desk. It was from the Academic Sanatorium Kotelnica:

"Hello! Is this Tatra National Park?"

"Yes, Department of Development, Les Porowski speaking. What can I do for you?" In those days, Les was polite even when somebody interrupted his work on the daily crossword.

"A wild bird crashed against our window, and we don't know what to do with it. Too small to be a hawk, but its claws are huge. Could you advise us?"

"Is it alive?"

"Yes, but it's lost consciousness."

When he hung up, Les shouted with enthusiasm and at a decibel level available only to young lungs:

"Who wants to ride with me to bring a hawk to the office?"

He was so loud that I even heard him in the restroom. Was he inviting the entire park staff, all thirty employees, for an emergency visit to save a bird? I had to disappoint them.

"We have no room for spectators representing other departments, nor was a car approved to take you with us," I informed the interested others. Les owned a fifteen-year-old bike, a Polish Junak 350cc, so we didn't have to use the Park's SUV. Better to avoid an accusation of spending government money.

The bike emitted an impressive guttural growl that increased in volume as we turned uphill. Les rode like a master biker. No car could outrun a Junak. We roared up to the impressive sanatorium building on the slopes of Kotelnica Hill, just outside Zakopane. When we pulled up to the portico, two long, loud "vrooooooms" followed by two short, loud "vrooms" thundered from his exhaust as Les performed his pre-dismount ritual before shutting off the engine.

As we strode to the door, two nurses ran out. They had been waiting at the window for the park naturalists to arrive: beautiful, young women in white, starched aprons, one with straight blond hair cascading from her nurse's cap to her shoulders, the other with dark hair and noble breasts. They excitedly told their story, one interrupting the other:

"It hit that window! We thought that it was a stone. But it didn't catch the bird!"

"I looked for blood on the glass, but no, nothing."

"Is it a young hawk? It is so small!"

"Will it survive?"

So many questions we couldn't answer. We knew as little as these ladies. Well, maybe a little more, because we recognized the species. It was a sparrowhawk. And it was tiny, so it was definitely a male because females are almost twice as large. But would he survive? In all Poland, probably, no one knew the survival rate of sparrowhawks that smash into windows in pursuit of avian prey. But as you will see, we created an important data point to help resolve this question, if anybody ever looks into it.

We pretended to be wise ornithologists and experienced foresters. We assured the comely lasses that we would do our best and let them know within a few days whether the bird had healed or not. Hearing the "not healed" option, their mood saddened.

Les took advantage of their distress. He immediately asked the one with large breasts for her phone number. She glanced at his right hand, saw his finger wasn't blemished by a gold ring, then quickly wrote down a few numbers on a piece of paper. With envy I looked at my younger friend. He could enjoy his bachelor status, but as for me, now already married three years and with a little daughter, I suffered the connubial complaints of Marta, who was dissatisfied with my salary. The current plateau on our family's climb up the socioeconomic ladder she attributed to my lack of initiative to "do something." Nope. I couldn't think about pretty girls. I didn't dare. Better to think about the hawk, Mr. Roman, not about nurses.

OK, back to the hawk: The smallest of the Polish birds of prey, the sparrowhawk, a fearless warrior, weighs less than an apple. An upstart crow could tear one apart. The sparrowhawk hunts only for sparrows, small songbirds, wrens, and finches. It has a healthy appetite and must catch at least two small birds a day or go hungry.

Tiny and agile, the birds are hyper-alert to any hint of a predator. When alarmed, they can instantly cut and turn in any direction.

Sparrowhawks don't have an easy time filling their bellies. Hence, the boldness of these feathered murderers has no equal.

We all regarded this miniature gangster lying almost lifeless on the grass. We surmised that he had chased his intended victim up to the sanatorium window. The escaping bird, lighter and more maneuverable, would have made a full U-turn just in front of the glass, but the heavier sparrowhawk would have bashed into it with its full weight of 150 grams. When I picked him up and placed him into a cardboard box, I didn't feel much life in the tiny body. But who knows? Maybe he would recover? Maybe he'd survive the impact?

We bade the nurses farewell and returned to our office with the box and its comatose contents.

We knew Director Mruk, through his spies, would sooner or later learn about it if we hid a wounded creature in one of the park buildings. Of course, it is much easier to hide a sparrowhawk than, say, a chamois. But if he found out we had a private agenda and were not following his agenda exclusively, steam would come out of his ears.

On our way back, we decided we couldn't keep the sparrowhawk anyplace frequented by staff. Les informed me that "somehow" he had procured the only key to a worker's apartment that was partially demolished but that had one serviceable room. Perfect! We left the bird lying in the open cardboard box, padlocked the door, and returned to work.

Cautiously we approached the office, waiting for some reaction against us. But no bad news came from Director Mruk. None of his minions had denounced us. We had successfully carried out our secret mission, and no one knew. Ahhh! Now we could loll at our desks, put water on for tea, and return to solving the "important matters" of the park.

"So what will we name him?" I started what turned into a heated discussion.

"Why name him?" the environmentally correct Voyteck objected, as always. "Naming a wild animal suggests you want to tame it."

"We will tame him and train him," Les cut him off immediately. He had already visualized himself as a falconer, showing his tame bird of prey to the pretty nurse.

"Train him?" Voyteck asked. "What do you want to teach him?"

"We'll teach him to chase and attack you. He will tear your hair out and pluck your ears to a bloody mess." Les already had a fully developed program for our bird.

"So from now on, Voyteck, you will have to wear a helmet at your desk," I riffed on Les's idea.

"Idiots! Nasty idiots! I'm leaving! I will not help you!"

Although offended, Voyteck didn't leave. Our tea was still brewing. He loved strong tea, and on top of that, on that particular day we were brewing leaves of genuine Madras tea. Unbeknownst to the rest of the park employees, this imported tea was given to us by speleologists from the West. Of course, we issued them a special permit to explore Zimna Cave. "A permit for tea?" you might ask. Well, the real engine of Communism worked far below the surface of administrative regulations. We played this game on a small scale—what's wrong with that? Of course, imagine applying for a permit to build a highway. How much Madras tea would it cost to obtain such a permit? An enormous amount! Is this why Poland had no real highways back then?

The tea was ready, and Voyteck filled his huge mug. I told him it had only been a joke. He wanted us to say "sorry," so we did—as always. He was basically a decent guy, and his anger never lasted. Voyteck knew that at times he was too serious and too hardworking. Such behavior is counterproductive. We never let management know that operations would be more efficient if our diligence equalled Voyteck's. We had explained to Voyteck more than once that working hard does none of us any good; it only increases output quotas. He couldn't turn off the diligent nature that was core to his being, though, so from time to time he suffered our teasing.

"We have to find some food for the bird. And his name is Otto," I proclaimed, changing the topic to more pressing issues.

"But what? What will Otto eat?" Les wondered.

"Sparrows, tits, finches." Scholarly Voyteck could list all the tasty birds preyed upon by our hawk.

"Bravo, Voyteck!" I exclaimed. "Then go outside and grab a few tits for Otto or maybe a few sparrows. What is it to you? It's easy!"

"Gimme a break! You guys stop talking nonsense. If you're so wise"—he looked at me sideways—"you'd go out yourself and bring back a piece of fresh meat for the bird. But not earthworms and flies, no. Something bloody, like a fresh steak. Well? Are you glued to your chair?"

I looked sadly at Voyteck. After more than two years of my being his mentor, instead of respect toward me, he showed arrogance. Arrogance toward me! I'd worked in the park two years longer. I had showed him the ropes. Eh! People … Never thankful. No virtue in their hearts! Disappointed in Voyteck, I got up, gave my colleagues a contemptuous look, and strolled proudly toward the door.

I walked down the hallway absentmindedly, ignoring what was going on in other offices. Still lost in thought, I left the building and walked mechanically toward a tiny cluster of shops a couple hundred meters from the park.

A piece of fresh meat. The thoughts I was lost in were full of vivid memories of food from the past: a Wiener schnitzel so huge that it was almost as big as the plate. Crispy crust, white juicy meat inside, or … smoked sausage with garlic, or … medium rare filet mignon … I couldn't stand it. This was too much! When was the last time I saw a piece of fresh meat? Not frozen, not stringy-bony, but an actual piece of fresh steak. A few years ago. But where? And when? I did not remember. Socialism had killed the memory of fresh meat in me. As if I were in a dream or a fairy tale, while my thoughts stayed on the injustice of

Communist economics, my legs carried me onward, through the empty streets, past darkened houses and a still-closed restaurant, up to the entrance of a butcher shop.

I opened the door and looked around.

It was empty. Of course. Middle of the day. Empty as only a butcher shop can be. With its entire floor and all of the walls, and even the counter, covered in white porcelain tile, it looked like a morgue, and for a moment I imagined cadavers lying cold and silent in the back room. Clean, white surfaces surrealistically reflected black hooks on the walls and a row of vinegar bottles on the counter. A dead store. A store that was alive for one hour a day after morning delivery, and then, once everything was sold, was deathly silent until the next delivery. A counter divided the shop into a section for buyers and a section for sales clerks. A few years ago, the iron hooks held halved cows and pigs, legs pointed to the ceiling. Now they were empty, and we could only pray to God to end this calamitous shortage of meat. But God was absent. No meat in Poland. Bottles of water-clear vinegar mocked us from the shelves. Their contents could not be drunk even by the thirstiest person, and no alcohol could be brewed from them, either. *Vinum acer* reigned unconsumed in the butcher's shop.

"Good morning." I greeted two saleswomen busily occupied with drinking coffee and smoking cigarettes. They looked at me with hostility.

"Who is this *dupek* interrupting our work break? Can't you see we have nothing to sell?" one of them snapped, briefly looking up from her women's magazine *Girl Friend*.

"Yes ma'am, I see that. I am very, very sorry. However, I would like to ask if there is any chance that you could have a tiny, tiny piece of fresh tenderloin?"

"What? What?! Do we have … tenderloin?" Both women exclaimed indignantly.

"This guy enters our store in the middle of the day and asks for ... tenderloin? Is this a joke? Did you bang your head on something?"

"Maybe he's on drugs, Ewa. What do you think?"

I waited for them to finish, and then I repeated my request.

"Tenderloin. I could take some other meat, even mutton—but fresh. Clean, fresh, never frozen meat. And it doesn't have to be much. A little bit, a tiny slice. Please don't look at me like I'm crazy. I'm a naturalist from the park. It's not for me. It's for Otto, a bird we rescued. It's for Otto the sparrowhawk."

The two middle-aged women couldn't decide whether to laugh at me or throw me out. They were confused. I didn't look like a madman, but I talked like one. They eyed me silently without fear. They were not afraid of turning away a crowd of a hundred hungry customers trying to break in. Why fear one nutcase interrupting their peaceful afternoon coffee klatch? Even if I were aggressively threatening, these robust *kaffeeklatsch* had meat cleavers and knew how to use them. Why not have some fun with the crazy imbecile? So no, they didn't show me the door. They chose to ridicule me, to amuse themselves at my expense.

"Who's the tenderloin for? For a bird?"

"Yes, he's wounded. If he doesn't eat today, he won't make it till morning."

"Where do you have that bird—in your pocket? Ha! Ha! Ha!" They laughed as one pointed at my nether regions.

"No, he's at home. I can bring him and show you how tiny he is."

"Wonderful! Please come back and show us how tiny your 'bird' is. Ha, ha, ha! This guy is asking for a piece of tenderloin. Because ... because—Ewa, I can't stand it!—because he has a tiny, tiny 'bird!' Oh, that's funny! Ha, ha, ha!"

"You crack me up, Krystyna!" replied Ewa, snorting to catch her breath between spasms of laughter.

They couldn't stop laughing at me.

I ran into the street. Biting back my anger, I walked to the park office. What an insult. What injustice! To make fun of me! Me, a master of science with a doctorate already underway. An employee of Tatra National Park. Me, with a salary of nearly three thousand zloties—forty dollars a month! And who are they? Two bumpkins without an education. They steal meat to sell to friends! They felt like queens because they have access to meat and others do not. They are more important than medical doctors, engineers, journalists, and ... me! *Wredne babska!* They're both ugly. And so fat! They eat so much, they're putting on weight while the rest of us get skinnier and skinnier!

I felt distressed, but I was not the type to fail. Not me!

I returned to the office and asked Les to come with me to the apartment because I needed Otto. He was surprised, but he didn't ask why.

I lifted the top of the box. The bird had recovered a bit. Otto no longer lay on his side, but he squatted on his bird feet. He did not try to escape.

"I'm taking him for a walk for several minutes. See you." I decided not to inform Les of the details of my quest.

I walked quickly to the butcher shop. It was still open. The ladies gossiped loudly over empty coffee mugs.

I brought the bird into the shop and moved toward them delicately, the box held before me like a chalice brimming with Eucharist wine.

They looked at me uncertainly: *Is this guy from outer space?* They could imagine all kinds of things—a volcano eruption in the parking lot, an appearance of Our Lady on the empty wall, Gierek's face on their morning toast—but they never expected me to return with a bird in a box.

I placed Otto's box on the counter. They stared, but neither dared open it. What had this crazy idiot put inside?

"Open it yourself," the one closer to me whispered.

Slowly, solemnly, I lifted the lid. They saw little dying Otto, breathing with difficulty. Desperately he opened his curved beak, as if making a silent cry for help. He looked up at us with large, green eyes.

"It's an extremely rare bird," I lied. "I feel sorry for him, dying of hunger."

"Yeah, but we don't have any steak. None." Yet they seemed concerned by the imminent tragedy of death.

"I understand." And I turned to leave.

"Hold on, please," Krystyna said, looking me in the eye for the first time. "Come back at five o'clock, after closing. Enter the backyard and knock on the green door, the one with the sign 'For Delivery Only.' Knock five times then wait. But remember, not before five."

"And be certain no one follows you because people are so uptight right now," added Ewa.

"It's worse than the German occupation," Krystyna blurted out. "At least then the Germans were the enemy. This time, it's our own Polish leaders who destroy our livelihoods. People are ready to denounce us to *Milicja* for a piece of meat."

"Terrible! People are heartless!" I agreed with my new friends.

I finished working in the office at 4 p.m. and went for a beer with Les to Smrekami's, a modest bar a few minutes' walk from the office. After a while I checked the time, drained my second beer, and said goodbye to my companion. Leaving the bar, I turned left toward the Wielka Krokiew ski jump landing hill, and after a few hundred meters, I made a U-turn and walked toward the butcher shop. James Bond couldn't have done it better. On the way, from time to time I stopped at a shop window to discretely look back to see if I was being followed, but the streets were empty.

I found the yard. I also found the green door and knocked the secret signal. A minute passed, two, three …

Over the backyard, in the attic, a window opened. And again, there was another stretch of waiting. I was about to leave when I saw light behind the door. A woman's hand deftly handed me a small parcel wrapped in *People's Tribune*, the official Party newspaper. Inside were two slices of fresh sirloin.

"How much?" I whispered before the door closed.

"Nothing. And come at the same time the day after tomorrow."

For an entire month, every other day, I brought fresh beef home for my family. My daughter, Katia, ate better meat than her classmate, Basia, whose father was the director of the Party hotel. My wife, Marta, stopped complaining that my salary was small. My coworkers in the office never found why, every other day, I stayed in the office later than usual or where I walked alone after work on those days.

But one day—oh, I remember this sad moment—the saleswoman Krystyna asked me to bring the bird to their shop again because she wanted to show it to her daughter.

Hearing her plea, I handed the packet of meat she'd given me back to her and tried to produce tears in my eyes.

"What's happened? Jesus and Maria!" She groaned, concern in her voice.

I was on the brink of telling her that the bird had died the day before. (In reality, it had died three weeks before.) Then I thought that, for all her goodness, she deserved something better.

"They took him to the zoo yesterday. I came to tell you about it, my dear Krystyna."

"Oh, my God!" she exclaimed regretfully. "We won't see our bird anymore, and, I am sure, he won't get such fresh meat in the zoo!"

She did not ask me to keep the packet of meat for my family. Oh, well.

ROXY STORIES

To his dog, every man is Napoleon.

—Aldous Huxley

THE ADOPTION

Five years after arrival to America, there were five of us. Let me start with Kasia:

Kasia was a teenager. We pronounced her name "KASH-yah," which is a diminutive version of the Polish name "Katarzyna." It is pronounced with the sound of sawing a piece of styrofoam and coughing at the same time.

Can you imagine an oversensitive teenage girl in the U.S. allowing her parents to call her a name like this? We were terrible parents; we called her "Katarzyna" in the presence of her American friends!

No wonder she not only cried but exploded and showed disrespect toward us. We patiently considered her behavior typical for an American teenager. We knew she needed time to mature enough to understand that her parents were always right. Our resolution not to change her name was firm.

"We are proud Poles," I told her. "By doing this, we are defending our fatherland, our culture, our parental authority, and our moral law."

Yes, our moral law held that we had to defend our morals in the new country. Our names were a part of what had to be defended. And our daughter's name, this beautiful "Katarzyna," with its so-Polish sound of "rz" in the middle, was a symbol of our patriotism, never to change and never to be lost!

Even the variant "Kasia" was Polish. Our pronunciation of "sia" falls somewhere between "sh" and "j," similar to the French "j" in "Jacques." It's a beautiful sound and a beautiful name for a beautiful Polish girl. Our teenager should have been proud of having a "sia" at the end of her name—a "sia" that not many Americans could pronounce but that every American would have liked to have. But no! She wanted to be "Katia."

I said we should be in awe of the moral law that each of us has within us. In our case, our morals had led us to believe that the smallest change was a concession. Merely swapping a "t" for the "s" in "Kasia" we felt was changing the natural order of the world and would result in something terrible: Maybe a volcano would erupt in Philadelphia? Invasion from Mars? Arrival of the Antichrist? Who knows? Better not to provoke God and the Rules of the Universe.

Because when a girl is baptized as Polish "Catherine,"—that is "Katarzyna,"—and her parents lovingly call her "Kasia," she should be happy with that name and eventually die as "Kasia." Amen!

So, we called Kasia "Kasia."

* * *

I have a feeling you want to tell me I've lost my sense of direction and, instead of giving you a dog story, I'm writing about something else. OK, this story will be—eventually—about a dog, but what is more important, a dog or your children? Children, correct?

Therefore, please pay attention.

* * *

I also had two sons: Patasz, pronounced "PAH-tash," was five; Piotruś, pronounced "PYO-trush," was two and a half. I know—by now you are thinking, "OK, enough Polish already!" I am a compassionate storyteller. I do not want you to have to twist your tongue to make strange sounds. Now that you know their *real* names, I'll use their American names, Matt (the five-year-old) and Peter (two and a half). And—the most important person among us—is my wife. In this story, she asked to be called "Marta" to gain your sympathy by not causing you to tangle your tongue.

And where is the dog?

Slowly. It is my story, not yours. Dogs do not appear *deus ex machina*, falling down from the sky in the middle of the TV room. One more paragraph, and some action will bring you closer to the dog.

Katia's life (she won the battle, of course, and now she uses this Americanized name instead of "Kasia," and I am not going to irritate her, so hereafter it's "Katia") was busy. She had many friends and many dreams, mostly about boys, parties, and clothing. Soon she would be going to college, and she did not yet know where. She loved us, and she understood the finances of our family. But she could not stop thinking:

"If only my parents were rich! Oh, if they were rich, but they are not. How do I live among such people? Not only do they speak English with heavy accents, not only do they work all the time and study all the time, but all they talk about is money and education, money and education, nothing else!

"My God, how weird. How boring! Even worse, how immigrant-like! And what are they, compared to my American friends' parents? Poor! Well, maybe not 'poor' poor. But, as if out of spite, they earn just enough money to keep me from getting financial aid for college but not enough for tuition in a good one. Why such bad luck? Why me?!"

No wonder Katia was often moody and upset. Wouldn't you be? She had no time for her spoiled younger brothers. They did not care. They didn't care what she did or thought because they had only one dream in all the world: Katia's brothers wanted a dog.

* * *

Aha! You were waiting and waiting. To keep you reading, I lied when I said only "one" paragraph, but now, finally, the dog is coming!

Soon, quite soon.

How was it possible that my young boys did not dream of a computer, a bike, or a swing in the yard, but they desired an animal above all else? It is simple. Computers were so expensive that, in that time, only three families—the Rockefellers, the Morgans, and the Carnegies—could afford a computer. The Vanderbilts tried to purchase one on credit, but the banks refused the loan. Yes! My story takes place so many years ago that Steve Jobs was a nice, shy, friendly young man who didn't need to shave yet. Bill Gates still preferred singing in the choir to programming.

Do I exaggerate? Perhaps, but I want to give you an idea of how long ago those ancient times were before the human race developed a special bone in the back of the neck to accommodate looking down at cell phones all the time. After all, a sense of history puts meat on the bare bones of a story.

If I were entirely honest, though, I'd admit that one reason Matt and Peter wanted a dog was because I had planted the seed of this dream in their still-innocent brains.

How could I be so vicious, to use small children to fulfill my selfish plans? Hmm, well, everyone needs love. And who could love *me*? My always-busy wife? My never-noticing daughter? My two noisy and fighting-with-each-other boys? No. Only a dog! If someone needs love, he cannot be dogless. I desperately needed a dog!

Familiar with Niccolò Machiavelli's recommendations in his instructive manual *The Prince*, I introduced my sons to the habit of walking with me every evening to the nearby school field, where dog owners gathered with their pets. We spoke to the owners and petted their dogs. We talked about how to approach Mama and convince her that a dog would be the answer to all our problems. We discussed which breed would be the best for us, what name would be the greatest, and what Mama would do if one day we surprised her with a dog as a new family member. There was no better topic than "our dog." My sons loved walking with me because I did not preach to them or scold them. We were the founding members of a secret society of dog lovers.

* * *

Mama had no clue about the conspiracy.

Ambitious and full of goals, Mama had too much work. A new member of the family might throw a wrench into her plans. No, she definitely did not want to add a dog to our already chaotic mix.

There was a moment when she—although she didn't know it— might have avoided a dog invasion. When Peter reached out to pet an unknown dog, the scared dachshund bit his hand. Fortunately, I successfully explained what had happened. I convinced Peter that "some dogs bite, but when you own a dog—when he's *your* dog—he doesn't bite you. Never!"

Weeks passed, and the boys could not go a single day without searching through books about dogs and discussing pictures of dogs. In addition to books with descriptions and photos of all the different breeds, I checked out several informative works of dog fiction from the public library: *Old Yeller, Because of Winn Dixie, The Incredible Journey,* even Stephen King's *Cujo*—so they could learn the amazing loyalty and ability of dogs but also know to stay away from rabid Saint Bernards. And they started sharing their interest with their mother.

"Oh, this one! Could we buy this one, Mama?"

"And look at this other one! Mama, can we have a poodle? It's so cute! And I am *sure* he loves children. Right, Papa?"

My wife looked at me and hissed: "You did this. Admit it—you did this!"

I never admitted I did it. I already knew the cardinal law of husbandhood: Never admit you did it. Never, never, never!

"Me? Don't you know that our property borders the school, and all the neighbors walk their dogs on the school field? If anybody is to blame that our sons want a dog, it's you."

"Me? How dare you! Why me?"

"Because it was you who found this particular house and you who insisted we buy it."

"I bought it because it was the cheapest one in this neighborhood!"

"But it was your choice. Admit it."

Thus I escaped blame with a clever Machiavellian U-turn. Now, she had to "admit" something.

But she was a tough warrior, and she always had to have the last word:

"In this family, you have a choice: your wife or a dog."

I did not say a word. I only thought:

"We shall see."

Then an amazing opportunity came along.

* * *

Marta was invited to join a group of experts working on a project in Italy to teach parents of sick Italian children how diet change could help heal their kids' health problems. That's what she did. She was a professional dietician who advised school systems. She knew that the chances of persuading pre-teen pasta gluttons to substitute veggies for carbs were tiny, approaching nil. Ah, but to see Florence, Pisa, and Rome? She would do anything, even leave her beloved husband home alone. She delivered her ukase: "It's only fourteen days. I'm gonna do it."

My mind quickly calculated sixteen days total. Pennsylvania isn't next door to Italy: one day to fly over to Europe, and one day to fly back. I ventured a query, desiring to clarify details.

"But sweetheart, what about … "

She used her schoolmarm voice to cut off any nascent protest: "Don't be so fussy!" Lowering her register, she assumed her syrupy tone, the one she used to show affection. "Not to worry. I'll make daily and weekly task lists so you'll remember your chores." Marta's long, black lashes blinked once, slowly, demurely, concealing momentarily the promise of her dark eyes.

The boys and I would be free. Free at last, oh Lord, free at last! Our hearts would fly like larks, our spirits would soar, our glasses would be rose-colored. At least, I certainly felt that way. If I understood Marta's orders properly, she said that I was obliged to *do everything possible to make sure that they eat and are healthy, and make sure nothing bad happens to them.* This meant that I should feed them regularly, avoid fires, protect them against diseases, and watch TV with them.

Not one "do not" in my wife's orders.

Good!

∗   ∗   ∗

Saturday morning. Breakfast. For the first time, I made French toast, and as you know, French toast–making is among the activities at which men, the first time, usually do not succeed. Because this story is about dogs, and I expect that children will read it by the thousands, I will not elaborate about other things men usually screw up the first time.

My two breakfast connoisseurs immediately started grumping:

"The toast is soft inside—I don't like it."

"My toast is burnt!"

"And not sweet enough!"

"Oh, my tummy hurts!"

"Why did Katia not have to eat this? Where is she?"

I didn't know where my daughter was. Marta told me to take care of the boys. Katia was already sixteen; she had an exemption from eating my food. She had spent the night at her friend's house. I trusted her not to do anything stupid and also that she would eat enough over there. I didn't have to worry about whether she was hungry or not.

Immersed in *The Philadelphia Inquirer,* I pretended not to hear my sons. Marta did not like me to read during breakfast. She was gone, I could relax and enjoy the paper.

My eye caught an ad: "Pets, Buy and Sell" and a subhead: "Dogs." Well, do not suspect that I intended to buy a dog. I was just reading. Silently, not showing any emotion to small children, I let them believe I was concerned about Matt's tummy, or nauseated Peter. In truth, I was reading, slowly and with great consideration, about dog breeds starting with the letter "b."

Believe me, I had no particular intent. I was far from the type of a husband who—if his wife goes to Europe for sixteen days—opens the sanctity of their marriage, the holy portals of their home to a ... boxer. No way! Marta could eat *cacio e pepe* in Rome, admire Botticelli's *Birth of Venus* in Florence, or sip a truffle-flavored espresso in the shadow of the Tower of Pisa—and I would never disrupt the harmony of our marriage. I have my moral principles!

About half a page of boxer ads were in this weekend edition. Somewhere in the middle I found this:

Roxy: Charming six-month-old girl, dark brown, housebroken, trained, obedient, spayed, and incredibly sweet. Loves children, other dogs, even squirrels. Selling due to moving. Only $300 (cash only!). Clymer Street, Philadelphia.

"Are you going to finish this breakfast?" I raised my voice.

"No, it's cold!"

"No, it's yucky!"

"Your breakfast is not as good as Mama's!"

"We don't like your food!"

"All right. If you eat everything on your plates, I will drive you to Philadelphia, and I will buy you a dog."

In two minutes, their plates were clean.

Didn't I do what Marta told me? *"Do everything possible to make sure that they eat and are healthy"*?

Rushed by my boys, I drove to Philadelphia like a madman.

"When will we be there? How many more minutes?" asked Matt, the elder of the two.

"Do you think—Daddy—they still have a dog?" lisped Peter. He was just two and a half, newly successful at combining words into sentences, so it sounded more like, "Dee tink—Dada—habba doggie?" Except it didn't sound at all like that because of course we were speaking Polish.

They were excited! But they were imagining all the boys and girls living within a hundred-mile radius of downtown Philadelphia, with their parents, driving, flying, or perhaps even rowing down the Schuylkill, to buy their dog. Already it was "their dog," the dog they needed, like air and water, to live and be happy.

I drove at top speed along empty Ridge Pike. It was 10 a.m. on a weekend, and in the suburbs people preferred to stay home. Few were out buying a dog with the cash hidden by their wives under the mattress.

"How wise it is that Marta left this cash!" I thought. "It's Sunday, so I wouldn't have been able to withdraw it from our bank account. But because of her foresight, I have it! What was she thinking, leaving me with so much money? Plumbing emergency? If one of us got sick, and we needed cash to bribe a surgeon? No! No longer do we live in Poland and have to "convince" doctors we should go to hospital. She knows that. She already knows and feels America better than I do.

"So, why? Did she think gangsters would rob the banks and steal everything, and the only money available for us—the Roman family— would be the cash hidden under the marital mattress? Or maybe she thought a thief, a cruel robber, would kill us all if there was not enough money in the house to pay for his expenses, for his gun and ski mask?" My thoughts were stupidly wandering, and my imagination was creating impossible scenarios. I did not know why I was so lucky. I had fifteen $20 bills in my pocket.

Whatever Marta's motives, purchasing a dog wasn't among them. Of this I was almost certain.

While I was gratefully pondering her foresight, Marta was probably simultaneously experiencing a severe hiccup attack walking across the Ponte Vecchio. Hiccups are—according to my grandmother—the reaction of a person talked about by others behind her back. Grandma was 100% convinced this was true.

We passed the statue of William Penn on top of City Hall, entered Broad Street with its expensive shops on both sides, and after several blocks, turned left into South Street. It was super crowded in the evenings, but today—this Sunday morning—almost empty.

"Are we there?"

"Is it this house?"

"No!"

I stopped for a moment to look at a map. After a minute, I drove on.

We approached the Italian part of the city. The clean, small row houses were inhabited by working-class descendants of immigrants from Calabria and Sicily. Pansies and lilies, along with dark green ferns and exuberant hostas, filled their fifteen-by-five–foot front gardens. It was a lovely neighborhood, even if a few blocks away were more run-down areas.

These Italians had pride. They maintained, expanded, and improved houses their parents or grandparents had purchased with their hard-earned dollars. These were second and third generations of Italian immigrant families who sweated, saved, brought up their kids, and ate well.

I pinpointed our destination on the map. Moving toward 12th Street, I turned right, and then I noticed a tiny park. Yes, here we are: Clymer Street! A magnolia tree bloomed in the grass strip between the sidewalk and the curb.

Certain I had found the place, I carefully, slowly, parked in front of a narrow row house. The boys flew to the door without touching the pavement. I read the name on a plate above the doorbell to be sure that I found the proper address:

Anthony Caralucci.

OK—that's him.

That's the guy who confirmed, when I called him, that they had the dog, and they would wait for us to pay for it and pick it up.

I rang the bell. Silence. Nobody coming, no barking inside.

I rang the bell again. The boys were silent, too, scared to death. I knew what they were thinking.

And then, when we started to get impatient, we heard somebody approaching the door, noisily opening it—and I saw him: Mr. Caralucci.

He was five, maybe ten years older than me, a hardworking man who liked to eat, who likely drank wine and sang with his friends, talked a lot, loved his family, and went to church every Sunday.

But not this Sunday.

Today he stayed home to meet a stranger. The stranger had arrived. Mr. Caralucci looked at me with some interest, but his face was sad. Did he have tears in his eyes? He seemed tense. Was this big man crying? Strange.

* * *

He led me and my boys through the tiny space where the family kept coats and shoes into the living room. There, in silence, the entire family waited for us: a despondent wife and three crying girls who were literally covering their dog with their bodies, trying to protect a poor animal from the oncoming thieves. Us.

My sons were much younger, much smaller than the girls, who were ready to defend their dog against any tiger or wolf. But toddler Peter had the sweet face, blond hair, and innocent eyes of a baby angel—a different story.

The three sisters relaxed a bit and revealed their hidden dog. We saw the intelligent face of a young female boxer curious to see new human friends visiting her home. Roxy slowly, carefully approached my younger son. Their faces were at the same height. Without hesitation,

Roxy licked Peter's cheek. Peter was on cloud nine. Matt moved his face closer to the dog. He also wanted to be kissed.

"She likes them," said the oldest girl.

"She thinks they are younger than she is," added another girl.

"She's not that stupid. Our Roxy is smart."

"But she likes them—that's good."

And the oldest girl looked at Peter and asked:

"What's your name?"

At this moment, Mr. Caralucci, reminded by his daughters' behavior, came back to life and shook my hand, introducing himself:

"Tony—Tony Caralucci."

I immediately decided to use my knowledge of his, or his parents', fatherland, and to use the original version of my first name:

"Romuald, Romuald Roman."

"But you are not Italian? And you have an Italian name?"

"You are right. I am Polish, but my name is Italian, after St. Romuald, the bishop of Ravenna, who was a great saint. *'Empty yourself completely and sit waiting'* is what he taught," I volunteered. "He practiced stillness and passivity in old age, but in his youth St. Romuald indulged in the pleasures of the world."

"Ah. That's nice." His face changed as I described St. Romuald. His eyes crinkled ever so slightly into a smile. "Nina—this is my wife, Nina—could you bring some cake for us while we talk?"

Nina smiled at me and silently left for the kitchen. The boys and girls had started telling each other their names, and Tony showed me to the family dining table.

Their house was a typical old Philadelphia row house, narrow and deep. Each floor was approximately fifteen feet wide and forty feet long. On the first floor there was a big living–dining room and, behind it, an open kitchen.

Spread about this open space, we created three groups busy with different tasks: children playing with the dog, two men talking, and Nina preparing us coffee and treats.

"So, you came to buy our dog?" asked Tony.

"Yes. Here's $300 for you." And I started counting my $20 bills.

"You don't have to"—he interrupted me—"I trust you. I would never sell this dog if not, … "

"If not what?" I automatically asked then realized I shouldn't have said that. But it was too late.

"You see," he started, "we live in my mother's house. It's a small place, and she doesn't like dogs or cats—even birds—so it was out of the question to buy a pet for my daughters. And they had always, always wanted to have a dog."

He looked at the ceiling to calm down. "As long as we lived with my mother, we knew we couldn't have a dog. But last year she moved to Florida, and she let us stay in her house because then she did not have to sell it immediately. We were—financially, you understand—not ready to buy something."

I nodded my head. I understood.

"Well," continued Tony, "I spent a few months to find just the right dog. It was not easy because I wanted a purebred, but I couldn't pay a lot. I did not need a certificate, the so-called AKC, you know. I just wanted a dog, a boxer, that would present all the virtues of the breed and be inexpensive at the same time."

"And I was lucky. Roxy was the last one born out of seven. The smallest, the weakest. And the people who sold her to me—I knew them; they were also Italian—they warned me that Roxy might not survive. But we loved her so much, and we took such a good care of her, that—Look, look at her!—she became this beautiful, healthy dog."

"The girls and Nina spoiled her with their love, so I had to be tough, and I trained her. And you know, now she is better trained than those dogs that had six weeks of obedience training. Your small son, Peter—his name is Peter?"

"We call him 'Piotruś' in Polish, but here in America, yes, he's Peter. It's easier for him and for us."

"Yes, you're right. So, your Peter, he can walk Roxy on a leash, and she won't pull. She would walk at his side, and even if a cat or a squirrel runs in front of her—she won't pull. And she doesn't bite. Not at all! The kids can take her favorite food right out of her mouth when she's eating—and nothing. She only looks at them, asking 'Why?' She's such a good dog."

"So, why are you selling her?" Why would he sell a perfect dog and deprive his children of their best friend?

"My mother did not like Florida. She's coming back next week."

"Did you tell her that you already have a dog and that her granddaughters love it?" I felt so much compassion for this loving family, I completely forgot that my boys should be more important to me than the Caraluccis and their kids.

"Yes. She said that if she finds Roxy in her house, we have to leave. 'Either me or your dog,' she threatened us. This is the reason I am selling Roxy."

"My God, that's terrible," I sighed.

"Terrible," he agreed.

We sat in silence—no longer strangers but two men perfectly understanding each other, two heads of families, overwhelmed with the revelation of how terrible a mother-in-law can be.

Finally Tony interrupted our silence.

"Before I allow you to take Roxy from us," he hesitated, "I have a few important questions."

"Go ahead."

"First, do you have all the … things … for a dog? You know, food bowls, toys, dog bed, books? Because you do not have to pay for those. We have everything. Do you want them?"

"Yes, of course."

He nodded his head.

I knew that that was not the "important question" he had in mind. I waited for something difficult to answer—and I was right.

"Hmm, I am not sure if I am in a position to ask about this, but because of Roxy, I will. Do you believe in God, Romuald? Tell me the truth. Do you?"

"Yes, I do."

"And what is your religion?"

"Roman Catholic. I have told you already, St. Romuald of Ravenna—even my last name is 'Roman.'"

"Thank you, God!" rejoiced Tony. "You see, our Roxy grew up in a Catholic home."

I sighed with relief. Hopefully no more personal questions, but who knows? This one was easy, but what should I say if this Italian man asks me if I had ever cheated on my wife? What should be the proper answer?

Thankfully, the next question was easier:

"Tell me Romuald, do you drink alcohol?"

And again I answered.

"Yes, I do."

And hearing this, Antony Caralucci smiled at me for the first time. Then, he called out to his wife:

"Nina, Nina! No coffee for us! Bring a bottle of wine!"

*   *   *

On the road home, our car was filled with loud noises of boys playing with Roxy. I had drunk half a bottle of Tony's wine, but I drove slowly and safely, fully aware of my precious cargo of boys and dog. I wasn't stopped by the police. We drove safely toward home.

I thought, "God likes people who are not afraid to confess their faith ... and their habits," feeling proud of how my honesty made Mr. Caralucci feel a little bit better about handing their dog off to an unknown family.

Then I remembered the tears I thought I saw when he opened the door for me then Nina's dour look when she first came into the room.

And the three daughters? I recalled how they hovered over Roxy, ready to protect her with their lives! No matter if we were "good people." It did not matter. They had lost someone they loved dearly.

Did God punish the Caralucci children by taking away their pet? Where is God's justice if three little girls must suffer terribly so two little boys could fulfill the dreams I had enticed them to dream?

Dogs do speak but only to those who know how to listen.

—Orhan Pamuk

THE RETURN

When she was a small girl, Marta was bitten by a boxer. Ever since, she has been afraid—panicky, even—if she sees this particular breed. For her, a boxer was as terrifying as the Dragon of Cracow. A virgin-eater, this vicious monster roamed the famous medieval city. Today, virgins are quite rare indeed in Cracow.

Other breeds were only slightly less frightening to Marta. The sight of a basset with its aggressively hanging long ears and scheming eyes caused Marta to stop walking and ask me to position myself between her and the beast.

Her opinion of dogs was unshakable. A collie? "Wild, unpredictable, looks like a wolf." Golden retriever? "Too big! It'd kill you if it got angry!"

Even a Yorkshire terrier, with its sharp teeth and four pounds of muscle, would make Marta tremble. If a Yorkie decided to attack her and bite her ankle, doctors would have to amputate her leg, probably up to her knee. Lots of pain, and who knows how her husband would react? Maybe he would divorce her. Abandon her with one leg gone and a pile of bills from psychiatric hospitals for treating "canine nervosus."

Consequently, whenever Marta suspected an unknown woman approaching might have a dog in her bag, she asked me to cross the street and walk on the other side. It's always better to be on the safe side than unexpectedly to come eye-to-eye with a hostile Yorkie.

*   *   *

Marta. What would she think? How would she react? What would she do? The sword of Damocles was suspended over our heads by a hair. The boys and I could do nothing. We couldn't call Marta to tell her we bought a dog. At that time cell phones didn't exist, and besides, we didn't know her schedule or the names of the hotels where she was staying. We only knew the date of her return home.

It was like knowing a date of the flood without means to build an ark. Even a prisoner waiting for the date of his death sentence still has a chance. A president, a king, a judge, or a miracle could save his life. We didn't have any option, except to wait.

Roxy was seven months old, not fully mature, but old enough to know right from wrong. Most often, she behaved like a happy, friendly pet. Her experience was limited to the Caralucci family, where she knew everybody loved her, and she loved everybody.

Her expectation of receiving love could get her into trouble, though. She'd been told many times that jumping up on people can scare someone who is not expecting it, so she tried her best to limit her expressions of love to licking human hands. Or, if you were close enough, she'd lick your face. And once she kissed you, your entire face would experience the warm softness of the boxer's pink tongue.

* * *

Marta. Marta, who was so fearful of dogs. Marta, who knew nothing of the important change in our family. Marta, who cultivated the art of makeup, whose moisturized skin tasted like nothing else.

Marta's reaction to being kissed on the face by a terrifying monster dog was instinctive. As hikers are told to do when attacked by a grizzly, she made herself into a stone. Roxy, therefore, had a lot of time for kissing.

But finally, the stone-still panic was over. Marta screamed.

Her first scream was full and loud. Peter covered his ears with his hands. Matt sat up in terror, eyes wide. I stayed immobilized, like Lot's wife—a pillar of salt. The terrified dog peed on the wood floor in our living room.

Marta screamed again, this time a long, blood-curdling shriek that expelled all the air in her lungs.

Then she stopped.

The silence was more terrifying than the scream.

The monster dog that had probably intended to tear her to pieces looked different now. Roxy stared down at the puddle she had made on the floor. Even if she had tried to be a decent dog, she'd done something terrible.

The worst thing a dog can do. Pee on the floor.

Roxy could not look the screaming lady in the eye; she could only look at the floor. She was only seven months old, still a "teenaged" boxer, and sensitive as only teenagers can be. She'd peed on the floor!

The dog waited for the human to punish her—maybe kill her, cowering as if she already felt the pain of this punishment. Crouched over, Roxy awaited her execution, to be performed by that terrifying, screeching human who, just moments ago, had entered her young and innocent life: "Off with her head! I'll use this handy sword of Damocles."

While Roxy cowered, Marta gathered strength to scream again. While inhaling for her next outpouring of existential angst, she noticed the dog shivering. Roxy seemed even more scared than Marta was. As if on cue, at this moment when Marta first truly saw Roxy, the traumatized creature flattened herself on the floor, trembling, and once more peed with fear.

At least Marta did not pee with fear.

In this confrontation between woman and beast, she—the woman—was a winner! She sensed that the young boxer was completely defeated. Marta stopped being afraid. The dog was begging for forgiveness.

Marta changed her reaction from fear to interest.

"What *is this?*" she asked Roxy with a voice that showed no anger.

"This" crawled to her, still trembling, keeping her head on the floor and her eyes shut.

"Are you so scared of me?" asked Marta, her voice shifting toward compassion.

Roxy raised her head. Marta saw guilt in the little dog's heart and how this poor animal suffered.

Then, still not sure if it was safe, Marta petted Roxy's head. And Roxy, still scared to death, licked Marta's hand.

And we could keep the dog.

If you pick up a starving dog and make him prosperous, he will not bite you. This is the principal difference between a dog and a man.

—Mark Twain

SUCH A GOOD DOG!

When our dog Roxy was young, we lived in Lafayette Hill in our first home, which we proudly named "Romanówka"—Polish for "The Romans' Home." We even painted a sign with the name so it would be like it used to be in Zakopane, Poland, where our house had its name, and all the other houses on our street also had names: Bright Palace, Friendly Home, Mountain Home, Maple Mansion, and so on.

We continued this tiny aspect of our past life. However, we had no idea that our colorful sign made all our neighbors believe that our surname was not Roman but Romanówka. No matter—we knew what it meant. Every time we saw our house's name, it brought to mind the old neighborhood we had left behind.

We were happy in Romanówka even if it was small and shoddy. We worked hard. Both Marta and I went to college to get U.S. college degrees. We aimed to achieve the same status that we had attained in Poland. Marta invited a few older family members—aunts, mainly—from Poland to stay with us. (Six months was the maximum permissible time for a tourist visa.)

Our visiting relatives helped us raise our children while we focused on education and on finding better jobs. Marta's aunts kindly watched over our brood, even though their tourist activities were limited to a few trips around Philadelphia. They knew that our race toward the American dream made life hectic. Ah, the benefits of extended family!

Gradually we succeeded on both fronts: children and work. Katia, our oldest, was a smart, promising teenager; the boys were following in her footsteps. Matt was an excellent student; Peter at age five was interested in ancient Egypt and conducted ritual burials for field mice. I imagined in the future one would become a scholar and the other would be director of a funeral home. Even our dog was a smart, caring family member with whom we could always safely leave the children, not only the children, but also an aunt from Poland, and even a grandfather, Grandpa Aleksander Rybicki.

The entire family in the U.S. called Marta's father "Grandpa Aleks." He was a big man: big head, big body, big, deep voice. He didn't care about Picasso or Spinoza, but he could talk for hours about metal crystallization, forge temperatures, or how to organize the 3,000 employees of Foundry Końskie into a winning workforce that set the pace for production and efficiency for all of Polish heavy industry.

How did Grandpa Aleks know so much? It went back to the German invasion of Poland early in the Second World War. When the Nazis occupied Poland, they looked around and saw lots of healthy, cheap labor—perhaps even free labor: all the teens too young to have been slaughtered in the Polish army. When Grandpa Aleks was sixteen, Germans forcibly deported him to Germany to work like a slave for the Reich. In all, he spent three years in Essen on the Panzer tank assembly line at the Krupp ironworks.

It was common Nazi practice to replace Germans fighting in the army with workers "stolen" from occupied countries. Many enslaved workers, like Aleks, had good luck, survived, and in 1945 returned to their countries. Russian prisoners of war and Jews, however, were treated differently. They were worked to death. And so Polish, Russians, and Jews all provided hard labor at almost no cost to the Reich.

In Germany, Aleks learned the rules and the importance of work. When he first reported to the factory floor, the manager said, "I don't know how much you know, so we're starting at the beginning. I'm going to show you the right way to hold a hammer." It was carved in Aleks's soul to care about quality and to follow best practices.

"The result of best practices," he thought, "is quality work, and good work makes you feel competent and proud." Even work in a Nazi tank factory. Even work for a new Communist regime. Aleks followed this philosophy of life and dedicated his entire life to work.

* * *

When Aleks returned to newly Communist Poland—eighteen years old, high school unfinished—he started as an ordinary worker, and in the evenings he attended school. With his punctilious work ethic, he soon became a technician and then a manager. As a manager, he excelled. He had the strength and energy to motivate his workers and, at the same time, to attend the polytechnic where he specialized in metallurgy. No wonder he rose like an elevator up and up through managerial positions. He had no interest in politics. His natural focus was on technology and on organizational management.

Aleks was far more creative and dedicated to work and than typical Communist factory managers were. Their goals? Promotion, more money and, of course, covering their rears and blaming somebody else for their own greed and stupidity. So Aleks's initiative and responsible nature stood out. Although young, his years of experience as a factory worker enabled him to talk easily with workers.

He discovered how to motivate with higher salaries. He accompanied the raises with open group meetings to discuss production flow, safety, management expectations, personnel issues, or anything else a worker might want to bring up.

The result? Everyone worked more efficiently, as part of a cooperative team. Increased production not only covered the wage increase; it boosted revenue and profits, too.

In his spare time, Aleks enjoyed introducing his own ideas of work organization and writing his own technical patents. Because he shunned fighting for status and money, and because of his generous nature, he did not have enemies trying to undermine and destroy him behind his back.

That is how Aleksander Rybicki became one of the key managers in Polish metallurgy. The Communist authorities promoted him to CEO of a complex of metallurgical plants with several thousand workers under his leadership. For such a high position, Aleks had to become a member of the Polish Communist Party, but in his understanding it was just a bureaucratic step required to promote him.

His obligation toward his kinsmen was not to be for or against Communists but to be an industry leader strengthening the economy for all of Poland. Boost iron and steel production in his factories, increase worker compensation, and improve technologies: that was his way of life, his morality, his religion. Every autocratic system needs such people. Orwell's workhorse.[3]

Aleks's wife Lena adjusted less readily to the Communist regime, however. A devout Catholic, she could not hold back her opinion. "Aleks, this is a sin—certainly a venial sin, maybe even a mortal sin, God will decide—but joining the godless Polish Communist Party is a sin!"

All the same, Lena found a way to get Communists to support a church ceremony. A big family wedding was coming up: Lena's niece and her wonderful young accountant were to be married in the beautiful red brick Cathedral Basilica of the Holy Family in Radom. Lena wanted the wedding to be grand in every way.

At the time, Aleks's high management position entitled him to a chauffeured Volga, a big, black luxury automobile from the Soviet Union like the ones that drove high-ranking party executives around Moscow. The company motor pool also had several brand-new 1978 Polonez sedans for the use of middle managers.

Lena called the director of logistics at the factory and said, "This is the wife of CEO Rybicki. We have an important family wedding coming up at the beautiful Cathedral Basilica in Radom. Can you please arrange for the Volga to pick me up at home? Then we'll go pick up the bride."

"Certainly, Madam Rybicki, yes, I certainly can arrange that."

"Oh, that's so wonderful! It will make the day even more beautiful. Say, by the way, could you also arrange for four Polonezes to carry the groom, the best man, and the bridesmaids? That would be absolutely grand!"

She likely fluttered her eyelashes as she was saying this last bit. Of course the logistics manager couldn't see that through the telephone. Nonetheless ...

---

3   "Boxer" is described as a hardworking but naive and ignorant cart horse in George Orwell's 1945 novel *Animal Farm*. He is shown as the farm's most dedicated and loyal laborer. Boxer serves as an allegory for the Russian working class who helped to oust Tsar Nicholas and establish the Soviet Union but were eventually betrayed by the Bolsheviks.

"Certainly, Madam. One Volga and four Polonez, coming up!" All was arranged.

Late on the afternoon of the wedding, Aleks received a call from the head of the provincial Communist Party, a big shot, almost equivalent of governor in the U.S.

"Comrade Rybicki, what the hell is going on in Radom? I've just had the report: a government Volga and four brand-new Polonezes parked right in front of the Cathedral Basilica. Jesus Christ! What are you doing? You a goddamn Catholic agitator?"

The crisis passed because Aleks was an extraordinarily valuable manager. Besides, he was not directly involved. He had plausible deniability.

In 1980, when the Independent Self-Governing Trade Union "Solidarity" emerged and gained power, things relaxed a bit, and Communist party membership was no longer required to be a CEO. Increasingly, workers were given power to get rid of industry managers. But nobody tried to replace Aleks. Even delegations from plants directed by Aleks years in the past stood in support of him.

One day, the local chairman of the Communist Party in Aleks's industrial plant entered his office:

"Comrade Director," he whispered into Aleks's ear, "several of your workers are walking from one facility division to another asking coworkers to throw their Communist IDs into a trash can. They already have hundreds of them. What should we do? Should we call the police? Maybe we should inform the government in Warsaw and ask for assistance from the ZOMO[4] special forces?"

"No. First have them visit my office. And tell them to bring me that trash can," ordered CEO Aleksander Rybicki.

---

4   Zmotoryzowane Odwody Milicji Obywatelskiej, a Communist-era paramilitary police created to fight dangerous criminals, provide mass security for events, and help in natural disasters or other crises. Ultimately, however, they were best known for their role in quelling civil rights and for brutal, often lethal, riot control.

"Yes, Comrade Director," agreed the local party chairman, with a silent sigh of relief. No longer was it his problem. The Party apparatchik knew that when Rybicki said something, he was serious. No jokes, no empty promises—just action. This CEO was like a bull, able to charge at the crowd and disperse it. Now, the comrade director would extinguish the revolt. Problem solved.

The representatives of the rebellious workers entered the CEO's office determined to defend their cause, even against the "big boss."

CEO Rybicki scowled at them. "Show me the trash can," he demanded.

Two men hesitantly edged forward to show him an ordinary plastic trash can, half filled with red-striped IDs.

"Come closer," Grandpa Aleks growled at them.

Although brave men, they hesitated.

"I said *closer!*"

They moved the trash can up to the CEO's oak desk.

Then Aleksander took out his wallet, removed his own Communist ID card, and threw it into the can.

"My ID should go with yours. Good luck, and now, goodbye!"

He had no time to talk to them. He had done what he had to do. He had done what he had always wanted to do. Now he was independent of that crazy, repressive political doctrine. He moved on to the next task. He had to make plans to remove an obsolete open-hearth furnace and accordingly modify the plant's workflow.

* * *

A few months later, General Jaruzelski imposed martial law in Poland. Three Solidarity activists from Aleks's plant were taken to secret prison camps. Where they were and whether they were still alive were open questions. Alerted to the news of martial law and the arrest of part of his staff, Aleksander responded immediately. He ordered his Volga chauffeur to drive him directly to Warsaw to the office of the Minister of Industry. After arriving, he demanded his arrested employees be freed immediately. He demanded so loudly that the authorities fired him on the spot.

It went something like this:

"CEO Rybicki, we don't need you any more. Your career is finished!"

Over. Done. No more managerial positions for Aleksander Rybicki. Fifty-four years old, in great health, full of energy, and—no work, no responsibility. The Communist anathema forced him to retire. No opportunity for rebellious CEOs in Poland! Like a plant with roots

exposed, a knight fallen from his steed, or a Polish Christmas carp removed from the bathtub, he was no longer in his element. Enough examples? I think so. You already sense how he felt. Imagine this bitter, disappointed man, trying to live through each day. No wonder his wife Lena—Marta's mother, a wise woman—sent him to the U.S. Better that he should move far away from his memories so he could recover and make a new life.

We eagerly cooperated with her idea and invited Grandpa Aleks to stay for six months in our home.

In a few months, Grandpa Aleks received an American tourist visa, and within two weeks he arrived at Romanówka. Now it was our responsibility to create a new life for him. Not an easy task. If he were an archaeologist, he could excavate our entire third of an acre. If he were an economist, he could start a chicken farm in the backyard. If he were a poet or a revolutionary–politician, not to mention a baker or a fortune teller—it was obvious there would be plenty of work for Grandpa Aleks. But a steel plant director?

We would gladly have offered him the position of CEO of Bethlehem Steel. But in 1989 this corporation was so close to bankruptcy, even our Grandpa Aleks could not save it. Running Ford or the IBM corporation would also have been a good job, but we did not know how to persuade their boards of directors that he would be the best candidate.

Consequently, we were his only potential employers. It was our responsibility to motivate Grandpa Aleks to work on something, if only to keep his temper under control.

He cooperated as much as he could. Once we introduced him to our household, he immediately started looking for some engineering work in our backyard. Unfortunately, no work even vaguely related to metallurgy occurred to us. The planned construction of a treehouse was canceled by Marta, who was afraid that the boys were too small to climb the tree.

Creating a vegetable garden would have to wait for spring, and fencing the backyard I had already completed, immediately before acquiring our dog Roxy, who was by now perhaps the most beloved member of our family. We had hoped that repairing an old lawn mower would give Aleks some work for a while, but he found the problem and fixed it in five minutes. He offered to sharpen our two axes. Marta said yes. He asked if he could use them to cut our trees. Marta said no.

And that was the extent of our ideas.

Sitting on the sofa, Aleks watched TV without knowing what was said.

"Do you have a TV program in Polish?" he asked.

"No."

"In German?"

"No."

So what could he do to occupy his time? Finally one night,

conferring in bed, Marta and I came up with something. In the morning, we asked him to build a wooden shed for our garden tools. This would be creative work, suitable for an engineer, we thought. Thank God he shared our opinion and started construction.

During this time, Grandpa Aleks and Roxy became friends. Not immediately, of course. A real friendship starts slowly. Roxy was a tactful young boxer. She did not want to automatically befriend every human she met. All Aleks wanted from the dog was for her not to interrupt him during his work.

For several days, these two lonely creatures were alone together in the wilderness of the backyard. Each developed new feelings. Every day, they discovered virtues in one another. Bored and tired of people who wanted to pet her or make sure she obeyed commands like "Sit" and "Lie down," Roxy noticed that Grandpa Aleks let her be an independent dog. He did not try to pet her or give her commands. He only worked.

Roxy saw that he did not work like the noisy guys who had converted the Romanówka garage into the apartment where Aleks now resided. Those two simpletons had worked automatically, without thinking, making loud rat-a-tats with their nail guns. Aleks, on the other hand, stopped often and thought, quietly. Was the construction of a storage shed more complicated than the remodeling of a garage? Roxy did not know.

But she observed the old man carefully.

After a while, he, too, noticed that he always had company. He started to share his thoughts with Roxy.

"You see, I try to connect those two-by-twos with nails, but they sometimes crack. How to avoid it?"

Roxy intensely thought about this problem.

"You don't know, yes? I understand. I don't know, either. But I'll tell you what we can do. I will check how American workers connected pieces of lumber. Let me look at those walls in the old garage. Maybe there will be an opening showing the inside."

He walked to the garage addition, only to face another dilemma.

"Walls are plastered in such a way that I can't see what is beneath this ... how do they call it?"

He looked at Roxy, who tried to understand each word by the tone of Grandpa Aleks's voice. Aleks took *A Concise Polish–English Dictionary* from his pocket and tried to decipher an English entry:

Why do they call it "*Kamienna blacha*"? But that's what they call it. But it is not "sheet"; sheet is made of metal. Or cotton. Or silk. So, maybe it is *płyta*? Now it makes more sense! *Płyta kamienna?* Maybe *gipsowa!* Sounds better. Well, close enough." He was content that at least he could explain what he needed to his family, who spoke English.

The look in Roxy's eyes, as she peered into his, revealed that she understood. She'd heard American workers call this construction material "sheetrock." She was more interested when they were talking about hoagies and hamburgers.

"But now, we have to find how to remove part of this *płyta ścienna*, Roxy. We should do it in such a way to avoid too much damage. My daughter would immediately show her disappointment. Hmmm, what do you think? Making a hole with a screwdriver would be too brutal, and too visible ... "

Roxy had no answer. She moved her head, pretending she saw a squirrel in the grass.

Aleks knew no squirrel was there. If a squirrel came near, Roxy would fly at it with supersonic speed, and in a split second, the squirrel might cease to exist. Roxy's enthusiastic pursuit kept squirrels from scampering around Romanówka, even though they lived elsewhere in the neighborhood.

So he knew Roxy was pretending. How tactful. What a nice dog!

But, he thought, she was against the idea of making a hole in the new wall. That's why she turned her head away.

Aleks returned to the shed site. He slowly measured pieces of wood and carefully cut them with a hand saw, all the time evaluating the pluses and minuses of destroying a tiny piece of the sheetrock in his room. He thought he might glue things back together after inspecting the uncovered pieces of wood. Unfortunately, he had no glue.

After a while, he became used to sharing each task with Roxy. Years ago, in Germany, he discovered how effective teamwork is compared with individual efforts. Roxy was his teammate. If only she could assist him—hold pieces of plywood, or carry the tape measure.

But at least she helped him discover the secret of framing lumber.

It went like this:

Aleks, with Roxy's assent, decided to use a screwdriver to make a tiny, tiny hole in the wall—a hole just big enough to see what was underneath.

He picked a spot at the height of his eyes, in the corner, and (literally) prying with his screwdriver, he "delicately" investigated the gypsum-like material.

As an aside, I must tell you that at that time, wood framing, sheetrock, and gypsum boards were unknown in Poland. We followed Big Brother's example and built everything with cement.

A few white pieces of gypsum fell to the floor.

"Oh! It's really very soft," said surprised Grandpa Aleks to Roxy.

Roxy wasn't sure. She approached him, sniffed the white dust on the floor, looked up, and scratched the wall below him with her paw.

"Oh, yes, of course!" exclaimed Aleks. He started scratching away sheetrock in the same place.

One of Roxy's favorite entertainments was to dig holes in the garden. She succeeded in this task and had wonderful results until Mama Marta screamed at her and forbade it. But maybe digging holes in walls was not forbidden, especially when her new human friend was doing this? She could help!

Together, Grandpa and Roxy enjoyed their common endeavor so much that they created a rather large hole. But they learned enough to know how to follow American wood frame wall construction. They decided to continue the work next day.

Unfortunately, that next day Marta found the terrible hole that Roxy had created just above the floor in Grandpa's room. She brought the canine villain to the scene of the crime. Roxy cowered, sensing an approaching scolding because of Marta's tight grip on her collar. "I try," Roxy thought, "but I must be the worst dog in the world! Please forgive me for my sins." But at the moment Marta started screaming at Roxy, Grandpa Aleks immediately stopped her.

It wasn't Roxy's fault. In fact, Roxy had demonstrated valor and virtue few dogs possess. She had tried to show him a mouse hole in the wall. She wanted to warn the family about mice coming from the yard into our house. He—Grandpa—would repair this hole, he promised. (Of course he had no idea how to do it, but this project could wait.)

Finally, he suggested that Marta buy mousetraps to solve the mice invasion instead of blaming an innocent dog for the calamity.

As her father knew, Marta had a deep fear of mice. She forgot about "Roxy's" hole and screamed out the important issue: "Mouse invasion!"

From then on, Roxy understood that Grandpa Aleks was her defender and best friend. He saved her. He was a powerful person. Even Mama Marta listened to him. This is how their friendship was sealed. And it grew every day.

* * *

The two watched TV together. Mostly old Westerns. They liked action movies the best. The ones with little—if any—dialog. They both looked at the screen. From time to time, at key moments when an evil character lurked behind a boulder, or when the hero decided to kiss the girl, Grandpa Aleks looked at Roxy, and Roxy immediately looked at Grandpa Aleks.

Widziałaś go? Tego drania za skałą? "Did you see him? That bastard behind the rock?" asked Grandpa.

Roxy stared at Grandpa intensely, then blinked her eyes.

"OK. Let's hope John Wayne also saw him."

They continued watching. Together they enjoyed the final exchange of gunshots, cheering on John Wayne, of course.

Construction of the garden shed progressed. In fact, it grew and grew. Work goes fast when a team cooperates. After three weeks, it was not a mere garden shed, but an extra storage shed as well. After five weeks, the project had become "Grandpa's House." It wasn't long before we had no more money to buy materials. But Aleks was happy. Besides his small room in the garage, he had a new place in the U.S. It was his private place to smoke cigarettes. There, no one reminded him that he smoked too much. He and Roxy loved to spend time in this shed.

Grandpa brought in an old armchair, a coffee table, and a blanket for Roxy. They talked about the future. Grandpa revealed to Roxy his plan to add a small kitchen and to bring electricity, maybe even gas to "their" shelter. He shared those visions with Roxy first, prior to presenting them to Marta. Roxy listened seriously, understood each detail, and unlike Marta, never interrupted Grandpa's talking. Finally, Roxy became such a good friend of Grandpa's that, to make him happy, she'd probably started smoking cigarettes with him. Maybe she shared a puff or two, who knows?

Marta, however, was not as thrilled. Her response to Grandpa's plan was different. She abruptly shushed her father and shut the project down. One shed in the garden was enough. Maybe Grandpa wanted to build a second shed, then a third, or, why not, a second-story lounge to better catch the breeze? We would not turn our backyard into a tool shed maze!

Once Marta declared construction terminated, Grandpa had an idea to "repair and improve" the bathroom in the attached garage we had converted for him. This bathroom had already existed prior to the garage remodel. We did not use it often and had never thought to spend money on its "modernization."

But if it was going to be another Grandpa project, why not? Maybe it would increase the value of our house? Marta, reluctantly opened her wallet to purchase necessary materials and said, "Yes, go for it." Why did she say yes reluctantly? Because she knew her father could calculate differential equations, and maybe even design a factory, but bathroom sink repair? He might have a problem. It was not a huge project, but he might screw it up. By the way, she had already inspected the finished shed. She said nothing, but she knew what she thought of his work.

Grandpa Aleks's "heart"—his eagerness to work—beat her "club" of resistance.

One Saturday morning, Aleksander Rybicki disappeared from sight and reappeared as a plumber. Metaphorically speaking, of course—no one noticed. Everyone ran in different directions: the boys left to play with a neighbor's son; Marta worked in the hospital ten miles away; Auntie Maria cleaned the kitchen.

And me? I was in bed studying physical chemistry or daydreaming, I forget which. "What about your daughter Katia?" you inquire. Would she, a teenager, return so early from Friday's sleepover with Jane? Romanówka was plunged into the Saturday morning bustle, except for me, at peace in the rare quiet. Nothing foretold the upcoming disaster.

At 10 a.m., Roxy burst into our bedroom and barked loudly at me:

"Woof! Woof!"—and she snuffled me with her nose.

"Woof! Woof!"—and she jumped on the bed with her front legs.

"What's going on, Roxy? Don't you like me studying chemistry?"

"Woof! Woof!"—the dog was shaking all over with nervousness.

I got up from the bed. I thought hard: What does she want? To show me something or what?

The dog ran away a few steps and ran back again, demanding I follow her.

She led me to the garage.

There we found Grandpa Aleks, sopping wet head to toe, wrapping a towel around a broken pipe with one hand and trying to stop a spewing stream of water with the other. He couldn't see anything through the spray from the pipe. All he could do was scream at the top of his lungs, trying to outshout the sound of water:

"Roxy! Roxy! Go get someone! Bring someone to help me!"

"I'm already here, Grandpa! We'll do something right now!" I shouted, attempting to calm him down. Then I ran to the main valve and quickly shut off the water supply.

Roxy watched me shut off the water, as if she too knew where the main tap was and how to do it. She would probably have turned it off herself, but it was a bit too high for her, and—as you can probably guess—too hard to turn off the tap with a dog's mouth. It's easier to get a human to do it.

After her quick action rescued him from his water-soaked dilemma, Grandpa knew Roxy understood everything. "Roxy speaks Polish, and English, and Human," he'd exclaim. "All of the languages spoken in the world. A canine Rosetta Stone!"

* * *

Time passed. Grandpa returned to Poland. After a while he found a job in private industry. When he called us, he always asked about Roxy. He never stopped believing Roxy understood him.

I have met many people who think their dogs understand human speech. It's really interesting. An educated person who behaves properly and shows no symptoms of mental illness will say, "I believe my dog understands words. Not tones of voice, but words. Even sentences."

Of course, many hide this wild conviction deep in their souls. They know to reveal it might expose them to ridicule or, at the minimum, make people uneasy. But if they feel safe, if they feel you too are dog-crazy insane, they'll tell you stories that *prove* dogs understand and think like people.

Some people talk to animals.
Not many listen though. That's the problem.

—A. A. Milne

DEATH OR DELIVERANCE?

Traffic on Ridge Pike never ceased. Day and night, hour after hour, two-ton hunks of metal filled with gasoline and—who knows, drunk teenagers, probably?—sped past our home. Their engines screamed into our ears like Luftwaffe Stuka dive bombers. We choked on exhaust fumes.

When a twenty-ton eighteen-wheeler would pass eighty feet from our windows, the entire house trembled like an old man with a cane walking on cobblestones. I swear the house groaned, feeling pain in each wooden joint and every termite-infested two-by-four. Built cheaply for working-class people who could not afford quality materials, our home proved the genius of carpenters hundreds of years ago who invented timber frame construction that moves, vibrates, even screams for help but does not collapse under attack.

Gradually we became accustomed to the sporadic earthquakes. Yet we were always a bit scared and annoyed. After each passing truck, we desired to move someplace safe and silent. "A few more years," we comforted ourselves.

In the morning after 6 a.m., the noise did not allow us to stay asleep. At night after 9 p.m., traffic flow diminished enough that we could watch TV. After 10 p.m., we could go to bed.

Roxy was curious about what kind of neighborhood existed on the other side of the street. Was it as noisy as ours? Was there another church and another field? New dog friends?

I sensed that if I let her loose in our front yard, she would immediately run toward the busy street, cross it blindly, and—if still alive—run farther and farther until she got lost among the identical houses that grew over there like mushrooms.

Trying to prevent such an event one day, I took Roxy for a walk along the edge of our property that bordered Ridge Pike. It was only thirty feet long because our property was a trapezoid, with the shorter thirty-foot side along the street and the parallel one-hundred-foot side in back of the house. The backyard was fenced so that the dog couldn't escape. The front yard, on the other hand, was open to thousands of cars chasing one another along Ridge Pike.

So on this day I took Roxy for an educational walk. The cars passed by dangerously, only three feet away. Roxy was scared of each of them. Seeing she was trembling with fear, I started my lesson:

"Cars do not see you. Not at all. They drive, and they do not care whether they hit you and kill you or not. Because they are not living creatures. No! They are machines. Terrible, dangerous killing machines. Do you see that dead squirrel in the middle of the street? You would be like that if you tried to cross this street. So you should never do it. Never! Do you understand?"

I moved my face close to hers.

"Promise me that you will never escape from home and that you will never run into the street. Promise?"

I hoped she understood and agreed with me.

After walking ten more feet, we were jolted by the roaring approach of a souped-up Dodge 4X4 pickup. As it passed just a few feet away, a blast of air hit us like an Oklahoma tornado. I gave my warning a second time.

"Did you see how big and heavy that truck was? With its noise so loud, it hurt? Yes? And the wind blew us away, like we were dry leaves. We were scared to death, weren't we? Can you imagine if such a truck hit you, Roxy? You would look like the goulash inside dog food cans. And your guts would spill out. So you already know what I am going to tell you? Never, never, never cross this street! You are a good dog. Not a stupid dog but a good dog! Promise?"

She licked me.

I took it as a sign of her promise.

Nonetheless, my confidence that this four-legged teenager would be responsible had limits. I repeated my lesson for the third time at home to the boys and to Roxy. I sat all of them on the living room floor, Roxy nestled between her brothers. Three sets of brown eyes gazed up at me expectantly. "Ridge Pike is a great danger to Roxy. You must be certain she can never, never get out to the street!"

I ordered them to always make sure the gate between the front yard and the backyard was closed. "The front yard is not for children and not for dogs!"

Six brown eyes looked up with rapt attention. The boys—and Roxy, too—were listening intently. I had my audience in the palm of my hand. A good time to elaborate with some specifics.

"Peter and Roxy do not know how to open this gate, and this is good. Matt, remember that before Roxy does her business, make sure the gate is closed. Peter, listen to Matt. When you boys walk with Roxy, keep her always on leash, so she cannot escape and be hit by a car."

Marta listened to my preachings and said: "Do you think they understand what you are saying?"

"I do," said Matt.

"I do, too," said Peter, even though nobody believed he did.

Nobody asked Roxy if she understood my words. Maybe we should have. Maybe it would have been good to slowly repeat the lesson one more time?

Eating dinner after I returned from work one evening, we were suddenly alarmed by strange noises from the street. Horns, loud traffic sounds—definitely something unusual was happening.

I opened the door and ran to the street. Within seconds I was on the scene and realized what had happened. Roxy lay on the other side of Ridge Pike. A white Mercedes with the hazard lights blinking was stopped in front of her. Nearby, a confused older woman was staring at the motionless (dead?) dog. All the traffic had slowed, and cars were gingerly circling around this spot, carefully passing around the accident.

I approached.

"Is the dog dead?" I asked the woman.

"I don't know," she gasped, visibly shocked. "It happened so fast. The dog appeared in front of my car. I wasn't driving fast—maybe forty miles an hour, I don't know, not fast. And the dog—oh, God! I slammed on the brakes, and, and—did I kill it?"

I approached Roxy. No blood. Warm body. The dog opened her eyes and looked at me, completely confused. I picked her up. Her weight, fifty pounds, was nothing for me at that moment. I sincerely apologized to the shocked woman:

"I am sorry. It's my dog."

"Oh! Don't be sorry. Is the dog alive?" She was concerned. Maybe she also had a dog? Poor woman, she might have killed a dog, had a serious accident, gotten hurt, or damaged her expensive car. All because of my stupid, disobedient dog!

"I think she is. At least right now she is."

For a rare moment, not a single car approached from either direction. I crossed back to our side holding Roxy, limp and unconscious, in my arms. I wondered if my dog was pretending to be dead because she would rather be dead than face punishment.

Telling the woman not to worry, I walked to the backyard gate—it was open—and took a few more steps. I placed Roxy on the grass next to the huge maple tree where I intended to build a treehouse for the boys someday.

Roxy lay there for a while. Then slowly, not sure of what had happened to her, she raised up and stood, shocked and confused, avoiding my eyes.

Meanwhile, the entire family had arrived in the backyard.

"Bring me the leash!" I shouted at the boys.

They ran to get it.

"What are you going to do?" asked a concerned Marta.

Matt brought the leash.

"I will punish her in such a way that she will never cross the friggin' street."

"Are you sure? The dog won't understand, and you will only teach our boys cruelty. Better to think a little than follow your anger."

"Do you want to see how I will punish Roxy?" I asked my sons.

"Yes! Yes!" responded the duet of future medical doctors.

"I am not going to watch! I do not approve of what you are doing," Marta opposed me in front of boys, and she reluctantly left the scene.

I am pretty sure Katia was in her room at that time, but she decided to keep her peace of mind and not participate in a barbarian ritual perpetrated on her dog by her dad. And she knew that if her mother couldn't save Roxy, her chances of doing so were nonexistent.

I attached the long nylon leash to Roxy's collar and tied it to a low branch of the tree. I removed my leather belt and wrapped one end around my right hand, holding the metal buckle inside my fist. I held the dog's collar firmly in my left hand and lifted my right arm.

I felt so angry. She had almost died! How could she do that to me? "I'll teach her a lesson," I thought.

"You bad, bad dog! You escaped. You ran into the street!"

Inches from Roxy's nose … Smack! The leather belt slapped the bark of the maple tree.

"Because of you, an old lady could have been killed. And she could have killed other people!"

Smack! Smack!

"The car could have mutilated you. You could have been dying in the street right now, surrounded by a puddle of your own blood, suffering beyond imagination."

Smack!

"We would cry and mourn you, even though you would not deserve our feelings!"

Smack!

"You will remember this punishment till the end of your dog life!"
Smack!

Again and again I whipped the maple tree with the leather belt.
Smack! Smack! Smack!

"You bad, stupid dog!"

Smack! Smack! Smack!

"And now, I will leave you here on the ground, so you can think about what you did and wait for my decision about what I will do with you."

She stood motionless, her head almost touching the grass. Was she crying?

"Don't even try to comfort this dog!" I snarled at the boys as they approached.

They did not listen to me. They waited until I disappeared, and—I was pretty sure—as soon as I entered the house, they rushed to Roxy. But I didn't care. I did what had to be done. I, the leader of the family, proved to everybody who was in charge of our household. Not Marta—but I!

"I fear not great ideas," I mused. "Nor do I fear boldly going forth to realize them. Like Napoleon. His army was disciplined! Was he afraid to invade Russia? No, he wasn't. Canines need discipline!"

At 9 p.m., I noticed that the boys had brought Roxy water and food. She did not touch it. She lay on the grass, her eyes closed.

Very good. Crime and punishment on Ridge Pike, Philadelphia. I hope she'd remember this lesson!

In the morning before I left for work, I checked on Roxy. She had not changed her position since yesterday. Did she even notice me walking around? She did not raise her head, did not open her eyes. Dead? Impossible! I touched her. She was warm, alive. What a great actress! Let me see how long she can pretend, behaving like this.

So off I rushed to work.

At noon Marta called to tell me she'd untied the dog, but Roxy continued to lie down. She didn't respond to words nor to attempts to lift her up.

"She will," I snapped. "She will."

At 6 p.m., I returned home. We had a family meeting to discuss what to do. My opinion was to wait till morning. The dog could survive thirty-six hours without water and food. Marta said that Roxy might be suffering and could die, and we should take her to the nearest vet. Katia, Matt, and Peter agreed with Marta. My reign as family Napoleon was overturned by popular revolt. When did families become democracies?

The five of us, carrying Roxy, climbed into our van. Everybody wanted to save the dog. They all knew it was my fault. I did something terrible to our dog.

I drove to the veterinary hospital in Plymouth Meeting. It seemed a modern and expensive facility. More a campus, really, with different buildings for different animals. We had nothing to compare it to because this was the first time in our lives that we had visited an American vet. Weterynarii Rzucidło and his Psi Butik on Stanisława Staszica Street back in Zakopane was nothing but a beggar's hovel, now that we'd seen America. Amazing!

An older doctor examined our dog and found nothing but dehydration. He recommended that we leave Roxy there until the next day so they could administer IV feeding with the best nutrients for her.

"How much would it cost?" I asked, thinking about our anemic bank account.

"Doesn't matter! It's for Roxy. To save her life!" Marta angrily whispered in my ear.

"The exam is $130, and for staying in the hospital under our care we charge $100 a day. Is this OK, Mr. Roman?"

"It's OK," responded Mrs. Roman so as to prevent a possible refusal from her soulless husband.

We returned home, and there was only one topic of conversation: Roxy. Everybody was optimistic, and everybody was against me. Katia especially gave me a logic-based educational sermon, pointing out my lack of respect for American morals and customs, my vicious cruelty, my many character flaws, and my primitive male stubbornness. How wonderful that I could leave them all and go to work the next day.

I did not call the hospital during the day because we had only one car. The family had to wait for my return from work to pick up Roxy from the hospital.

At 6:30 in the evening, our team arrived to get Roxy. We met Dr. Gordon, and he told us that there was no progress. Yes, they were able to keep the dog alive, and they hadn't noticed any sickness. But, probably because of the shock, the dog had not recovered. According to their experience, one more day of staying in the hospital should return Roxy to life.

So we left Roxy for a second night.

"Three hundred and thirty dollars," I calculated in my head.

Our home without Roxy was not the same. I was pissed off that everybody blamed me for Roxy's ill health, but remembering their voices, I began to understand that I had overdone it. I punished myself, regretting how I had punished her.

I hoped the next day would bring change for the better.

Unfortunately, the next day—or, to be precise, the next evening—brought no change.

Dr. Gordon had no idea what was going on with our dog. He thought that unplugging Roxy's IV permanently would kill the animal. When he unplugged it for an hour and encouraged Roxy to eat, offering her food and water, she did not respond.

"We can keep the dog alive intravenously for a long time. Don't worry," he assured me.

"Yes, please do," I said, quietly thinking that I had already spent $430.

The next morning, I called the bank to ask about our balance.

Then I made my decision.

Once I came home after work, I announced to the family:

"I am going to pick up Roxy and bring her home. If she wants to live with us, everything will be OK."

"I will go with you," insisted Marta.

The boys stayed home with Katia.

We arrived at Plymouth Meeting. I handed a $530 check to Dr. Gordon, who looking at our old van, realized that the Roman family had paid him up to our limit. Marta and I wrapped Roxy in a blanket we had brought from home and carried her to the van. The dog was quiet and did not move.

We drove in silence. I did not tell Marta, but during the drive home I decided where to bury our dog. At the corner, next to our neighbor John's property. There were no trees, only bushes over there, so it would be easier to dig a deep grave.

When we entered the driveway, Roxy awoke from her trance and started merrily barking. I opened the van's sliding door, and she jumped out. Without waiting for us, she ran toward the gate to the backyard. She stopped at the tree where her food and water bowls had been filled by the boys and started eagerly eating. Nobody would guess she was the same dog who lay dying in the hospital for four days in a row. No, Roxy was a happy dog, just returned home from vacation and heartily welcomed by her human family.

What were the results of this intense episode? Well, at least Matt and Peter learned something. All the way up to the time that they started their residencies as young physicians, whenever I asked them to do something, I would start undoing the brass buckle of my belt. They'd smile and politely comply, so I wouldn't beat their favorite maple tree again.

Did Roxy learn her lesson? I don't know. She had surely felt my anger as I belted the tree. It had been enough to make her sick with guilt and shame. For four days. Since that time, she never crossed the road alone. So I could say that I won that battle of wills. And she won back her health.

On the other hand, Roxy did show her sly genius. By playing sick for three days, she manipulated the whole family. She cost me 530 bucks! As she cast her innocent gaze into my eyes, I knew in her heart she must have felt like the champ.

The higher the heels, the closer to heaven.

—Anonymous

ITALIAN SHOES

Roxy lived in a Catholic family for the first months of her life, so she continuously nurtured feelings of guilt, and she worried a lot about sin. She remembered that time when, as a baby, she was tortured by a stranger who cut her long ears into triangular stumps. Worse was the loss of her long tail, chopped short as a rabbit's.

Roxy remembered these punishments, but she wondered exactly what sins had caused people to be so cruel. What had she done that was so bad? At the time, she had been living with her mother and her sibling pups. Like Job, Roxy suffered without knowing why. Thinking of the penalty for her unknown sins, she trembled. Sometimes the fear was so unbearable that she would shake, lose control, and pee a little on the floor.

This reaction, this terrible reaction, caused even more fear in the dog's heart. If her masters noticed that tiny puddle, they might cut off another part of her body—a toe, a paw, maybe even the head—and they would have good reason because she was a terrible sinner.

Dog owners know that their pets' faces show feelings. A dog can smile at you with amused nonchalance, her head tipped at a quizzical angle. If a dog has a difference of opinion with you, her head straightens, the smile disappears, and she looks you right in the eye. When she's scared, she frowns; when ashamed, she lowers her head to avoid your gaze. No breed shows shame and sadness as convincingly as a boxer.

Roxy was a sensitive girl from a Catholic family and in the past, had been seriously mutilated and punished by being deprived of ears and a tail. She had been exiled to a new, foreign environment. So she worried.

Afraid to breathe, Roxy awaited her destiny. She didn't want to offend the masters, so Roxy avoided our eyes—even the big, round eyes of small tots who continuously hugged her as they tried to nap with her on the floor.

Over time, Marta's dog-bite dog phobia had slowly disappeared, and her curiosity had grown. She wondered, "This creature is so sensitive and delicate. Can I trust her? How can I be sure that nothing bad will happen to my children? She seems friendly, but she's still a wild animal. Can I trust a wild animal?"

The New Complete Book of the Dog by Joyce Robins was a book we had bought without her knowledge before Marta had returned home from Italy. She spotted it on the shelf one day. Intensely curious, she opened it and read avidly. Unfortunately, she found that the author did not like boxers. Or so she deduced because Ms. Robins did not mention them among "breeds with the reputation of being affectionate family dogs, good with children." And she had listed terriers in this group! "Everybody knows that terriers bark a lot, have big teeth, and bite," thought Marta. "And our dog is more dangerous than a terrier? Oh, please!"

But nothing terrible happened. Increasingly in her encounters with Roxy, Marta grew into a comfortable role to which she had long aspired: absolute ruler. At last! Roxy responded immediately to every change of her tone of voice, even the tiniest lilt.

We started taking Roxy for walks outside our fenced backyard. Mr. Caralucci, her first owner, assured me, "Roxy knows how to walk on leash and responds to 'Sit,' 'Down,' and 'Come.'" Pausing to think, he added, "Only use 'Come' when the dog is unleashed."

During our first walk with Roxy, I was the one holding the leash. Katia walked next to me, not excited by walking with a dog, and thinking that walking with blond-haired David from her school would be much more interesting. Matt and Peter had tried to hang onto Roxy, like baby opossums on their mother's back. Roxy walked slowly, as if she understood the importance of this trial of her walking skills.

Our house was located on the highly trafficked Ridge Pike, where car after car sped by at more than fifty miles an hour (even though the speed limit is officially thirty-five). This dangerous proximity to the busy street limited our walks to the grounds of the St. Philip Neri Church, those of its Catholic school, and the athletic field. There were always people around the church and people with dogs on the grassy baseball field.

In the afternoons once the students had departed, dog owners allowed their pets to run on the field, play, and chase each other. The dogs were happy and friendly, but we did not let Roxy join them. We did not trust her yet. Instead, we watched carefully to see how she would react to dogs and strangers.

She did not react. They did not exist for her. She knew she was to walk with the boys and take care of them. No outsider mattered, not even another dog.

I observed her dedication in caring for the children and said to myself, "Roxy—what a great dog!"

The next day, Katia told me that she was too busy to walk with us. So we had a group of four: Roxy, Matt, Peter, and of course, me, responsible for the whole tribe. After half an hour, when there was nobody around, I gave up my stronghold of power and allowed Matt to hold the leash for a few minutes.

The dog noticed that a little boy was now in charge, but she did not change her behavior. She walked slowly, at the same pace as the boy. She was careful. Roxy had not pulled on the leash even once. It was as if she knew that would make Matt fall down. "That's really something," I thought, admiring her for what I had witnessed. "This dog knows she is responsible for Matt." Meanwhile, Peter was crying:

"Now, my turn! Let me walk Roxy! Please, please!" But I was firm. No way.

If Marta knew what I was doing, she would have an attack of apoplexy. Nonetheless, in a few days the boys were taking turns holding the leash. I was there only to protect them if the dog were to suddenly change her behavior. But even though she was only seven months old, Roxy was like a mother to my boys.

We walked like this every day. We did not care whether it was raining or not. Well, I am wrong: When it was raining, the boys insisted that they should take an umbrella to hold over Roxy. And that was a beautiful sight: two small boys, barely bigger than their pet. Matt, taller and stronger, holding the umbrella and the leash. And Peter, on his tiny legs, trying to stay between the dog and his older brother, pretending he was also walking the dog.

My parental protection lasted for maybe a year, maybe longer; I do not remember. But the time came when the boys were walking the dog without me. And never, never did Roxy cause any harm to my sons. Because *Roxy was such a good dog.*

Oh, really? Not so fast. Walking safely with the children was important, but what about Roxy's friendship with my wife?

Marta always had been elegant. When we met at the university, she wore trendy, sophisticated clothing, displaying better taste than the other girls. Whether at university in Poland, or later in Austria, or finally (at last!) in the United States, Marta always looked more elegant than her friends.

Don't think I am telling you this because she's my wife or because I love her (did I just say "I love her"?). I state this as an objective truth. Marta has always been chic. Amen. Two plus two is four. Marta is chic. There are some unquestionable truths in this world. Marta knew how to be elegant. Her natural sense of style allowed her to be glamorous without being rich.

But it is much easier to be chic if one has the money or at least when one has a special opportunity to make a super deal on a bankruptcy sale.

At that time Marta worked as a dietician in several nursing homes in Philadelphia. She drove all over the city. Her geographical skills were incredible: She drove without a map through unknown neighborhoods, and she was never lost.

One day as she drove along in a poor and dangerous neighborhood, Kensington-Allegheny, a hand-lettered sign caught her eye: "Women's European Shoes. Bankruptcy Sale." Stopping on a dime, without thinking—during the time she would spend looking at shoes, somebody could steal the battery or tires from her car, for example—she boldly entered the storefront of a narrow row house. It had seen better days, and there was an odor of recently sautéed onions; was there a kitchen behind the shop?

And inside … inside, a woman twice as big as Marta was organizing boxes of women's shoes.

"What is your shoe size?" the plump proprietress asked. No "Hi," "C'mon in," or "Good afternoon."

"Thirty-six, sometimes 37," answered Marta shyly because her size was not common in the U.S.

"Ha!" laughed the woman. "That's the only size I have."

Marta opened the first box. With wild surmise, suddenly she understood how Ali Baba felt at that moment when, after saying "Open sesame," he entered the cave to behold the treasures of forty thieves.

"Italian shoes! All of these shoes are Italian?"

"All of them."

Marta tried two, five, ten pairs. There were red, and green, and yellow. Each was different, and new, and trendy, and … her size. A bag of gold could not have impressed Marta as much as those shoes.

"How much are they?" Marta asked.

"Ten bucks a pair. Well, depends on how many you buy."

At this moment, Marta experienced an illumination: "If they can spend $300 on a dog, I can spend the same amount on shoes."

"How many do you have?"

"Twenty."

"I can pay you $100 for all of them."

"No. You pay me $120. And that's it—$6 a pair, my dear. No bargaining. Their original price was $40."

"OK," said Marta. She opened her wallet. Half an hour before, she had cashed her weekly paycheck. She had enough—more than enough—but only twenty pairs of those marvelous shoes were available.

She'd have bought a hundred pairs! Well, maybe not. At that time, Marta's salary was not impressive.

I don't know how long it took Marta to try on the twenty most beautiful pairs of shoes, but I do remember that the whole family on that day was scared that something terrible had happened because Marta should have been home and wasn't.

When she arrived, she did not sit down to eat dinner with us. Instead she sat in the living room to do something far more important. First she had to try on each pair of shoes, one after another. Then she had to do it again and again, turning her feet to see each shoe at different angles. Marta hardly looked up. She was engaged in an immersive activity.

We soon tired of watching her. We left her with her shoes and watched TV until bedtime. Only Roxy remained, glued to the floor close to Marta, watching her and sniffing the exotic aromas of Italian leather. Marta finally finished and left the pile of shoes—some in their boxes, some in the closet downstairs. She left the closet door open.

Do you like to read the criminal stories? The good, old ones? Agatha Christie, Arthur Conan Doyle? Do you like them? OK. So, as I said, she left the door open.

The next day, Marta went to work wearing brand-new burgundy suede shoes. She felt ten years younger. New shoes have this special ability to subtract a few years when a woman wears them for the first time. Marta had nineteen more pairs; she could be 190 years younger if she wanted.

In the evening, Marta found great enjoyment looking at all of her new shoes, together like an array of defilading soldiers. First black, then brown, navy blue, and green. Then she organized this shoe parade into two rows, then four rows. Then she found there were …

Nineteen pairs! Not twenty pairs but nineteen! Had the shoe lady shorted her a pair of shoes? Maybe she had left a pair of beautiful Italian shoes in the car? Some people probably think it's not a big deal to lose one pair when you have twenty, but this stupid thought is likely from a person who has never tried to find top-quality Italian shoes in size thirty-six.

A day passed, and Marta decided to move all the shoes upstairs to our bedroom. While carrying the shoes, she found only eighteen pairs to bring upstairs. Roxy was absent during this counting. I and my sons, and Katia, too, were made to swear that we were not playing a stupid joke, hiding Mum's shoes. The atmosphere was tense. Somebody was lying.

But the third counting of Marta's shoes—we all witnessed the process of counting—found only seventeen pairs. Fear fell upon us. What was this? Space-alien thieves with spike-heel fetishes? A rare phenomenon of dematerialization taking place on Ridge Pike in Philadelphia? Total confusion reigned for a few horrible moments.

"Where's Roxy?" Matt suddenly asked.

"Roxy is so sad," Peter said.

"She doesn't like to eat," Matt added. "Why doesn't she like to eat our food anymore, Mum?" At this moment, Marta, the smartest person in our family, screamed:

"Ooooooh! That terrible dog! It's her!"

Within two minutes we found that, in the darkest corner of the garage, Roxy had organized her own "Open Sesame" treasure cave. There was a colorful pile, the remains of three pairs of Italian shoes, size thirty-six—pale pink, light yellow, and robin's egg blue. Clearly, Roxy's taste ran to pastels.

Since that time, the Roman family has always stored shoes on shelves at least five feet above the floor.

EPILOGUE

"Old soldiers never die, nor do good old dogs" is a quaint folk maxim I often heard as a youth, when I wandered Zakopane hillsides among shepherds and woodsmen. A soldier gains eternal glory through war—a dog, by being good.

This was Roxy's last story. But don't worry! Roxy will return like General MacArthur returned to the Philippines in October 1944. By the way, is it true that he borrowed our Zakopane maxim for his retirement speech to Congress?

You may find Roxy in small roles similar to the pipe-clenching general's well rehearsed, camera-ready leap off of his whaleboat into the waves and onto a Leyte beachhead under fire. Great PR for MacArthur but otherwise without meaning and luckily without consequence. Similarly, if you find Roxy's brand publicized in future cameos, rest assured, Roxy herself won't affect the story line. She's a "red herring" if it's a mystery story.

An Australian military historian (Gavin Long, if you must know; you can look it up) opined that the American public, uncertain what lay ahead in that dark period of World War II, "desperately needed a hero and wholeheartedly embraced Douglas MacArthur—good press copy that he was. No other human came close to matching his mystique, not to mention his evocative lone-wolf stand—something that has always resonated with Americans." Roxy never smoked a pipe; nonetheless, she has her own mystique.

Genetically, she's far closer to a lone wolf than the late general was. He's "evocative"? Not compared to the vivid feelings and memories Roxy evokes in every developmentally challenged child[5] who cuddles with her on the rug. In that moment they experience warmth, closeness, and love that's remembered for a lifetime! She is less vain than the general and more compassionate, too, so I rest my case: Roxy is a much greater hero than Douglas MacArthur. I trust you've enjoyed getting to know her. I hope she resonates in your heart and that you'll be delighted to bump into Roxy again.

To err is human; to forgive, canine.

—Anonymous

---

5   Because we lived near an outstanding psychological center for developmentally challenged children, our home had sheltered many families during the children's treatment visits.

MARTA STORIES

Am I not a man? And is not a man stupid? I'm a man, so I'm married. Wife, children, house—everything. The full catastrophe.

—Nikos Kazantzakis, Zorba the Greek

MIKIMOTO PEARLS

Our twenty-year wedding anniversary was drawing close. I had no gift for Marta. I had already decided to buy her a string of beautiful pearls, but ignorant on the subject of pearl-buying, I hesitated to finalize the purchase.

Every string of pearls serves the same purpose: to elegantly adorn a neck. Fifty-dollar pearls can fulfill this function. Or you can spend hundreds, even thousands of dollars.

Like watches—a shiny Timex shows the same information as a gilt Patek Philippe. But each watch has its own brand, and different brands tell different stories about their owners. Knowing Marta, I didn't dare offer Timex pearls for a Rolex anniversary.

But how to buy Patek-like pearls that didn't cost so much? I couldn't afford such a huge expense. I started figuring out how to afford, let's say, Tissot-level pearls and not overpay for them either. And I couldn't be fooled into buying a fake.

It's so hard to buy high quality cheaply!

So I waited. I waited and hoped for a miracle. Why not? Jewelers could have bankruptcy sales; the TV program *Antiques Roadshow* was full of people who had bought precious jewelry at garage sales; women might lose jewelry on the sidewalk. And I always look carefully at the pavement, ready to find something precious.

So, why rush my money to the nearest jeweler instead of waiting a few more days?

I have to add that at that time I worked at the corner of Chestnut and Market streets in Philadelphia, bordering so-called Jewelers' Corner, where each shop glistened with pearls, diamonds, and Rolex watches. Owned by Russian Jews, those shops sold expensive jewelry. Others, owned by Asians, sold cheap jewelry. No judgment here. The best way for immigrants to slot into the economy? Move fast into neglected niches. It's all a matter of timing.

Wait a minute. You're already wondering, where's the animal in this story? Think carefully: Where do pearls come from? An oyster is definitely an animal. A sacred animal, at least for Mikimoto pearl lovers. There. You have your animal. You'll have to settle for an oyster in this story.

Could Marta distinguish jewelry made in Antwerp from jewelry made in Seoul? If it were about cloth, she'd know, but pearls? Every day I passed a jewelry store with an "Asian Diamonds" sign in the window, full of bright and shiny objects. Another sign said "Real Pearls" were available for $100 to $300. Did these pearls change color with time?

Did they break during frosty winters? What was wrong with them? Would they be good enough?

But still, it was safer to wait. Speed is good only when catching flies with your hand.

One day I stepped off the train from downtown. Walking toward the car, I remembered that Roxy's canned food supply was almost gone. ACME grocery store was half a mile away, so I drove to the store and found extra large cans of dog food on sale at 50% off. What a bargain! Stores don't have dog food sales often. Once a quarter, maybe. And today I was so lucky! Without thinking much, I bought sixteen huge cans. Happy as a child, I drove home.

As I pulled into our driveway in front of Romanówka, I noticed we had a visitor. I recognized a new Honda Civic with the license plate "ELALAW." It was our Polish-American friend Ela. She'd left an internship with the U.S. Environmental Protection Agency to join a private law firm downtown. Probably, returning from work, she had stopped by to chat with Marta.

I removed my shopping from the trunk, two double plastic bags, sixteen pounds each, and proudly entered the house.

* * *

The aroma of veal stew met me. There is no other entree I love as much as veal stew with a creamy, red paprika sauce. I stepped into the kitchen and sampled a spoonful. Then a couple more spoonfuls. The stew was delicious. I had no doubt that this dish would be served that night. I looked around: White tablecloth, huge bouquet of white lilacs (Marta's favorite flower) in the middle of the table, nearby a bottle of champagne in an ice bucket …

An animated Marta entered the dining room in her best blue dress. She had a new haircut, she was wearing some lovely blue Italian high heels to match, and she had the aura that "now something wonderful is about to happen." Ela followed her. Both women watched me as if I was the main actor in this event. What did they expect from me? I had no clue what was going on. Why champagne? Why the veal? Or the tasty-looking torte on the buffet?

I stooped to put the sixteen large cans on the floor, making a clinking noise like the collapse of a construction crane. Winded from carrying my burden up the flight of stairs from the driveway, I gasped, "I bought [gasp] sixteen cans [gasp] of food for Roxy [gasp] on sale at ACME [gasp]."

Silence.

I pointed at my shopping as if they could not see the bags of cans. More silence.

After a while, Marta slowly approached me. With each step, tears brimmed in her eyes. Looking straight through my eyes and into my soul, she whispered:

"So you remembered the dog. But not our twentieth wedding anniversary?"

Ela looked at me with the steely eyes of a prosecutor facing a murderer brought in shackles in front of the jury. Marta had a key witness to my Crime Against the Holy Sacrament of Marriage.

* * *

I didn't utter a word. I ran to the car. Without checking to see if I had enough gas, I started driving. The car was a metallic blue Chevy Horizon with 170,000 miles on it and six previous owners. The warning light that would glow if I didn't have enough gas was dark. Good!

I drove to King of Prussia. At that time King of Prussia Mall was the third-largest mall on the East Coast. The most prestigious stores were there: Nordstrom, Neiman Marcus, Lord & Taylor, and others that only sheiks and oligarchs knew about. And I drove to this mall. Twenty miles. Like crazy. Rusted metal sheets of Chevy Horizon that rattled when flying down the highway at seventy miles an hour now made a sound like a police siren. Other cars mistook this sound as a chasing police patrol, slowed down, and let me pass them. Police patrols, if there were any between Plymouth Meeting and King of Prussia, must have thought that I was one of them, only disguised as an ordinary car to catch some special criminal. They too allowed me to speed along the highway.

Within twenty-five minutes—record time—I was parked at the King of Prussia Mall. On my left side was a Mercedes S500 and on my right a Maserati Biturbo. I parked without pausing to think about if I was too close and, when opening the door, the Maserati might damage my car.

In front of me—Fate's choice, not mine—was glassy Nordstrom's. I entered. Thousands of lights surrounded me in every direction. As I moved through the store, hundreds of aromas assailed me. They came from perfume bottles proffered by elegant ladies eager to spray something on me and others. I sniffed their expensive perfumes, and they sniffed my veal stew aroma and looked at me surprised because the strength of my fragrance eclipsed their Chanel No 5.

I walked in further, looking for the jewelry department. Here it was! An older gentleman wearing an immaculate suit and crisp white shirt evaluated me with his experienced senior shop assistant's eyes.

"Sir," he said.

I knew what I wanted. I was only uncertain that I could explain it properly.

"I want to buy—I want to *purchase* ... " I corrected myself, knowing that I was in a store where each item was so expensive that the word "buy" was not adequate.

"I want to purchase a string of pearls. A single string of pearls, but of very high quality."

"You are in Nordstrom, sir," he interrupted me, and when he said "sir," the tone was not very genuine.

"Yes, I know, but I've heard that there are Japanese pearls that ... "

"Mikimoto pearls, sir?"

"Yes, Mikimoto pearls! Do you have these?"

He did not say anything. He opened a drawer, took out three strings of pearls, and spread them in front of me on a black tray covered with fabric. Fingers against the black velvet, he gestured at each string of pearls separately. They glistened like treasure from *One Thousand and One Nights*. Hesitantly, I picked up the smallest string.

"Excellent choice, sir." Good sign: an expert confirmed my choice. "An extraordinary value. These pearls come exclusively from Mikimoto oysters, and Mikimoto oysters come only from the oyster beds created in the Shinmei inlet by Mikimoto Kōkichi, who chose the best possible place to grow outstanding pearls. The Shinmei River runs for thirty kilometers over a limestone bed. Its high level of calcium bathes the oysters day and night as the seeds grow into pearls. How would you like to pay for your purchase?"

"With my Visa card," I said, taking out my wallet.

"Does this card cover the entire purchase?" he asked, and there was no "sir" at the end of the sentence this time.

Oh, you, you pushy shop assistant! You who probably noticed I wore jeans and my faithful sweater. You think I cannot afford your overpriced pearls? Listen, stupid:

"My Visa limit is sev-en thou-sand dol-lars," I said, accenting each syllable.

"And the rest? Do you have another credit card to pay for the entire purchase?"

Momentarily I was mute. I looked at him like a surprised calf.

He moved "my" string of pearls up to his eyes and read:

"Ten thousand, four hundred and eight dollars." He stopped reading. "Sir."

This "sir" was different. This "sir" showed the triumph of a Nordstrom shop assistant over a tentative client who did not belong in his circle of clients. This "sir" was my punishment for buying sixteen cans of food for Roxy on my wedding anniversary.

* * *

There was no continuing my chat with the senior shop assistant. I made a U-turn and, without saying a word, walked out. I continued walking until I entered Macy's, where my brisk stride took me to the jewelry department.

A statuesque African-American lady with green eye-shadow was warm and friendly as she talked with me about pearls. She helped me select a beautiful three-strand necklace, held by a gorgeous clasp set with tiny diamonds. Tiny, but real. And the pearls were also real.

Seven hundred dollars.

And beautifully wrapped.

I drove slowly. This was the time to enjoy "mission accomplished." This was the time to make my entrance, see Marta's happy face, and savor how Ela would envy Marta, who had received such a wonderful gift.

I parked the car. Ela was still here. She had to see what I bought.

I entered the house. Roxy welcomed me, demanding to be fed.

(They did not open any of the cans. The dog was still hungry.) But I didn't heed my dog. I approached Marta and gave her the beautiful package. Then I was kissing her, and she was kissing me, and Ela was exclaiming:

"Unwrap it, unwrap it! What is it?"

Marta opened the box. Both women whispered with admiration:

"Oh, how beautiful! Not one strand, but three! And the pearls are so big!"

And now was the time for my reward. Reheated stew, cold champagne, happy wife.

Ela, eying my gift, wanted to know how I met Marta. After enjoying a second glass of Sauvignon Blanc and a warm smile from Marta, I began our romantic story:

"It was a cold Saturday. I didn't want to study. Who likes to study on Saturday? Instead, hoping to meet a pretty girl, I decided to go to the disco. The nearest student disco was in a dorm called Piast. Remember, Marta? How I remember our wedding day! The eighth of November, 1971, I ... "

"The fourth of November," Marta corrected me.

"No, Marta. It was the eighth." Channeling Zorro pulling out his sword to stop a hanging, I pulled at my wedding ring to prove the truth. Wed to my finger for twenty years, like Marta, it wouldn't budge.

"Check your wedding ring," I said because I had forgotten that, many years ago, Marta had lost her original ring. (How one can lose a wedding ring without losing a finger, I don't understand.) We had replaced it with one that had no engraving of the wedding date inside.

"You know mine has no date." She was indignant. "Check yours. Use soap."

So, at the kitchen sink, I lathered my hand with dish soap. After some struggle, I pulled off the ring, rinsed it, and read:

"Marta. Nov. 8, 1971."

"Impossible!" screamed Marta. She snatched the ring from my hand.

"Let me see it, too!" demanded Ela the lawyer.

"And today is ... today is November fourth. I had four more days to buy an anniversary gift for Marta. Do you agree?"

They did not.

They told me to eat the stew because it was best when hot.

After dinner, Marta asked me:

"Do you have the receipt from Macy's?"

"Yes," I said and handed it to her.

You can guess why she asked, yes? Four days later, on our real anniversary, Marta approached me with a smile on her face. From her neck hung a beautiful jade pendant.

"Do you like my necklace?"

An intelligent husband always knows how to respond.

"Oh, it is truly beautiful! How marvelous! Where did you get it?"

"From you, sweetheart. It's perfect with this pink silk blouse. Thank you so much!"

Frigates are tough old birds, literally. They live fifty, sixty years, a long time for any creature.

—Anders Gyllenhaal, Flying Lessons

FRIGATE BIRDS

Marta and I are on entirely different wavelengths. She's down-to-earth, and I'm a tosh-thinker. You don't know the word "tosh"? It's British, and I think it's close in meaning to the Polish word *banialuki* (our word for "fudge") and the English word "nonsense."

I am such a person that my thoughts jump from nonsense to fudge to rubbish, and each thought has no practical use. What would happen to me left without direction? Thank God that Marta, who doesn't see clouds, can spot a speck of dirt on the floor. Sometimes I wonder, if the two of us sat quietly in a room together doing nothing but thinking, would our two thought-waves ever intersect?

I hope this would not happen. If she read my thoughts, her circuits would overload, and I would be in deep trouble.

Thus, the best place for me, a lazy husband, is a Caribbean beach. There, Marta would read inspirational paperbacks, drink margaritas (no sugar, please!), and nap in the sun. There, she wouldn't bark housekeeping commands at me. And nobody thinks deeply at the beach. What better distraction than to get on a plane and, after a four-hour flight, enjoy the sand and the warm blue sea?

So here I am. Thirty kilometers from Cancún, Mexico.

Marta is under a huge umbrella, sipping a margarita. I'm under another umbrella, sipping local rum. My eyes watch a huge bird majestically soar up into the sky. It's a frigate with black plumage and a long, deeply forked tail.

I notice that Marta is immersed in both her book and her margarita, unlikely to discover my thoughts by connecting her wavelength to my wavelength. I am safe. I can imagine anything! She won't ask me to repair a faucet, rake leaves, drive to the grocery store, or do anything else requiring immediate attention. At last, time to think!

I relax. On the beach in Puerto Morelos, with the Mexican staff to follow Marta's orders, I am as free as that bird. Slowly, without intent, I muse on the turquoise ocean and two puffy white clouds, feeling in love with the moment. This evening, I would eat fish and tropical fruit, and perhaps a smiling waitress would compliment my broken Spanish.

* * *

Two frigates float motionless above. How I *love* to watch them hang in the air so effortlessly. It's almost as if they're asleep on the waves of warm air rising over the ocean. Warm air offering loving support to great, soaring birds.

I sink into a reverie of useless facts stuck to my brain—not serious facts that I could actually use. But then, following the birds in the sky, I am glad that I know many useless facts about this amazing gift of creation. I am proud to be a naturalist, even though that was forty years ago and in another country. In any case, I can tell you: *Frigate magnificens* lives in Florida, the Caribbean, and the Galapagos Islands.

They say that frigates are relatives of pelicans, but I find that hard to believe. Compare the clumsy flight of a pelican, flapping its wings like a sick crow, to the smooth glide of a frigate, at ease between the clouds and the sea. A frigate expends little effort in the air. In concert with the wind, it plays with hidden ripples and invisible currents. It's almost as big as an eagle, the frigate bird, but it would take three of them to weigh as much as one single eagle.

Their lightness of being is bearable, though; it allows them to float in the heavens. Their black tapered sword-wings slice the sky smoothly. The seven- or eight-foot wingspan, in proportion to a frigate's body length, is unequaled. Even an albatross cannot boast such perfect dimensions. No wonder the frigate can float on air without landing for a week. It swings about, playing on the wind, first slowly forward, then a high-speed sideways turn. At times it flies so high that it is barely visible in the sky. Then it will swoop low again, close enough to see a red spot on the neck and the long beak ending in a curve. What a beautiful bird!

* * *

My lazy thoughts slide into old memories. Many years ago in Zakopane, I taught biology at a school for adults. My students were shop managers, police officers, nuns, activists—all kinds of people. My job was to teach them about evolution. I explained every detail twice to the militia, I did not mock the nuns who believed "God created everything, amen," and I allowed tired workers to sleep during my lessons. I conveyed what the curriculum required, but at the end of each lesson, I usually added a few sentences. For instance, "It's a fact that the Church does not deny evolution but accepts it as following God's direction. So, dear nuns, it is not a sin to listen to the teacher." Or, when attempting to move cops or party apparatchiks toward spirituality, another favorite was this: "Can you see the beautiful simplicity of evolution? We can only stand in awe and wonder at creation—its majestic grandeur, its microscopic granularity." It sounded profound to me, and who knows? Maybe they became more humane.

I taught others, but how could I myself know what to believe? Should I wait for a "burning bush" to show me the path or simply stroll down the road from Jerusalem to Damascus until a moment of enlightenment radically altered my belief system? Surely I could look to science for truth. Scientists decipher the mechanism of protein synthesis. With the electron microscope they look inside the cell—indeed, inside the atom—so how could I not believe in all of the phenomenal scientific discoveries? Is there any reason not to posit a Creator of evolution, now that we have science?

Yet I was skeptical of the boasts of overconfident Soviet scientists as they claimed discovery after amazing discovery. "Skepticism" turned out to be the right response. The Soviet announcement that they could create live protein in a test tube was indeed nonsense. Soviets were not the only scientists to be deceptive or at least to deceive themselves. Most American scientists' "discoveries" about cold fusion were simply lies or distortions.

Finding my beliefs to align with neither pure religion nor pure science (at least as practiced by overambitious researchers promoted by the government), I developed my own theory. The "curtain theory" goes like this: We experience existence as if we sit in an opera house before a heavy curtain. You can't see anything through it, but you can hear the orchestra tuning instruments, the faint sound of people talking. We think, "Oh, if they raise that curtain, we'll see the whole scene." Then the curtain rises! Unfortunately, behind the first curtain is a second one. At least it's not so thick, we note. The sound is not so muffled. Is that someone walking on the other side, billowing the material? No matter how much we see or hear, the view is still as if from Plato's Cave. So we ask, "Please, please, unveil the rest … "

The second curtain rises, and again, things are not as we expect. This time, there is a more transparent curtain. You can clearly see the play of lights on the stage and the figures moving across it.

By now, we are almost sure: If they raise that one final curtain, everything would be revealed!

Curtains behind curtains. We still don't know what's really going on.

Self-confident, pompous science. That's pretending the curtains don't exist, that everything is crystal-clear and squared away. But how could *anyone* ever be fully knowledgeable of *anything*? Like Achilles in pursuit of the tortoise, we get nearer with each step, but we never arrive. A tiny rift left for God.

Stephen Hawking said that he no longer needs God. I am not as wise as he; I cannot visualize neutrinos, so I'd rather return my thoughts to the sky and the soaring frigates. My inspiration. How beautiful they are. How perfect!

For me, this bird suspended in the blue sky is an avatar of the unspoken truths we may never know. Emily Dickinson may not have been the first to point this out, but few rival her lapidary wit:

> I hope you love birds too.
> It is economical.
> It saves going to heaven.

Immanuel Kant opined, less succinctly, "The more often and

steadily we reflect upon them, these things fill the mind with ever new and increasing admiration and awe: starry heavens above and moral law within me."

Through my imagination, I know the starry heavens. Now, where's that moral law Kant mentions? I'm up in the clouds. Is a *cirrus* crime in progress? Did I mention my mind wanders … lonely as a cloud?

* * *

OK, OK, enough vagabonding. "On with the story!" you demand. No problem. I'm down with that, as my American-born son would put it. He's an ER physician, by the way.

Now, where was I?

Oh, yes. We're at the beach, and no thought occupies my mind. I'm one with the moment. I fly, a bird aloft. I feel the soft touches of the Gulf Coast breeze. From time to time I doze to the murmur of surf on sand. But Marta's voice interrupts a stolen moment of bliss:

"Look, instead of lying here, you"d better walk to Puerto Morelos. There are interesting shops there. You could buy presents."

"And they have nothing at the hotel? No gift shop?" I mutter reluctantly.

"Nothing at all. And expensive! Their prices are crazy! No, you need to go into town to the silversmith shops. Get a thin silver choke necklace for Katia, and silver cufflinks for your boss. He'll love that. And maybe a little surprise for little me? Well, what're you waiting for? Are you gonna walk along the beach to town or what?"

Hmmmm. Didn't really feel like it …

On the other hand, it would be good for me to walk. For my health, my weight—she's probably right.

"But it's five kilometers one way." I was not yet convinced.

"Exactly. It will do your heart good! Put on your hat. Smear your neck with SPF 50. And take money! Find the most interesting silver jewelry. Look for it; don't buy just anything. Be careful with our money! *Jezu Zmiłuj się!* Put on your T-shirt. Not inside out!"

As you can see, my wife has a gift. She can convince even a tosh-thinker to follow her "recommendations."

* * *

I walk the seashore. Puerto Morelos lies to the south, in the direction of Cancún. The sun is warm. From my left, flooding waves tickle my feet again and again. On my right, hotel guests sprawl on deck chairs under umbrellas, staring at me because I must be crazy to walk in this afternoon heat. Above me, the frigates roam the sky, still refusing to flap their wings.

On and on I go. Boring. I take my iPhone out of my pack and search for a book to listen to. I find Wayne Dyer and Deepak Chopra's *Creating Your World the Way You Really Want It to Be.* At the beginning, both gentlemen introduce themselves as scientists, they say how many books each has published, and they list what successes they have each achieved. I get bored and angry as I listen because they remind me that these days, no one reads my books anymore, few people like my blog, and even mild praise is a rarity.

I skip a few chapters. Now Dr. Dyer is telling me how he met an old native on an exotic island who knew how to summon clouds or chase them away. When there is a drought, the villagers go to the cloud whisperer, and he looks at the sky and talks to the clouds. Then the rains come and water the village fields. Too much water? No problem. The natives go to the old cloud man, he talks to the clouds again, and immediately the sun pops out. That's exactly what Dr. Dyer says. I wait for Deepak Chopra to interrupt and blow the idiot away: "What are you saying, Wayne? You're so childish! You actually *believe* this nonsense?"

But no. Deepak pays careful attention to the whole story without comment, and then he says to us poor innocent bystanders:

"Now I will tell you something interesting that may not surprise you because, if you are listening to this recording, your eyes are already open to the wonders of the world. Well, imagine an English scientist researching whales. One whale this scientist has never seen, and he wants very much to see it. Unfortunately, the whale hardly ever appears, and when it does, it's only off the coast of Bali. It is a rare whale—almost extinct. The scientist goes to Bali."

Deepak went on to tell us he walks Bali beaches for a month, two, three, and … nothing. He becomes so sad that the natives notice. They approach him, curious.

"Why are you so sad?"

"Oh, because I've wanted to see a whale for three months, and the sea has been empty."

"What whale?" The natives ask.

"The rarest whale," he replies.

"Aha! You want to see our whale?" They rejoice because the Balinese secretly despise the Aussie bloke tourists who support their economy.

But a scientist who comes to study their rare whale? That would bring a higher level of tourism: scientists, naturalists, and tree-huggers instead of loud-mouth surfers and beer-swilling "mates."

"We will ask our little girl, and she will call our whale for you."

At this point Deepak takes a theatrical pause.

"This is exciting—don't stop!" Dr. Dyer demands. "Tell me what happens next."

"Well," Deepak continues with an insider's tone, "a twelve-year-old girl comes to the beach, speaks to the waves in her native tongue, and then tells the English scientist that the whale will arrive at nine the next morning. Next morning, the whale appears as promised. It's now the scientist's turn to rejoice. How great! The rarest of rare whales in view!

"But that's not all. The whale draws near to shore then launches himself up onto the sand as if he wants to shake the scientist's hand with his fin to welcome the eminent Englishman to his habitat. The distinguished scientist examines him and takes a few skin scrapings for DNA samples, and then the whole village gathers around the whale to push him back into the water."

Deepak finishes his story. I wait for Dr. Dyer, a psychologist who has listened to many irrational people, to respond appropriately to what has clearly been a bizarre fantasy. "Deepak," he'd say, "whatcha been drinking today, brother? Wow! More than a couple of Stolis, I bet. Do you need an intervention?"

But no! Dr. Dyer praises the story. It proves, he concludes, that there is more to heaven and earth than we imagine. After exchanging a few smarmy compliments, the two doctors move on to the next chapter.

I'm angry. Why? The entire world buys this pap. Nobody protests; everyone takes this bunk at face value. Is it permissible to publish bilge under the guise of self-help? Well, I guess so because that's how they sell millions of copies.

* * *

I walk. On the left, waves break onto the sand. On the right, beachgoers repose under umbrellas. I muse that ripe young women haven't noticed me for decades. I pass by as if in stealth mode, producing no signal on their male–female radar. To register on their screens, I joyfully trot over to retrieve a ball, or I help a crying toddler up from the sand. Look, young mommy, what a gentleman this old man is!

The view on the right becomes less attractive. Stray animals eating dead fish can't compete with tanned girls under umbrellas. The hotels have ended. Only a vagrant dog looks at me, staring from the shade under a bunch of dune grass. "What's that oddball doing, walking in the afternoon heat, wandering off to who-knows-where," he thinks as I pass.

Discarded melon rinds, torn plastic bags, crumpled newspapers, and rusted cans litter the dunes on my right. As I proceed, I see stray mutts prowling the shoreline discards. These Mexican dogs, I discover, unlike young women, do notice me. They regard me stonily. My subconscious fear that one of them will sneak up behind me and chomp off a big hunk of my posterior soon transforms into real fear.

Stay alert, I think. I look more closely along the beach. Maybe find a stick or stone to protect myself?

The dogs make no move. They don't care about me after all, or maybe they're too smart to exert themselves in the blazing afternoon sun. To the southwest, I see thunderheads darkening the horizon. I no longer need be on guard to my right. Looking left, I notice two rows of dark pilings sticking out above the waves, probably the remains of a long-ago collapsed pier. On them are an assortment of seabirds: a pair of clean, white gulls; three pelicans; and three big, ugly birds.

Pelicans are weird but cute. Gulls amuse us with their bold thievery. But these three black birds? What are they? What are they doing? They are notably larger than the gulls and slightly smaller than the pelicans. They sit dark and hunched over, like the witches in *Macbeth*. Their beaks are long with a cruelly curved tip, their feathers sleek, and …

Oh, what a nasty peck! No fair! What's going on? Two of the black, misshapen, skulking birds gang up on a poor gull. One pecks the gull's head with his long, sharp beak, while the other goes low, trying to bite off a leg.

He succeeds. The gull loses balance and falls into the waves. The three dark fates resume their vigil on the now vacant pilings. The gulls and pelicans have all fled the bullying mayhem I witnessed. The wind picks up and froths the waves.

Suddenly I notice the red spot on the neck of one of the nasty birds. That stops me short. Could they be frigates? My frigates? My soaring avatars of freedom, truth, and beauty? Impossible!

I observe the birds on the piles for maybe an hour. As I watch, the realization creeps up on me that, once again, life has tricked me: One moment I find divine inspiration in frigates, and the next, the scales fall from my eyes when I see the same birds, sitting on pilings, pecking and harassing their neighbors.

It's the same with people! You watch someone dance or sing, and you see them as a symbol of love and health and beauty. You imagine this person's other attributes—that they are wise, noble, creative, and God knows what else. You think that your ideal is before you. Then comes the wondrous day when your dream person sits beside you, and—a tragedy! Inanity, a heartless attitude, moral blindness, a mean streak, bad breath, always something you would never have expected.

* * *

I return to the hotel at dinnertime feeling exhausted, yet triumphant. I've walked ten kilometers, no mean feat by itself, and I found everything Marta wanted—even a small silver iguana for her surprise. She praises me for a wonderful shopping experience. I am proud to be a great shopper. And it was not too far. Not at all.

Back in our room, I open my laptop. The illuminated apple offers me another bite of knowledge. I google "frigate birds."

Alas, I am right to believe what I had seen with my own eyes this afternoon. Frigates are murderers and thieves! The can't swim. Frigate feathers soak up water, and if frigates get submerged, they drown. They can't walk, so they conspire for days about how to break eggs, eat chicks, smash turtles with their beaks, or steal fish from gulls. Such an attitude toward life even has a name, I found: "kleptoparasitism," a combination of being a thief and a parasite.

A witch disguised as Botticelli's Venus: that's a frigate aloft. On the ground, it's merely a witch.

Oh well, as old as I am, I've survived disappointment before. I have Marta at my side. I'd love to soar freely into the sky, but Marta is consistent, and practical, and a great cook besides! Maybe for a while I'll plant my feet firmly on the ground and keep my nose to the grindstone. That will make Marta happy.

Live in such a way you would not be ashamed to sell your parrot to the town gossip.

—Will Rogers

MY ENEMY ALBERT

I've lived in the United States for decades, and no one has ever truly hurt me. Sure, there was the rogue I encountered one night on Allegheny Avenue who took a few dollars from me. Oh yes, also, that malicious foreman who, in my presence, told Polish jokes to our fellow workers to wind me up. But no person has wanted to completely destroy me. Never!

However when I say "never," I refer only to people. A creature once hated me. He lived for one purpose only: to make a hole in my skull. Albert. You'll soon see what I mean.

At fourteen, my older son Matt began to exhibit open irritation at my existence. It hurt. Convinced that I did not deserve this from my son, I had no explanation of his behavior, of what caused him to be so far off base. I was angry as a kid, too, but my father never hit me. I certainly didn't want to hit my son.

Searching for guidance as to how to respond, I remembered what my eighth-grade teacher Mrs. Wójcik told us: "Never guess; look it up!" She would proudly point her finger at the long row of *Wielka Encyklopedia PWN* volumes in the bookcase along the side of the classroom, as if to say, "It's all there, at your fingertips!" I searched Google. I searched Wikipedia. I searched in books I had read years ago, books I kept in my library because they included underlined paragraphs I had considered important when I read them. What to expect from my son? How to relate to him? What is most important between father and son?

The internet provided me guidance. Under "family relations" I found an interesting term, "filial piety," so I clicked on it.

Wow! My needs were modest and mild indeed, compared to the practice of traditional Chinese filial piety. Nothing close. I counted ten commandments in the article:

1. Be good to parents.
2. Take care of parents.
3. Engage in good conduct outside the home to maintain respect for one's parents and ancestors.
4. Show love, respect, and support.
5. Display courtesy.
6. Ensure male heirs.
7. Uphold fraternity among brothers.
8. Wisely advise one's parents, including dissuading them from moral unrighteousness.
9. Display sorrow for their sickness and death.
10. Bury them and carry out sacrifices after their death.

All ten? No hope for that. The first was all I needed. The last would be nice, too, I thought, wondering what my sons would choose to sacrifice in my honor.

Disrespect and antipathy continued, however—grew, even. "Life is painful," I thought. "My oldest son! Emotionally walking away from me, and I can't stop him. Worse, his brother Peter, still a little boy of eight, is watching Matt with admiration, learning from him how to reject a parent."

Matt was seamlessly shifting his attachments from home to the outside world. This shift in attachment made a great leap forward one year when my wife Marta decided to send both boys to an exclusive private school. "Even if I raised them badly," she told me, "the school will mend my mistakes and fix their character."

We wanted the best for our sons. We sent them to a school where they would be surrounded by the cream of society. Alas! Not intellectual cream; it was financial cream. What we didn't know as we proudly enrolled them was that the students and parents at The Academy were all members of a cult that worshipped money and sports. Our boys suddenly had to reconcile the vast difference between our family circumstances and those of their classmates. Money? We lived paycheck to paycheck. Sports? From the boys I soon learned that the sports I liked were stupid.

I suffered. Even if our sons were super smart (they weren't) and even if they worked like ants (not with my genes!), they would always seem worthless to their classmates. Their parents were poor. Poor and different. And weird. Unwanted outlanders.

I needed to counter this unfortunate trend. I tried to establish shared activities, to spend time together to teach my sons important skills and values. "We can have fun together!" I'd say. They didn't listen. Why should they?"

"We might barely be able to afford a ski vacation, but tennis is a sport I like and could teach you easily," I told them. But skiing and tennis were not the macho sports of their alpha-male classmates. The peak of Academy success was only accessible via the swim team or the team for what they called "football."

A Polish immigrant, I didn't even know what to call that spheroid the monstrous giants carried, threw, and caught on the field. They call it a football? Seems like the spheroid rarely touched a foot. "Handball," "airball," or "runball" would be more suitable names. I didn't grasp the rules of this brutal game. The famous players and weekend scores meant nothing to me. American football? I had no desire to learn this misnamed sport in the middle of my life. Real football, where the ball can only touch the feet but never the hands, Americans called "soccer." At The Academy, soccer was a game only for girls.

How could I compare with the other parents in The Academy? Where I grew up, in the Tatra Mountains, we had no swimming pools and no deep rivers, just shallow mountain streams. Yes, we had mountain lakes, but they were covered with ice for most of the year. So, where would I have learned how to swim—in the puddles in my muddy backyard?

I grew up in a poor country, isolated from the West. We ate cabbage, pierogies with farmer cheese, and gołąbkis, our stuffed cabbage with tomato sauce that I considered the height of Polish cuisine. Delicious! Until arrival in the U.S., we'd never seen a lobster, mussels, or a tasty hamburger. We sang Polish Christmas carols instead of rap.

But at this socially prestigious private school in a Philadelphia suburb, my sons were surrounded by rich kids. At the time they started attending the renowned Academy, they couldn't help but compare our Romanówka with the large brick or stone mansions with sweeping green lawns where the other students lived. Our ten-year-old Toyota Corolla looked silly next to the Mercedes, BMWs, and Audis the other parents drove. Matt put it this way: "You can't keep on dropping us off in this crate! We should buy a new car."

The boys continued to denigrate our lives versus "everybody else's life." Their disloyalty to our family, our country, and our language rubbed me the wrong way. *"Jakbym miał drzazgę w sercu!"* I told Marta. English does not use such a phrase because the English have never suffered the deep pain we Poles have endured. But it means something like, "As if a splinter pierced my heart!" My boys felt ashamed of our Polishness and our poverty.

Other parents brought their sons to Philadelphia Eagles games. We had no idea if those Eagles played basketball, or hockey, or something else. Money-spewing American parents were like gods for Matt and Peter.

My sons turned their backs on their heritage. Our Polish accents and unfamiliarity with American customs annoyed them. No wonder both began to show that they were ashamed of their parents. For them, we were the main cause of their school misfortunes.

Our daughter was different. Katia was older—a teenager. She knew our financial situation, her mum's ambitions, and the fact that there was not enough money to send her to a prestigious college. She never tried to demand the same money that we spent on the boys for herself. When she applied to Swarthmore College, she did so knowing that her parents had no money for tuition. Even so, we'd insist that she go; we would pay for it—and our debt would soar. So when she received an acceptance letter, she didn't say a word. She knew it would put us into an awkward position and force us to pretend that money wasn't a problem. "Your education is all that matters," we told her, many times. But she understood that the college of her dreams was even more expensive than private school for her brothers and more than we could handle. She knew that we, her parents, still had debt from our own American college loans. Katia grew up quickly. She suffered, but she did not protest.

To compensate our sons for their stress and to imitate other American families, we decided on a one-week vacation to Florida, to Disney World. We knew that each American child must eventually go to this place. So, let the children have joy! They have to see Disney's miracle town. It's obligatory. We can't let them be inferior to other kids. Of course, the other kids had been to Disney World when they were small. For Peter, Disney World was still cool; for Matt, no. As it turned out, Matt had zero interest in being photographed with Mickey Mouse.

After twelve hours of driving, we found ourselves at the cheapest Holiday Inn in Florida. It was located many, many miles from Disney World. The only attraction was a cage hanging from a tree at the hotel entrance. Yes, a huge metal cage. It was surrounded by a crowd of children who were admiring a bird sitting inside. It was a small, gray parrot, looking not unlike a Cracow pigeon. Its only colorful markings were two purple-red spots on the chest and tail. Nothing special in appearance. Inconspicuous—more modest than those huge, colorful Amazon parrots you encounter with beach photographers and street organ grinders.

But what I didn't know at the time was that this was an African gray parrot. Its value was not in its beauty.

Matt stood in front of the cage and looked at it without much interest. The parrot turned its head and considered him as a potential interlocutor.

"Hi," said the parrot. "What's your name?"

"Matt," my son replied automatically.

"You are crazy! You are crazy!" the parrot yelled.

Matt jumped back. Having never before been taunted by a bird, for a moment he froze in shock. He had barely come to his senses when the parrot spoke again. This time, however, she spoke not with Matt but with the passing cars. Exposed to moving traffic all day long, she had mastered the cough of an engine starting, the growling rush of a speeding car, even the blare of a horn. The bird enjoyed playing car for a while. Then she noticed that Matt was still there and said:

"My name is Judy! My name is Judy!"

"Hi," said Matt.

"Hi," said Judy. "What's your name?"

"Matt." He introduced himself for the second time. Then, Judy couldn't hold back her depth of feeling for my son.

"I love you," she squawked.

From that moment, day and night, Matt dreamed of an African gray—a parrot–human cross-species love-fest. We watched for an entire week as our son, uninterested in Disney's special effects or trained orcas, wanted to return to the hotel to "talk" with Judy. Seeing this fascination, I asked at the hotel where to buy such a bird and how much it would cost. I thought, maybe a hundred dollars—well, maybe two hundred?

(Do you remember? My knowledge of American life, and especially American prices, was imperfect. I thought that a bird must be less expensive than a dog. It was logical, wasn't it?)

African grays are birds that can remember thousands of words. They cost, depending on age and breeder, one to two thousand dollars! Or more! One month's salary for a bird!

So we both dreamed, Matt and me. He dreamt about a miracle because it would have to be a miracle for his poor parents to buy him that bird. And me, I dreamt that my Matt would open his eyes and discover what is most important in life. "Possessing money and things, having fun, being admired for your status—none of that brings happiness, son," I wanted to tell Matt. "Do good things for others, be a noble person, make the world better for other people—that is how to be happy." It's a simple, self-evident idea. Why couldn't Matt be a loving person? Why didn't he realize how much we loved him? Why didn't he return our love and stop rejecting us?

Days became weeks, weeks turned into months, and life went on. During that time, we had finally saved enough to move to a much bigger house, which we named Silverstone. We redoubled our efforts to eat less, buy nothing, and save as much money as we could. Marta and I had a goal. We were saving for something sure to cure our son of his mistaken attitudes. We wanted a happy, loving son.

Finally, we had saved enough. I found advertisements in *The Philadelphia Inquirer*, telephoned a few of the numbers, and made inquires. I had hope.

Just before Christmas, I said to Matt:

"Get in the car. We're going to Coatesville!"

"For what? I don't have time," he grunted.

"Get in! This is an important day for you. When we get there, you'll be surprised."

We went to Coatesville, found the African gray parrot breeder, and bought a young bird. I wanted the bird to be only a few months old because a young bird will become emotionally attached to its owner. Let Matt have the chance to raise his parrot to recognize him as its master. Let him teach his pet different sounds and words. Let him enjoy his new feathered friend.

I paid for the bird, the cage, the toys, the food, and the water bottles. God … I paid, and paid, and paid. Why didn't Matt dream about having a cow? It would have been much cheaper! And we would have free milk. But we bought the parrot anyway.

Filled with wonder, Matt could hardly talk. He whispered quietly, "I'm naming my parrot Albert."

We drove forty miles home. I waited. I had no idea why, but I had a feeling that, after receiving such unimaginable proof that we loved him, Matt would do something, would say something to me. What? How? I waited.

At the least, I expected that Matt would talk to me about Albert, how we would raise him, teach him, feed him, train him, talk to him, but he sat silently, staring at the bird as though at a picture, not responding to my encouraging questions. God, was it possible that nothing would change?

In Silverstone, the whole family observed the shy parrot:

"Looks like Judy!"

"Only smaller."

"Of course, he's younger."

"What's the first word we will teach Albert?" asked Peter.

"Something easy. Maybe … 'Hello'?" suggested Katia.

"How about 'Do your homework!'?" I said, provoking my kids.

Marta immediately looked at me with disapproval. "No! First we will teach him to say 'God bless America!'"

Albert turned his head to the side as if he were interested in what was to be his first word in the English language.

Everybody looked at the bird.

"Shit!" said Albert.

Apparently, he had already had a lesson. Maybe even more than one? Hopefully, no more obscenities. Confused, we looked at our children. The boys and Katia laughed at Albert's first word.

Albert was nearly an adult, slightly smaller than a pigeon. A spot on his chest was intense purple. His feathers were fresh and shiny, his piercing eyes watchful and sharp, and the skin of his feet young—not yet hardened, like an old hen's. Albert fulfilled our dreams: Matt's dream of having his own parrot, and my dream of filial piety. We leaned over the cage, each of us trying to get close to the bird to see him better.

"Well, enough torment for the poor thing," Marta finally stated. "Let him have some rest."

We reluctantly agreed with her and covered the cage with a dark blanket, and Albert went to sleep. We did not. We talked for the rest of the evening. So many things to discuss: We needed to buy a larger cage and more toys, so he would not be sad, but he would know that we liked him very much. We planned who would feed him and when (every child wanted to do this), who would wash the cage (nobody volunteered), and who could trim the feathers on Albert's wings (Matt perked up at the thought of being a bird doctor). OK, let him. He likes animals, so maybe he would become a veterinarian one day.

You expect me now to say something like, "Albert grew and got smarter every day."

Well, based on the excited comments of Marta and the boys, he apparently did grow for a few months, but it wasn't so obvious to me. As for his intelligence: Did he gain knowledge and become smarter? I don't know, I don't know. Surrounded by a crowd of Albert fans, perhaps I also should have displayed excitement and admiration for our newest pet. But how could I enthusiastically exclaim that Albert was un-be-lie-va-bly smart and learned things quicker than a border collie when he seemed, well, more like a pigeon than an intelligent bird? I had had much higher expectations for a bird that cost more than three boxer puppies.

Albert had "lessons" with Matt every day. The boy sat in front of the cage and kept repeating:

"Albert! Albert! Albert!" And again, with emphasis, "ALBERT!"

Albert tilted his head back and forth, regarding his increasingly exasperated teacher, but he didn't utter a word. Nothing. Not even his famous "Shit!" Albert did not like school.

Matt pretended he wasn't upset that his parrot was dumb. After all, Albert behaved tenderly toward him. Albert liked to perch on my boy's shoulder and "kiss" Matt's ear and cheek. He let Matt stroke his feathers and carry him from room to room. He even made Matt his confidant, talking quietly and continuously in his ear in a parrot tongue.

Peter rarely approached Albert because he was afraid that his older brother would scold him for trying to steal his pet. Katia didn't care about Albert. She lived the life of a teenager, and in her life there was no room for a parrot. All the space was already taken up by her friendship with Jane, her attraction to David, and her plans for going to college. None of these three areas could be improved by gaining Albert's friendship. Consequently, for seventeen-year-old Katia, the parrot was not cool but useless.

I tried to engage Matt in conversation about Albert. I began ineptly:

"I think Albert likes carrots very much."

"Uh-hm."

"You know, yesterday when you went to school, Albert said 'Albert.' Your mom told me."

"I know."

"If we let Albert out of his cage, I'm afraid he would go out the window, don't you think?"

"He wouldn't."

"I wonder, is Albert a boy or a girl?"

"Hm."

And so we talked.

More and more, I realized that Albert's presence added to my household one more living being who didn't care about me. I had spent more than a thousand dollars on a bird. It did not help me get any closer to my son. If Matt had in his heart any capacity to love, this space was now taken up by a parrot.

Turns out I was wrong to think that Albert didn't give a hoot about me. On the contrary, he considered me an important figure in our home—important enough to be worthy of hatred. He despised me so much that after a while it was clear Albert was a bird on a mission to kill me or at least to cause me severe wounds. Let me describe the arc of our relationship.

When Albert was young, he wouldn't let me pick him up or pet him. He protested, breaking away and screaming. This made me angry. Didn't I have the right to play with him like the others? The answer was a resounding "No!"

Albert excluded me from *his* family. He whispered sweet words into Matt's ear and touched his cheek with his beak. He watched Marta with great interest, rode on her shoulder, and animatedly squawked sweet nothings in her ear. He even tolerated Peter stroking him. He even acknowledged *Roxy's* existence. But as for me? He hated my guts. And for what? For buying him? Moving him from provincial Coatesville to cosmopolitan Philadelphia? For providing him food, water, and shelter?

What explanation is there for unearned hatred? Maybe reincarnation? In a previous incarnation I apparently got under Albert's skin. He must have recognized me in his current bird life because as soon as he grew up and started flying around the house, he declared absolute war on me. With planning and precision, he took revenge for something from a previous lifetime that I didn't even remember. Was I a parrot in a previous life who attacked his prior self or perhaps stole his mate? Maybe he was originally human but was demoted to birdhood for this life because of bad behavior. Yes, that seemed the likeliest explanation to me. He had been human, I had been a kind and loving parrot, and he was jealous that my good behavior had won me *human* reincarnation, while he was demoted, reincarnated once more as a mere bird.

I'd return from work, tired after ten hours in the office, and open the door to a dark house. Albert waited in hiding, fully prepared to launch a guerrilla attack. He would hide in the dining room, behind a curtain, inside the kitchen cabinet, or if the was door ajar, in the front closet. He stayed hidden until I let my guard down. As I relaxed and sat down to read in a comfortable armchair, he'd emerge from hiding and, with a screech like a Messerschmitt attacking a B-17, Albert would fall on my head, peck my skull painfully, then instantly fly away. Every surprise attack threatened to give me a heart attack! You think I exaggerate? Oh! Please, take a look at photos of those African gray beaks. Disproportionately strong and sharp! And look at me: the hairless top of my head is shining in the sun. People think it is baldness due to genetics or to debauchery in my youth, but no! No, my friends. It's from Albert's pecking at my head and tearing out my hair.

I was defending myself, violently waving my arms to scare the attacker away, when I heard Marta scream:

"What are you doing to that poor bird? LEAVE HIM ALONE!"

Albert was protected from my anger. He knew he would always go unpunished. It was safe to wage war because his "mother" was there to protect him from me.

This nasty bird treated me as an enemy but considered me his equal. He despised poor Roxy, a stupid, subservient dog. Albert was not only nasty toward the old dog but devious, as well. Roxy had a favorite pillow in the hall and loved to sleep on it as much as possible, even twenty hours a day. Poor Roxy. As the old boxer stretched out on her back on the soft bedding, belly up, and showed her sleeping, dreaming doggy face, Albert would fly over her nose and shout at the top of his voice: "Good morning! Good morning!" The terrified dog might leap to her feet looking around for someone to defend her or to complain to, but Albert was too sneaky. He made sure no one was around.

Roxy grew nervous. She was afraid to fall asleep because she knew Albert's attack was inevitable the moment she dozed off. She was no longer young. Her squirrel-catching days were long gone. Her metabolism had slowed with age; she loved to sleep. And now … this new flying creature! This awful bird with the character of a wasp! Float like a butterfly, sting like a bee—wasn't that Muhammad Ali's technique? Albert was the Muhammad Ali of parrots. The old dog couldn't catch him, chew him up, and spit out the feathers because, even if she had had her youthful exuberance back, Albert was owned by the same family. Roxy felt sad that the family liked Albert, seemingly even more than they liked her, although she'd been with the family many years. No longer could she slumber away the afternoons on her pillow. She suffered. Everybody except Roxy's master—that is me—preferred the feathered screamer to the old dog. But Roxy could see I despised that gray feathered rat!

The persecution of Roxy and me went on for a year or longer. We experienced a series of humiliations and painful episodes. Neither of us could truly relax in our own home. How I suffered! Worse, I had to watch happy Marta when the bird greeted her every day with shouts of "Thank you, Mama! Thank you, Mama!" Amazingly, the bird loved the melodic sounds of *"dzień dobry."* To say "good morning" in Polish—if a parrot can do it, so can you—say this: "zen doobie." He ecstatically repeated this to himself, again and again, every morning until he was bored. Then this nasty bird imitated the ring a telephone to invite Marta to come downstairs and keep him company. His sweet "I love you" whispered in my wife's ear drove me mad. He looked at his second love, Matt, with a warm expression, and made faces at him, opening his beak wide to display his narrow black tongue. The tongue had pink highlights, Marta noticed, and this meant he was in excellent health.

Exposing his healthy tongue showed how much Albert loved Matt. The bird would do this right in front of me, yet if I came near him, I'd get a nasty peck. Albert was a horrid representative of the *Psittacus erithacus* species.

Well, you have to live, somehow. I lived, humiliated and furious, and I didn't strangle that former reptile or break his wings. I waited … for an opportunity.

One morning at the beginning of summer, little Peter said to me:

"You know, Papa, other birds eat from the feeder outside the window and chirp and talk, and our poor Albert only looks at them from inside the house. He probably would want to … "

"Hm … ?"

"But you will be angry."

"What about, my son?" I showed no emotion, but my heart beat faster.

"You won't yell at me?"

"No. Just tell me what you did." I already felt an anticipatory lifting of my spirits at the good news my beloved son would soon announce to me.

"I took him outside to the birds to play with them, Papa."

As if on wings, I flew to the window.

I strained my eyes to scan the yard. I wanted to enjoy this view. Ah! My dream was taking place before my eyes. Birds populated the feeder area: a few sparrows, a wren, a shy red cardinal on a branch, and a hummingbird dipping his long beak into the red honey-water container. Above all of these birds, on top of the feeder, Albert sat twisting his head. Then suddenly, our African gray parrot spread his wings. I felt my heart quiver with hope that Matt had neglected to trim his feathers. Albert flapped his wings a few times, then flew like a drunken eagle to the trees.

"Peter, what have you done? Albert escaped!" I cry with mock horror.

"Jesus Maria! Albert! Everyone get him! Save Albert!" Marta screamed louder than ever before.

People flew out on to the lawn: Marta in a bathrobe; Katia with a butterfly net; Matt, still sleepy; Peter, scared because it was his fault; and me, an actor playing my dream role: a man broken by the loss of a parrot.

We wandered around the perimeter of the yard and shouted:

"Albert! Albert!"

We spotted Albert, up in the treetops:

"Albert! Albert!" He remained motionless. Did he feel threatened? Did he know where he was? Was he afraid of heights?

Louder and louder, we called out his name. Then Albert tried to fly to Matt, but at the moment he was about to land on the boy's head, he panicked, then flapped and wobbled back up to a treetop.

We let out groans of regret—mine sounded quite real—then continued to cry out.

"Come back, Albert! Come on back!" we encouraged him.

His wings spread out wide, and then he was in flight again, farther and higher than before. He was already above the neighbor's house, heading for the huge pines on Newton Street. We followed him, saw him in a tree, and screamed encouragement for him to come back to us. He wanted to—wanted to come back very much—but he didn't know how, I thought. He couldn't fly downward; he didn't know where to go, or how to land on a large, flat surface, because he had only experienced sitting on a perch, a branch, or the sofa, where his tiny talons could find a grip.

The bird squawked louder than we'd ever heard. It seemed a desperate cry for help.

"Albert! Albert!" we called again to him.

I know nobody will believe me, but Albert flew around like this until late afternoon. He never flew over the property behind us—our neighbors', the Bergmans'. I suspect that, approaching their property, he picked up their hostile aura because he returned immediately.

For the next two hours, he unsuccessfully attempted to land on our lawn. He would fly down, and then, at the last moment, he would fly back up and away.

Matt cried. Marta desperately set out bowls of water to entice him to come and drink. She placed chairs on the grass to encourage Albert to perch on the back of a chair. He couldn't! He tried, but he couldn't. He would fly in an arc, drop down, almost touch his talons to the arm of the chair, and then fly up again to a tree, where he'd sit squawking despondently. A bird bereft of hope.

Maybe in his previous life Albert was brave Lieutenant Thomas Selfridge, who died flying with Orville Wright in 1908 when their aircraft crashed at the Fort Myer army base in Virginia? Maybe one hundred years was not enough to erase the memory of hitting the ground—the sounds of broken wood, torn fabric, smashed metal? Yes. Once again, only reincarnation could explain Albert's behavior.

"Albert! Albert! Albert!" We continued to call out to him. He let out fearful cries, made three or four attempts to fly down, and … no success.

I grew optimistic. Endless flying would exhaust him to death, I thought.

Wrong.

About 4 p.m., Albert ran out of strength and fell onto the grass near Marta's chair. Crying happy tears, Matt carried him to the cage.

Damn it!

With this joyous ending to Albert's escape, everyone's love for him redoubled—everyone's except for Roxy's and mine. Albert warmed to Peter, who stroked his feathers for several minutes after his return to his cage.

On the contrary, Albert hated me, if possible, even more than before. He used methods developed in Cuba and Peru by Che Guevara:

hide, sudden attack, then disappear. Maybe Albert had actually been Che Guevara. Maybe as a medical doctor he knew the most painful spots on the human body and used this knowledge on me?

At that time, I didn't like being home at all. At work I was easily irritated. Even walking down the street, I'd automatically cover my head with my hands if I heard the whir of pigeon wings. Anyone witnessing this kept a distance from me. My health deteriorated. Optimism evaporated. I observed Matt regularly, every month, shortening Albert's flight feathers so that my enemy could not fly more than two or three meters—not far enough to fly away but far enough to bite my ear.

Have you read Hermann Hesse? Remember Siddhartha? He is desperate to find his runaway son when a wise ferryman urges him to let the boy find his own path, much as Siddhartha did in his own youth. Listening to the river flow by, Siddhartha realizes time is an illusion. As Buddha taught, all feeling and experience—even suffering—are part of a great fellowship of myriad things that interweave in the cyclical unity of nature. Applying this wisdom to my situation, it was better to wait and let nature take its course. At the same time, according to Buddha's advice I should also fast to cleanse my soul. Unfortunately, stress made me eat compulsively, but waiting? That I was good at. I waited, and waited, and waited … almost like Buddha.

And one day, finally, Matt forgot about his obligation to shorten Albert's long flight feathers.

Oh, I remember this glorious day! It rained. It was cloudy and cold. Autumn weather. A gloomy day for everyone else. But not for me!

On that day, someone (Not me. I swear to God—not me!) forgot to close the front door, and the bird flew away. Away! He did not even stop to sit on the bird feeder. No. He continued his beautiful, long flight like Lindbergh over the Atlantic. Like Icarus toward the sun. Albert flew over Stenton Avenue to alight on one of the trees in the park-like campus of the Institutes for the Achievement of Human Potential.

"Oh, God! Oh, God!" My family screamed.

"Save him! Do something! Call the police! The fire department! The White House!"

We called for help. We even climbed a few trees in an attempt to grasp the bird and take him home. I almost had him in my hand at one point, but he jumped up again and flew over the buildings, farther and farther, into the forest beyond the gardens. He was gone. We searched the woods for hours til it became dark. We saw birds, even a few hawks, but no Albert. He was no longer in my life. My nightmare was over.

Am I happy now? Have I come to myself? Not entirely. African gray parrots can live over one hundred years. Albert escaped in 2003. He might come back. I can only hope that he hates me too much to return.

And Matt? I let him down by not capturing the bird. He was pouty and unpleasant. But I'm an optimist. Eventually my sons will learn filial piety. Maybe they'll even bury me and carry out sacrifices after my death.

PHILADELPHIA STORIES

I once spent a year in Philadelphia,
I think it was on a Sunday.

—W. C. Fields

GOD'S REVELATION TO JAN THE HUMAN

When we bought our new (old) house, Silverstone, in Chestnut Hill, many, many things needed repair. At that time, most of the contractors we used were from Poland. At least, the contractors we knew were from Poland. We were Polish, and they were Polish. Why look further?

Some nationalities, after they come to America, automatically become involved in particular professions. We have gas station owners from Pakistan and laundry entrepreneurs from Korea. Rockets are built by Germans and houses by Poles. At the end of the twentieth century, the absolute best handymen in Philadelphia were from Poland. Unfortunately, sometime later, the creation of the European Union caused a contractor drain, similar to the American brain drain in the 1960s. The best Polish contractors moved to England, Ireland, and France. The niche was immediately taken by Mexicans, and we, Polish-Americans, now employ Mexicans.

But at the time of this story, you could often hear the Polish language in my house.

That's when I met Jan. This contractor could build anything and repair everything. Such talent! No matter if it was a watch or a refrigerator—no machine held secrets from him. When he started working, nothing could stop him. He was efficient and methodical, hour after hour, like a robot from Cracow.

As you know, we humans are animals. In fact, we're at the top of the food chain, ahead of lions and tigers—until we die, that is. Then the flies and maggots take over and eat us. The reason I bring this up is that I am including one human animal in this bestiary and an interesting specimen indeed. Mr. Jan.

Unfortunately, Jan had a character similar to Robert Louis Stevenson's Dr. Jekyll. When in his Dr. Jekyll body, Jan worked. When in his Mr. Hyde body, he was an alcoholic. Jan-the-Alcoholic could follow his boozy impulses for weeks, even months. Jan-the-Worker worked for ten hours every day for the whole week and did not drink a single drop of alcohol, not even beer. On Sundays, Jan changed into his third character: Jan-the-Gambler. Wasn't Stevenson unimaginative, to assign only two personalities to his character?

Anyway, on Sundays he would take all his cash and board the free gamblers' bus to Atlantic City. His gambling lasted up until his last dollar. Jan-the-Worker would then show up to work again Monday and work hard for a couple of weeks, telling stories of how he almost won hundreds of dollars, sometimes even a few thousand dollars. Almost.

From time to time, Jan tried to change. He fought his bad habits. But despite his many resolutions, it was failure after failure, relapse after relapse. A benevolent employer, I tried to help him. I had to convince him that what he was doing was bad:

"You spend 24 hours in the casino surrounded by cigarette smoke that destroys your lungs and your heart."

"You think the food in the casinos is free, and you like it. But what kind of food is it? Fatty food? Lots of salt? Sweets? Yes! As a result, you have high cholesterol. Soon you will have a heart attack."

"You'll earn much more if you work on Sundays instead of losing money from the rest of the week in casinos."

"Sooner or later, those casino thieves will steal all your money!"

"Have you no compassion for your wife, who cries at home while you lose money in casinos?"

And finally, the ultimate argument you can try to convince a Pole:

"Gambling is a mortal sin."

But he only laughed at me. "Ha ha, I do not go to church. I have no sin. You—you are the one who should not go to casinos, and you should not stare at beautiful girls who hand out free drinks. Because you go to church, you see your mortal sins everywhere. I leave God alone, and God also allows me to do whatever I like."

It was January 2007, a time of construction and repairs in our house. Pipes were rotten. Electrical cables were 150 years old. The roof was leaking. The sewage system did not work properly. And in this difficult time for us, Jan lost his drive to work. Maybe he started drinking again? Maybe he finally won big at the casino? I don't know. I called him. I left many messages, begging him to come help us. I even appealed to his honesty, reminding him that he already took money for one of the jobs he never started.

Nothing. No response.

At the time, no other contractors were available to work for us. That year was such that there were more jobs than handymen in my neighborhood. And to make the situation even worse, my wife, because of some family problems, had to go to Poland, and I was left with all the troubles and with all the unfinished work.

Oh, God! Remodeling a bathroom, fixing the leaking roof, not enough money, two spoiled sons who didn't want to listen to me—and I had job problems to boot. I worked twelve hours a day in the office. Now, on top of everything else, I had this unwanted responsibility to complete construction work in the house. How could I deal with all of this?

My wife, who is a motivational genius, practiced a policy of stick and carrot. To make my life easier in the upcoming hard times, she gave me two "carrots": the key to her new Volvo and her new iPhone. The Volvo S60 was a nice car to drive but the iPhone? I wasn't convinced I wanted one.

"Remember," she said, pointing her finger at me, "you must respond to every call. Especially every business call. This is your most important duty. Our income depends on it. Your attentiveness is a must. Any call could be the call that brings us money. Now, the financial fate of our family is in your hands!" She left and flew to Poland. I was alone.

Saturday turned to Sunday. Nobody called. The house was empty and bleak. I decided I needed help. The Our Lady of Consolation church was nearby. I needed consolation.

I went to church. I found it a good atmosphere in which to sink deeply into thought. The preacher preached, the organ played, and my thoughts wandered around the pipe that still leaked in the basement because contractor Jan forgot about me. The monotonous sermon created a tranquil atmosphere. I slowly became sleepy, very sleepy, and drifted off feeling completely consoled. In my dreamy meditation, sounds of the mass and organ music created a comfortable aura of spiritual grace. The priest did not sing too loud, and the people in the pews did not sing at all—only the choir, but the choir was far away. I was lost in this heavenly mood of religion and peace of mind. Then the iPhone started ringing.

Like a rattlesnake.

I removed it nervously from my pocket. Immediately I noticed my neighbors were looking at me with anger. I could see they considered me a criminal. I immediately pushed the button that my wife told me was the "off" button. I expected it to stop ringing—but nothing happened. I mean nothing stopped. The phone rang like crazy. I desperately poked at many other buttons and, again nothing. The ringing continued, maybe even louder! At this moment, heads across the entire church turned to stare at me. Parishioners signaled to me with their hands and their faces, insisting I should turn off my telephone. Right now! In my desperation, I put this vicious phone deeply under all my clothes. Under my coat, my jacket, my shirt. No use—iPhone ringtones are designed to pierce through many layers of clothing. The priest paused the mass. He stood motionless, looking at me with unconcealed disapproval. Evidently, he was waiting for me to do something. Stiff posture and a deep frown revealed his anger. We're going to halt this mass until this creature in our midst stops this unholy disruption of a sacred rite.

I got up from my pew and ran from the church. Upon exiting, I pulled out the phone and desperately pressed all the buttons.

By the time I reached the street, this stupid phone, without any reason, stopped whooping and shrieking. But no, this was not the end of my disasters that morning because when I panicked and left, my nerves sent signals to my digestive system and irritated my bowels to levels resembling those on Mount Vesuvius in AD 79.

I had to find a toilet. Now! I jumped into Marta's Volvo S60. Whirrrrrrrr ... that 200-horsepower engine. Finally, I could put it to good use! I drove like crazy. I was Bobby Unser in the Indy 500.

I entered my driveway. Go! Go! Go! I sprinted into the house. Now, the staircase. Hurry! Two steps at a time, I flew upstairs. And there I was. Finally sitting on the throne. Victorious. What a relief!

Life was good. I posed like Rodin's *Thinker* and contemplate in leisure everything I survived. It could have been a disaster, but I reached my goal in time. Lucky me!

That's when I heard a weak, trembling voice coming from my pocket.

"Mr. Roman? Mr. Roman?"

"Who is it? Who's talking to me?" I shouted, not remembering that I still had my wife's phone in my pocket.

"It's me, Jan."

"Jesus Christ, Jan, you scared me."

"I scared *you?* What can I say? You scared me to death! Just imagine. I was in the casino, Caesar's, playing roulette. I just put ten bucks on black, and then I heard this organ ringtone play. A portentous voice, in English, started talking about punishment for my sins. In the moment, I thought that God had called me to chastise me, right there in the casino. I was so scared, I froze. I didn't dare breathe. I couldn't move. I couldn't utter a word. I have no idea if the ball stopped on black or on red. A few minutes later, I heard the roar of an engine, then some strange noises and flushing water. You know ..."

"Hm. Well, we're just humans, Jan. What can I tell you?"

"Nothing. I'm glad that you feel better because I am still shaking."

Suddenly I realized that I had a chance to reform Jan.

"Jan, maybe all of this was a reminder that you should stop going to the casino. Don't you think? Maybe instead of gambling, you should repair the broken pipe in my basement. I asked you to do it over a week ago."

"Do you think it would help me? Jesus, I'm so nervous. I can't gamble anymore. OK. I will visit you at 7 p.m." Sometimes it's good to have God as your ally."

Jan arrived at 7 p.m. and repaired the leaky pipe. Three days later, the pipe started leaking again. Plumbers should not be shaking with fright when they solder pipes.

But I could not hold his shaking against Jan, not when God has read him his rights! That's enough to make anyone tremble. So I forgave his lapse. He continued to do many jobs for us. I never tried to discourage him from gambling again. His Jekyll-and-Hyde, on-again, off-again way of life was who he was.

Q. Why don't ducks read directions?
A. They prefer to wing it.

—Unknown

What are you going to gain from my tale? Confirmation that humans—so certain they know everything—hurt nature? Assurance that humans do not think but instead follow impulse or imagination, often making wrong decisions?

And the poor animals. They have to live around us. And suffer.

My son Peter, all grown up now, was celebrating his departure to Cleveland for his first professional assignment. He was going to start residency in a hospital he liked. Stressed and happy at the same time, Peter was spending time with his friends drinking beer. Beer—that amazing fuel that allows young people to do nothing for hours without being tired or bored. When the beer ran out, one of them drove to the store to buy a new six-pack of trendy IPA. Becuase the distance to the store was half a mile, chances of being nailed by the police for a DUI were minimal. And because my Volvo was parked next to the veranda, Peter's choice of a vehicle was obvious.

During this beer run, my son successfully avoided any police traps. When he returned to the veranda, he flourished the six bottles but also, somehow, lost the key to my car. How was it possible that, upon his arrival home, the key—the tiny piece of plastic and electronics that gets the car to run—"evaporated"? Keys have no legs, no soul. They cannot move. So, where was this blasted key? Where?

It was not until the next morning that I realized the key to my car was gone. My desperate announcement was interrupted by Peter's "Farewell, my parents. I'm sure you'll find the key sooner or later. Goodbye!" With that, he left for Cleveland. My wife Marta and I were left with the conundrum of the lost key.

It was not on the floor and not on the garden furniture. It was not on the tray with the glasses and not in the trash. We used deduction like Sherlock Holmes, checking all of the possible scenarios. After a while, we had no more places to search. Then Marta had an idea:

THE LOST KEY AND BALBINA THE DUCK

I like ducks. They are sympathetic, industrious creatures. Always busy, interested only in themselves, first eating something under the water—I don't know what but definitely something tasty—then proudly parading their ducklings around the pond. They do not care about us. Their focus is solely on the world of ducks, and because of their continuous puttering around doing their duck-business, they look happy.

After this introduction, you might expect a story full of humor and with a happy ending. No. This is a story about a tragic mother duck, stupid people—yes, I was one of them—and a friendship likely lost.

Maybe you should not read it?

"We should ask Saint Anthony for help!"

Saint Anthony's specialty is to help people who lose something. You pray to him: "Saint Anthony, help me, help me find the key. For this I will say three 'Our Fathers' or three 'Hail Marys,' or even both. You decide." Then, *deus ex machina*—the lost item will appear.

Following this ancient knowledge of our ancestors praying to the saint along the banks of the Vistula River, we said three "Our Fathers" plus three "Hail Marys" for good measure, but this time Saint Anthony was helping someone else, not us.

"Maybe the key is somewhere near the wall of the house," I thought in a moment of great intuition. "Remember? We were sweeping the floor. It could have fallen down from the veranda into the bushes?" I felt proud. Probably Saint Anthony had chosen me and whispered this idea into my ear.

I started methodically. Slowly I moved each flower and pushed aside each branch of the bushes along the stony wall. On my knees I slowly progressed from the entrance steps toward the end of the veranda.

Halfway down the length of the house, where the densest bush touched the wall, my hand suddenly felt the warmth of a living creature. Rabbit? I delicately pulled back one branch, and I saw something. It was a mama duck sitting on her nest—invisible, melding with the colors of the surrounding brown leaves, not moving, like a piece of a dead tree.

This is how I found the duck hidden under our bushes. One less dedicated to key-searching would probably screamed:

"Duck! Duck! I found a duck!"

Not I.

Some people would spread the news of this discovery, run to tell their families, talk to their neighbors, write a story for the local paper, or call the TV station. No, not I. Fully focused, I continued to search on my knees, inch after inch, to the end of the stony wall. Saint Anthony likely watched me and wept because I did not find the key. Finally, hope exhausted, with nowhere left to search, I told my wife about the duck in the bushes.

She was upset.

"Why didn't you tell me right when you found her?"

"For what?"

"So I could take care of her."

I don't know if she had an impulse to protect the mother duck against attacks of foxes, raccoons, or other enemies, or maybe she wanted to replace the duck in her motherly duties and become a surrogate duckling mom. My wife had read a book by Konrad Lorenz,[6] who became "a father" of an entire generation of lovable geese. Had Marta already envisioned herself teaching several cute ducklings how to swim and fly?

I knew that I had to cut those thoughts short. Marta was an angel, true, but an angel who could not fly. And ducklings need a proper flying coach, not a Polish grandmother.

However, opposing my wife with a flat "no" had historically proven risky. I needed somebody with unquestionable authority to support me. Thanks be to God, I knew a man who would be on my side: Dr. John Grant. He had written his Ph.D. on the history of the early Roman Empire, and so he must have been an expert on geese[7] and probably also on ducks. To boot, John was the best amateur ornithologist among our friends.

I called John and briefed him about my discovery, and he enthusiastically agreed to visit and become our chief consultant.

---

6   Konrad Lorenz, a biologist studying instinctive behavior of animals, worked with geese to investigate the principle of imprinting, the process by which some birds, if they leave their nest early, bond instinctively with the first moving object they see within the first hours of hatching.

7   Geese saved Rome in 390 BC when the Gauls secretly scaled Capitoline Hill in darkness. Sleeping Roman commander Manlius, roused by relentless squawking and honking of the sacred geese of Juno as the Gauls approached, rushed his contingent of Romans to defend against the clandestine attack.

Now, let me tell you that this story took place early in the COVID-19 pandemic. Some people immediately followed instructions to wear masks and keep a six-foot distance between persons—so-called social distancing Others disliked masks and did not remember to wear them every time they met somebody. In our home, we belonged to the second group.

John arrived within minutes. He wore a mask, and with an outstretched palm he showed me that I should keep my distance.

"Keep social distancing," he added unnecessarily during the inspection of the bush.

"Sorry," I agreed and pulled my mask up. My glasses immediately fogged over and made me half-blind.

John walked to the bush, spread some branches, and immediately spotted the duck. She did not move, staying almost invisible among the dry leaves and dense foliage, maybe invisible for foxes but not for Dr. Grant.

"It's a mallard," he said.

"Are you sure?" I stupidly asked, as if it made any difference to me whether it was a mallard or a pintail.

"I'm sure," he confirmed with the certainty of a man who has seen many mallards in his life.

"So what should we do now? Bring a container with some water? Spread some bread on the ground?" asked Marta, watching from the veranda.

"No. Do nothing. Listen. Please, leave the duck alone."

"And if something happens?" she continued shyly.

"Call me."

Because my wife could not do anything to assist our duck, she gave her a name: Balbina. Balbina the Duck was a capricious heroine in the Polish cartoons that we had watched as children. Giving the duck a name made her our pet, and from this moment, Balbina became a significant part of our everyday life. She was different from other pets we had had in the past. She was like a ghost that inhabits a house: Everybody knows it exists, but few see its shadow. We wanted to see Balbina walking to and fro, flying, coming back to the nest, but we never saw these events.

Once one of our guests asked, "Do you have ducks on your property?"

"Um," I responded with surprise. "Why are you asking?"

"We saw a she-duck in your driveway. Is there any pond around?"

"Not exactly."

Yes. Not exactly. The nearest pond was more than half a mile away, and it was separated from our property by a four-lane highway and another highly trafficked road. Balbina probably flew to us from there, but did she intend to return with her children? It would be suicide.

And knowing this, we waited on tenterhooks for Balbina's babies.

I found on Google that after hatching, little ducklings need twelve hours to dry and get stronger, and then they must follow their mother and walk to the water. How much time did we have? How many more days until they hatched?

Meanwhile, the COVID-19 pandemic had become such an everyday phenomenon in our lives that we had the habit of visiting with friends sitting on our veranda without masks. The fresh breeze and the distance between our chairs protected us. How could you drink cold Chardonnay with a mask on? How could you speculate about Balbina's future with a mask squeezing your face?

At that time in New York State, Governor Cuomo had just "unfrozen" some sectors of everyday life. His brother had recovered from COVID-19 and returned to CNN. No wonder that when Consulate General of Poland in New York City needed volunteers to count votes for the Polish presidency, we decided to spend a day there to help. In our subconscious we were driven by a hope that our assistance counting votes would help our candidate, Warsaw's liberal mayor Rafał Trzaskowski, become the president of Poland, not that smiling frog, our current president, Andrzej Duda.

We left home for NYC at 3 a.m. on Saturday and did not get back until Sunday at 8 a.m. This experience was twenty-four hours of nonstop, time-consuming work: opening every envelope, checking each name against the registry, and recording votes. No breaks, no rest—just work, work, work. At the end, we had to check protocols again and again because the votes didn't match. We did a recount and checked again. When did we finish? 5 a.m. Sweet Jesus! Our eyes were so tired that we could barely see the highway. Nonetheless, we put our fate in the hands of Providence and drove home to Philadelphia, exhausted and blinded by the early-morning sun—and all of this to find that our candidate came in second in the first round of voting.[8]

We drove into Philadelphia dead tired, no life left in us, to crawl upstairs to our bedroom without talking to anyone to fall onto the bed like logs. To sleep—that was our only desire.

We pulled into the driveway.

On the veranda, we met the friend who had stayed in our home while we were in NYC. She said with a trembling voice:

"Balbina's ducklings hatched."

"Great!" Hatched or not hatched, leave us alone. We have no interest in ducks. We want to sleep!

"Balbina left, and they are alone. It's ninety-two degrees out here. They could die," she continued, with growing concern.

"Well," I felt that if I stood in the blazing sun for even a few more minutes, I was going to die myself. There was no way that the tiny birdies could survive this heat.

---

8   Two weeks later we found that he lost the second round too.

My brain was exhausted by our all-night work marathon, the disappointing election results, the drive back from NYC, the sun's searing glare—and now, a life-and-death emergency. I couldn't go to bed. Not yet.

So I called John.

"John, the ducklings hatched."

"Very good."

"But their mother left. What do we do?"

"How long they have they been alone?"

"A few hours? I don't know."

"Not good."

"Do something."

"What do you expect me to do?"

"You promised to help."

"I know, but first call the Schuylkill Center Wildlife Clinic and ask what they think about it."

I called the clinic, but it was Sunday. There was no vet and no experienced staff. I talked with two young women who consulted with each other back and forth but couldn't decide what to advise. They finally agreed on one thing: They would call me back.

Meanwhile, time passed. Balbina did not come back. The temperature rose to ninety-five.

My wife—who could not watch the disaster and do nothing—brought a blue baby bathtub and positioned it three feet from the little fuzzy ducklings. Then she connected the edge of the bathtub with a piece of wood almost touching their nest. Finally, she filled the bathtub. Now, the ducklings could safely walk to water and stay there as long as they wanted. But they were silent, sitting squeezed together, without watching the construction of their swimming pool.

After an hour, John called.

"Did you call the clinic? What did they say?"

"They said that they would call me back."

"Aha. When they do, call me."

Another hour passed. The temperature rose to ninety-seven.

The lady from the clinic finally called.

"Sometimes a mother duck abandons her children, and then they die. If she has not returned, she won't. Please catch the ducklings and bring them to us in a box."

"How should I catch them? Cover with some fabric? I don't want to hurt them."

"Catch them with your hands. Please hurry. We will be waiting."

I looked at Marta. She looked at me.

"Call John," she said.

I called John.

"The clinic wants me to catch the ducklings and bring them over."

"That's what I expected. Can you do it?"

"We will try. Maybe … maybe you could help?"

Silence.

"John. Are you there?"

Silence.

"Is he coming?" asked Marta.

"I don't know."

But he came. They both came—John and Anna, his wife. They were wearing masks and clear plastic face shields. Anna stayed in the car while John walked around our property, checking bushes and combing through flowers to be sure that Balbina was not hidden somewhere on the property. No Balbina anywhere.

After completing his search, John started catching ducklings and placing them into the blue plastic baby bathtub. I clumsily attempted to help him. But when I approached the area, both the ducklings and John bolted from me as if I were a leper. Probably because of my presence, one duckling escaped into such a dense bush that even John gave up searching for it. Once six ducklings were inside the tub, John and Anna took them to our car and left them there for us without talking to us. Why? I looked at Marta. She was thinking the same thing. We both realized it at the same time.

"We were not wearing our masks! We forgot social distancing!"

True. We had completely forgotten about COVID-19.

I drove the ducklings in the tub, covered with one of my T-shirts, to the clinic. I also wore a mask. They were received immediately, and I left for home.

Home! Finally! It was 2 p.m. when I fell asleep.

And 6 a.m. the next day, I awakened.

When I walked into to the kitchen to get my morning coffee, I noticed that somebody—our friend, the same one who had stayed at our house—had left a note on my door:

"At 6 p.m., Balbina returned. She checked her empty nest, walked to the middle of the driveway, and looked at the veranda where you usually sit. Then she noticed me sitting in the gazebo, approached me, and stared into my eyes for fifteen minutes in silence, as if asking, "What did you do to my children?" I could not stand it. She spent two more hours walking around."

When I came outside to the veranda, our friend was there, looking out. In front of her, in the driveway, was Balbina. The duck looked at her with an angry stare, and then she stared at me. I was not afraid of a duck. But she seemed unafraid to lose her life, now that she had already lost her children, so I did not approach. She stood and glared reproachfully, like a statue of a mother duck confronting the murderers of her children.

I ran to the bedroom and woke Marta up. The three of us stood watching Balbina.

Our friend was a soldier, a colonel who had fought in Afghanistan. When her gaze met Balbina's, she started to cry. Marta did not hesitate to do the same. I noticed my own eyes seemed to have suddenly sprung a leak as well. Balbina waddled to her empty home and sat among the broken shells for a while.

I called the animal clinic:

"The mother duck returned. She is sitting in her empty nest."

"Let me look into this."

Half an hour passed. We stopped crying and kept wondering. Finally, Balbina left the nest and flew away.

The clinic returned my call after an hour:

"Is she still there?"

"No, she already left."

"Let us know when she returns."

But Balbina never returned.

A week passed. My wife had posted a photo of us at the consulate counting votes in New York on Facebook. I wore a mask with Polish colors, and Marta had an American flag mask on.

The next day, John called us:

"Were you away in New York the same day that you asked us to help you with the ducklings? With that crowd of vote-counters?"

"Well, to tell you the truth, we were."

Silence.

More silence.

Was this the end of our twenty-year friendship? It's not only the disease that creates COVID-19 victims. No, because COVID isolation preys on people's fears, and fear can overpower even a long friendship.

CHOMIK THE HAMSTER

One of the pets you have to purchase for your children is a hamster. When your child is tired of an ugly hermit crab, is repulsed by huge Cuban cockroaches, doesn't like mice or rats, and is afraid of snakes, it's hamster time.

Hamsters are the last stage before parakeets. And after parakeets, as everybody knows, only cats, dogs, and boyfriends and girlfriends remain.

So, what's so special? Why do people like hamsters more than rats, boas, or gerbils? And speaking of gerbils, what exactly *is* a hamster, anyway?

*My nephew asked me the difference between a hamster and a gerbil
and I told him I thought there was more dark meat on a gerbil.*

— Bobcat Goldthwait

OK, Bobcat's a comedian, but my questions are serious. Sometimes I think pets enter our lives in a fixed sequence, something like this:

I. Cockroach: Did you know that the Madagascar hissing cockroach—it hisses at you—is black, can be up to three inches long, and can live up to four years? You can get a starter pair on Amazon for $12.99 and breed your own colony.

II. Crab: A pet hermit crab costs only $7.85. But the Live Pet Hermit Crab Complete Starter Kit, shipped with two Live Crabs, will set you back $35.

III. Rat: Amazon has some standards and does not sell rats, but Petco sells the domesticated form of *Rattus norvegicus*, the most common species of rat kept as a pet.

IV. Hamster: Keep reading to learn more about hamsters.

V. Onward and upward, including the lovable parakeet, until finally you reach boas, iguanas, and mammals larger than a shoebox.

My family was different. We started straightaway at stage IV. You blame us for neglecting a part of our sons' growth experience and causing future psychological problems? Perhaps you're right. Going directly to an advanced pet in lieu of working through lower species likely gave Matt and Peter unrealistic expectations about life.

Anyway, my two sons dreamt about a hamster. This dream about a hamster was like chicken pox. There's an age when all kids get sick. A whole first-grade class catches chicken pox from each other, and you have to suffer, knowing that after a while, this nasty sickness will be over, and it's never going to come back—irritating, but not life-threatening. As you'll see, hamsters are very much in the same category as chicken pox. Our hamster was certainly irritating, and when he left, he never came back.

The point is, you still have to suffer all of the symptoms of this disease, even if it doesn't kill you. "Hamster disease" is caught from other children. Once infected, your kids become repeatedly, incessantly importunate.

"Mommy, Daddy, I would love to have a hamster. This guy, he's got a hamster; the other one has a hamster; everybody has a hamster. But I don't have a hamster. Please, please buy me a hamster. Mommy, a hamster is not expensive, and it's so cute."

"Give me a break. I'm not going to have rats in my house," a father might respond, but to no avail because a kid bites into your defenses like a tick goes under the skin, and it is winning.

"A hamster would be so nice, and it's silent, and it's not expensive, and it doesn't stink. And I would love to take care of a hamster."

Then the kid's mother comes to his rescue, and she starts changing the father's anti-rat attitude. "Did you hear? Did you hear what your son told you? He wants to be responsible. Responsible for an animal. We must develop his instinct to take care of others. Every child needs a four-legged friend. You cannot refuse this request."

So I did not refuse. If a refusal is not allowed, I cannot refuse.

We visited the nearest pet store to buy a hamster. Along with this hamster, we bought a cage, toys, some spinning wheels, an obstacle course so the hamster would not be bored, food bowls, water bottles, and three books about hamsters. Even if the animal was not expensive, with all the other stuff, we spent a fortune. But what the heck, all good things must cost something.

We told ourselves that we did something wise—something that we needed to do. We bought an animal. This animal was going to improve our family life and make our children more responsible. Now they would also be interested in nature, like their father.

"Let's name him Chomik," I suggested. "Chomik the Hamster."

Our kids were so happy with the hamster that they played with him for an entire two hours. They watched the hamster eat. They watched how this tiny guy would run in the metal spinning wheel. But after two hours they got tired, and they went back to their favorite hobby: watching TV while playing computer games.

Such is the fate of parents. Every parent must take care of a hamster. So now I was one of them because, as I expected, after a few days, our boys had had enough of the animal—especially cleaning the cage, changing the water, and providing food. The entire pleasure of having a hamster was ours.

OK, this was more trouble than we bargained for. The kids no longer had any interest in Chomik. After all, a hamster's repertoire is limited to running, eating, pooping, and sleeping. But how to get rid of Chomik? To get rid of a hamster is much more difficult than buying a hamster. It's almost impossible to escape from a pet hamster. You can't give it to somebody. To whom? To your neighbor? To the pet store? To the SPCA? Nobody wants a used hamster. A hamster is not a homeless dog or cat. Even most branches of the SPCA have no interest in one. You can only *buy* a hamster. Then you own a demanding monster you must take care of up to the moment it draws its last breath and its eyes snap shut.

Well, of course I could have poisoned Chomik. I could have cut off his head with an ax. But people do not do this. Probably they are afraid of gossip, and they are right. Imagine what your friends would say if somebody told them that Mr. Smith poisoned his daughter's hamster. Or, "Heard about that sadist, Mr. Novachek? He finished his hamster off on a chopping board using his Shun Classic eight-inch sushi knife with a pakkawood handle." This kind of gossip would stick to a guy forever.

So it is better to clench your teeth and live with your hamster, waiting for the moment when your child leaves for university. Then you catch it, toss it to the toilet, and flush twice, causing this vile creature to vanish. Or is Chomik now too big to flush into oblivion?

I did not protest when my family made me responsible for feeding Chomik as well as cleaning his cage regularly so we'd have no stinky smell. My boys gradually changed their position from hamster lovers to the hamster inspectors, checking whether I remembered my duties. What could I do? My only reward was that my sons spent a few minutes a day watching Chomik run around inside his cage. I always silently hoped Chomik would overextend himself and have a cardiac arrest, but our hamster was apparently as healthy as a horse.

Maybe I'm wrong, but I think mice must communicate with hamsters. That fall, Chomik must have invited his mice friends to our house because we had an invasion. I do not recollect any time that we had so many mice in our home as during that year. Mice ran everywhere in the kitchen, the pantry, and the cupboards. They were not afraid of us.

And wow, were they ever smart! I installed six mousetraps in different places around house. Cheddar cheese didn't work as bait, so I spent a lot of money experimenting with tastier treats that mice were certain to like: Parma ham, blue cheese on a celery stick, Manuka honey on sourdough bread. But hardly ever did I catch a mouse.

One night I woke to the sound of a mouse caught in the trap hidden at the bottom of our wardrobe: the "smack" as the trap tripped. Then, a different sound emerged—a high-pitched "Shrwuguwu, shrwuguwu!" I heard thrashing sounds, as if the rodent, trapped at the neck, was trying to escape.

Well, it will die very soon, I thought. But I didn't want to wake up, get out of my bed on this cold night, and deal with a rodent corpse.

I tried to lie still, but the mouse kept moving. What a nasty mouse, refusing to die. But I would not move. Let it fight, I thought. The noise didn't matter; I was going to get my sleep. And I fell asleep. I slept but barely rested, tossing and turning because somewhere, I still heard the rodent struggling for its life.

In the morning I woke up, walked to the wardrobe, and opened it. With his neck squished by this high-performance mousetrap, there was Chomik. He was still warm.

How did he escape from his cage? I don't know. I only remember my sons' eyes when they noticed, a few hours later, that the cage was empty. When they asked me, "Papa, what happened to our hamster? Why is it not in the cage?" I had my one-word answer prepared:

"Escaped."

"Where is he now? Nothing bad happened to him, right?"

"Oh, of course not. Now Chomik is free and happy! Now he can run around the meadows chasing butterflies, or he can walk through the forest, where he is sure to find good friends to play with."

"Oh, that's good, Papa. He is so lucky now because he was a bit depressed in our home."

My two sons are now adults, and they still believe their hamster chose freedom and found happiness. Please don't tell them the truth!

If you chase two rabbits, you catch none.

—Confucius

WALTER RABBIT

No one in the family knows how Walter came to us. We had moved to a big, big house—so big that we could not reuse our old house's name, Romanówka. We had to invent a suitable new name. Calling this new house Romanówka would be like calling an immense aircraft carrier "The Pussycat." Not serious enough. After brainstorming ideas, we named our new home Silverstone. Why? It was built with Wissahickon schist. The tiny specks of mica on the surface of the stone glimmered silver in the sun. Silverstone sounded dignified and, well, American. We enjoyed the new name with the intense feeling of immigrants who wanted to blend in, to be indistinguishable from the rest of society. The

Polish name of our old house? It no longer suited our high status as the proud owners of Silverstone Manor.

One day when I was walking around the yard, I spotted an immense gray rabbit regarding me from a bush. I crouched, stuck my hand out toward him, and started calling him with a childish voice:

"Rabbit! Rabbit! Rabbit!"

I don't know when or where I first heard this, but growing up in Zakopane, I knew well the folk belief in good luck if you repeat the word "rabbit" three times.

The rabbit was big. Never had I seen such a huge rabbit. Staring at me, he blinked once slowly, as if considering how to respond, and then ... he hopped *toward* me.

That's how we met.

You can see that we did not buy Walter. He chose us and entered our lives all by himself. Where from? Why? I don't know. Maybe he was scared of the old tomcats who patrolled my neighbor Esposito's house? Maybe he got sick of eating exotic plants in the meticulously manicured flower beds of my other neighbor, the unfriendly lawyer, Kratzer? Or maybe he crossed Stenton Avenue, ran between the speeding cars, and, after miraculously avoiding death, crashed into our lawn, so scared that he promised himself to permanently settle down on our property?

I didn't know. I never would.

But this I do remember perfectly. I spoke softly to the animal, soothing it. Then my sons arrived and excitedly asked me to let them adopt this giant bunny because "since we found him, he must be ours." Walter Rabbit had nothing to say on the subject.

I agreed. I had never had a bunny as a child. Observing my boys' enthusiasm, I realized that this furry, innocent being would provide never-ending pleasure to our family.

At least that's what I thought at that time.

Why did we call the rabbit Walter? I am not certain. Was it the influence at the time of my boss, Walter? He got under my skin, so it gave me joy when I scolded our new favorite pet and called out: "Walter, you clumsy fool, you! Look where that carrot fell. Come on, man. Get to work. Find the carrot!"

Walter staunchly gorged himself on carrots, cabbage, bread, and butter—anything he was given or found in the garden. He grew. He never stopped growing.

We placed Walter in a fenced yard at the back of the house in front of the kitchen window. With about seventy square yards of grass, not to mention the flower beds and a row of young, conical cypresses lining the fence, he had more private space than we had when we lived in Poland. He was an American rabbit. Everything's wonderful in America! In America, even rabbits have more living space.

Walter's territory had chain-link fencing on two sides. The gates were constructed with metal pipes and wire mesh by the previous owners of the house. They probably kept their dog there. Along the border between us and the Kratzers, "Walter's garden" bordered on a wooden sectional fence. We put Walter in his new home, certain he wouldn't get away. This allowed the boys to "own" him, get used to him, and become friends with him. Oh—and this is probably the most important thing—we decided to keep the rabbit safe behind the fence because we feared Roxy would treat him like a big squirrel, and then … you know.

And so Walter lived in front of the kitchen window, and he grew fat and happy.

We tamed him. All you had to do was to enter his area and call "Walter," and he would come out of his hiding place in the bushes or the new burrow he had just dug, stand in front of you on his hind legs, and silently plead for a carrot. And he let us pet him. And he hopped so ridiculously. He was so funny! Wonderful!

*   *   *

Back then, nearly all of Silverstone's visitors were patients of the Institutes for the Achievement of Human Potential, a nonprofit organization serving developmentally challenged children. Some of those children could walk, and their parents would lead them to Walter, where they would shout, "Walter! Walter!" Smiles lit haggard faces as the funny, fluffy bunny, standing on its hind legs, ate proffered cabbage leaves loudly and greedily, then asked for more and more. Walter knew that as long as the kids petted him, hugged him, and whispered into his ears, he'd be fed tasty vegetables. He did not protest, If they had food, they could play with him. No food, and it was hop, hop, and away.

Now, Roxy. I mentioned Roxy's presence at Silverstone. By now she was a middle-aged boxer who felt empathy for every visitor and every inhabitant of the house. She let developmentally challenged children treat her like a teddy bear, even visit her on her pillow on the floor and stay for a while, hugging her. She would even allow them to sleep with her there. Why not? Children are warm, and Roxy had already started feeling arthritic pain. Unfortunately, some parents of those friendly children did not like their kids sleeping on the floor with a big dog.

But outside? A rabbit?

Roxy did not care. Roxy pretended that that rabbit did not exist. At one point we allowed the two animals to meet, and nothing happened: no interest, no reaction. Good, because I feared our boxer's reaction would be to grab this monstrous squirrel-like creature and deprive us of our newest pet, all in a fraction of a second. Well, I underestimated the smart dog. At first, Roxy showed uncertainty as she watched Walter: What is that? Can I chase it? Can I smell it?

But when I "explained" that Walter was ours—that he entertained the children, so she, Roxy, wasn't allowed to break his neck—she understood. On the contrary, I continued: She should look after Walter because he was part of our responsibility; we owned Walter, so *she* owned him. Roxy grasped this concept immediately. Wise dogs understand the complexity of human life.

From then on, Roxy treated Walter like a member of the household—albeit the stupidest one. She looked at him with disapproval, as if he had come to live in our house solely so that she, the old dog, would have even more to do. But I admit, while she wasn't thrilled with Walter, she took her responsibility seriously and, as she appeared to promise, looked after him well.

She proved good in this role. More than once, Roxy was crucial to rescuing Walter:

He loved to escape. (Maybe that's how we got Walter in the first place?) Two walls of his enclosure were over three feet tall and made of dense mesh. The wooden fence on the Bergmans' side of his enclosure was even taller: six feet high. To Walter, it was El Capitan. In the history of the world, no rabbit ever jumped so high. Rabbits who could realistically evaluate barriers would have happily stayed inside.

A few highly evolved rabbits, however, have learned that if you can't fly, you can dig. Who would have guessed that Walter was highly evolved?

Tunnels appeared under walls and fences. As far as I know, Walter never watched Richard Attenborough, Steve McQueen, and James Garner tunnel out of camp Stalag Luft III in *The Great Escape*, but he knew how to design the tunnel in such a way that humans would discover neither the entrance nor the exit. And Walter, unobserved, created underground passages leading to the other side of the iron net, where Freedom and Space awaited him. And, from time to time, hop, hop, hop … he was gone!

When someone noticed our prisoner had escaped, every household member joined in the action. No matter how much we called, poked around, and peered into corners, the only one who could ever catch the fugitive was Roxy. So we learned to begin the search by calling:

"Roxy! Roxy! Walter escaped! Look for Walter!"

Roxy would run along the house, trembling with excitement, jump into the bushes, and pretend to smell rabbit tracks. As a boxer, her sense of smell was weak, but she trotted and sniffed the garden like a bloodhound! She charged about like a Polish hussar assailing the Turks at the Battle of Vienna in 1681, encouraged by loud calls from the family and any nearby Silverstone guests:

"Look for him, Roxy! Go, go!"

In her enthusiasm, like a rampant bull, she trampled Marta's flowers and damaged our nearly-ripe tomatoes. She left the tiny cucumbers unharmed; apparently they were beneath her notice.

Then, in a few minutes, you'd hear the dog barking:

"Wow, wow! I have him! Come quickly! Wow, wow!"

We'd run like crazy to feast our eyes on the proud boxer standing astride a pretend-dead rabbit. Afraid to breathe, Walter stood stock-still as Roxy pressed him to the ground. Roxy knew dog-judo or perhaps dog–jujitsu; in any case, she could hold him firmly without using her teeth.

That's when—I loved to make this performance in front of spectators—I'd grab Walter by the nape of his neck and carry him back triumphantly, modestly nodding and smiling at my audience. The whole world could see, with Roxy's help, we were able to get the fugitive back into his garden prison. A few peaceful days might pass, then again:

"Roxy! Roxy! Look for the rabbit!"

* * *

We lived through the whole summer and fall this way. Then winter approached, and we had to "do something about Walter." No easy solution. We had to make part of the basement into an enclosure. We removed broken furniture, boxes of God-knows-what, skis, Christmas ornaments, garden tools, and, you know, all of the other stuff you never use but don't want to throw away. I put it all on the street for the trash men.

Finally, only bare walls and a cement floor remained. We brought Walter down to the basement—our brave, optimistic bunny. He tried to dig the floor with his rabbit claws, as if he could break through a ten-inch layer of nineteenth-century concrete and get to the soft earth.

Poor prisoner! Our fluffy Count of Monte Cristo!

Poor?

Prisoner?

O naive one, you have no idea what a rabbit is capable of! To this day, I fail to comprehend how what happened happened. The concrete under my house was not hardened like Hitler's bunker but still. It was cement.

Was Walter a mutant with diamond-tipped claws? How did he pierce the cement floor like a 45 slug shot into gelatin at a forensics laboratory?

Despite my desperate attempts to fill the holes with cement, Walter somehow created a complex of underground tunnels. Once he went underground, he disappeared. He left his dark kingdom only to eat, after which he would return to his labor of love: extending his subterranean maze.

Imagine if our house collapsed, undermined by a rabbit! A huge three-story Victorian house, ten bedrooms, six bathrooms, two staircases, and a stone tile roof. And, like the Twin Towers, suddenly nothing would be left but a cloud of dust!

Fortunately, that did not occur. Spring saved us. We moved Walter back to the garden. The part of the basement where he reigned all winter could not be used; it looked like Warsaw, October 1944. We reminded him every day that we'd have to pay a fortune to repair his damage. Did he understand? Perhaps …

* * *

Now let me give you two options as to how this story might end.

Option One is for people with soft hearts:

Perhaps Walter was overwhelmed with guilt for tearing up our basement, or perhaps he wanted greater challenges in his life. We'll never know why he left. But one warm spring day, Walter was no longer among us. He'd run away. He'd felt the morning sun upon his back and the soft, dewy grass under his furry paws. Spring energy coursed through his veins, and thoughts of new lettuce filled his brain. So he ran.

He ran away from pellet food and wire fences. He ran toward a brighter future. He ran and ran—so far away that Roxy could not find him—only stopping when he found a farm, with delicious cabbages and not-too-shabby heirloom carrots, where he was adopted by adorable farm children who played with him on the lawn. He had found his new home.

Option Two is for people who like thrillers:

Since then, from time to time at night I awaken to a strange sound: "HOO-hoo-hoo! HOO-hoo-hoo!"

I tell myself it's the sound of the great horned owl who lives in a hollow in the old oak between us and the Espositos. Certainly, it *could* be an owl. But, I wonder, is that really an owl?

The cry, carried by the night wind, is eerie, more moan than hoot. A cry of despair perhaps? A cry for help? And where *is* Walter, anyway? I imagine him pushing his way through his maze of tunnels, hopping slowly, then hardly moving at all, then motionless. Silent and alone, nose twitching in the stagnant air, he searches for a sign, for any clue about what direction he should go. Sensing the faintest wisp of fresh air, he moves cautiously.

Suddenly the air is fresher. He finds the source: a vertical shaft left behind when an old gatepost was removed. He stares up the shaft, his bunny brain deep in thought. Rabbits may be good at tunneling horizontally, but have you ever seen a rabbit climb a tree? He tries to hop straight up. He wants to leap upward out of the dank, dark ground, but no. There is no way he can ascend to the open air above, where breezes carry ever-changing scents. Gradually he realizes his fate is sealed. He is trapped forever in a prison of his own making.

He stares upward, sees a circle of starry night, and begins his slow and solemn dirge: "HOO-hoo-hoo! HOO-hoo-hoo!"

One ending is true. Which one? That's up to you.

Inside the calm minds, great ideas swim serenely like the morning geese of the misty lakes!

—Mehmet Murat Ildan

MOTHER GOOSE AND HER GOSLINGS

On my return from the trails of Fort Washington State Park, where I walk almost every day, I crossed a long bridge over Wissahickon Creek. After the bridge was a parking lot and my car. I was at the end of a long walk. I had worked out for more than an hour and a half, and by using my Nordic poles, I had burned more than 500 calories. That made me proud and content. Once the bridge had appeared before me, my excursion was almost complete.

I started crossing the bridge and noticed I was not alone.

It was a long bridge, very long—115 of my steps. It was also high—more than forty feet above the creek. It was like being on the third or fourth floor of a building and looking straight down. Constructed of timber, the bridge had high railings, and the outer side of each railing was covered with a dense, metal mesh, such that maybe mice could squeeze through, but a chicken, even a small chicken, no. No way.

OK, so stepping onto this bridge I saw, exactly in the middle, a mother goose and six tiny goslings. Mother Goose was nervous; she felt uneasy on the planks of the bridge. They were squeaking and vibrating with the heavy tread of a human, and there was no place to hide.

When she tried to escape to the left or to the right, the metal mesh did not allow her to go. The goslings sensed her fright, and they, too, were scared. They huddled together and pushed against each other as they crowded closer and closer to Mother.

I stopped. I waited. I was waiting for this stupid goose to reach the far end of the bridge. But she had a tiny goose brain full of fear with no room for reason. The flustered bird was not able to make a decision. She took a few steps forward and then returned back to the middle of the bridge.

This lasted for minutes. I waited patiently. Sooner or later, something was bound to happen, but clearly the goose did not know what it would be. Would she walk forward, her goslings straggling behind her, or would she return to where she started?

She struggled with her emotions. She hesitated. She could not make up her mind. A goosy she-Hamlet! Would she suffer the slings and arrows of outrageous fortune and bow to the dictates of fate? Or would this lone matriarch proudly take arms against a sea of troubles and lead her brood to safety?

Poor creature. This way, that way, as if her decision-making center had a pendulum and nothing else. And her children? They looked at their paralyzed mother and trembled with fear.

At this moment, a young woman entered the other end of the bridge. It was too far for me to call to her. She was running fast, as if she was not on legs but on springs. She held her head high, eyes scanning the horizon, never once casting a glance downward at the path beneath her feet. She floated along with long, graceful strides, blissfully unaware that her youth and her speed were making me feel old.

Surely this blithe spirit wouldn't stop for a bird family. As she approached, the goslings stopped their peeping and fluttering. They snuggled into each other and stayed still as death. Mother Goose was protecting them, positioning herself toward the approaching runner. She was ready to die defending her children.

I thought: Could this bird withstand the pressure or not? When the runner got close to her, would she panic—run away and try to escape? And what about the children? If they squeezed under the railing they would fall forty feet down into the Wissahickon's currents? Then what? They could not fly. Were they going to die?

But I was still too far away to warn the girl by yelling: "Stop! There are frightened birds on the bridge. An entire family! Let them go first."

I waited for the decision of the Fates to be revealed. Clotho had spun the threads of life for these tiny goslings. Would Atropos wield her shears and cut their threads short seconds from now? Or had Lachesis measured them a lengthier allotment of life?

The runner, eyes on a distant goal, ears thrumming to Taylor Swift, was not looking at her feet. But as she neared, I saw her feet. They were shod in thick Nikes that pounded and resounded on the bridge timbers like Chopin's "Marche Funèbre." She almost trampled my birds. She jumped away at the last moment when she saw them, laughed, and continued her run with a smile on her face, oblivious to the near-catastrophe her passage had almost caused.

Whew! That was close. This time the geese survived the stress, and they did not try to escape.

However, I continued thinking: "It looks like walking people and even runners are not dangerous for 'my' geese. But what's going to happen if a dog enters the bridge? There are a lot of dogs, and often they run without a leash. Well, I have to do something. I have to help those poor geese."

I approached the birds gently, as a goose shepherd would, to herd them slowly to the end of the bridge.

Mother Goose tried to cover her children. She didn't want to move her kids and expose them to an approaching human giant. But I was diligent. I used Polish words to prod the geese: "*Sioh! Sioh! Sioh!* Move! I don't want you here."

I played a gooseherd. Slowly, slowly, they started moving toward the end of the bridge.

I herded my flock to the spot where the metal mesh ended. Outside the railing was a cement bridge abutment, and beneath that was a narrow slope leading down to the stony bank of the creek.

If Mother Goose—as you may have guessed, by now I was calling her that in my mind—moved across the bridge two yards further, she would be able to descend a grassy slope and enter the water. That would probably be safe for her and her children, so I made the grassy slope the target for my flock.

Maybe I yelled too loudly, or perhaps she did not remember the configuration of the slope. Like the benevolent king in the old story, I may be a good man, but I'm a lousy gooseherd. I would never know why Mother Goose left the bridge too early. "Let God decide whether I save my family or not," she probably thought. "I am too tired to wait."

And yes, she was impatient. Like General Lee at Gettysburg, she acted too early and moved at the wrong place. Goslings following, Mother Goose walked out onto the flat top of a cement pillar. She stopped, looked at the abyss, and without a thought about what would happen to the goslings, flew down to the stream and started swimming in circles. She looked up to the bridge and loudly called the children to follow her.

I didn't understand it. Those tiny birds were no more than two, maybe three days old. They were alone. They couldn't fly, and there were ten, maybe fifteen yards of air between them and their mother.

I stood close to the goslings, so I saw how incredibly scared they were. Maybe I should have retreated? Probably. Until this day, I do not understand why I did not move a few yards back.

The goslings listened to their mother, and one after another, they jumped. Some did somersaults in the air. Others seemed to float down like balls of down. With luck, they landed in the safety of the water below.

Do goslings have a pecking order, like chickens? The first to jump was definitely brave and confident. It took a true leader to be the first one over the precipice. Only the last one dropped too close to the pillar, and it landed on a stone.

It didn't scream, didn't cry. It was such a tiny creature that its voice likely couldn't reach me. Mother Goose climbed up onto the stone, and she began to lament. First there were honks and barks as she poked at her offspring with her beak, then hisses when it did not move, and finally a high-pitched oboe-like keening that seemed to capture all the grief in the universe.

My worst fear was confirmed. It finally hit me that now only five goslings remained, not six.

For days I heard the voice of the crying mother, like an advertising jingle you can't forget, Mother Goose's lament dug itself deep into my brain. No matter whether human, dog, or bird, a crying mother's voice is unforgettable. This voice stayed with me.

But, maybe I exaggerate what is a mere grade-school skit into a tragedy by Shakespeare. Maybe I am oversensitive. It was only a goose.

A bird. A stupid bird. And this bird was guilty, not me. And by the way, she still had five children. And I had good intentions. How long one can bother thinking about such a trifle?

Our gods were like possums. You go a lifetime without seeing any, but once you find one, you've found the whole damn family.

—Charles Journeycake (1817–1894),
Chief of the Lenape Wolf Clan

SOJOURNER POSSUM

During the long, hot summer of the year 2020, COVID-19, nasty spotted lantern flies and our president attacked America simultaneously. This was bad for humans but good for our vegetable garden.

Locked in our "social bubble," Marta and I could have bickered and complained like normal people do. But for some reason, with nothing to do all day, we both found solace in gardening. Our vegetables were our pride and joy!

Lettuce sprang forth from the dark earth, offering up tender, thin leaves wet with dew in the early morning. In full daylight, our green beans grew tall and proud, while spinach proliferated recklessly. I swear the squash grew all night; each day they appeared fuller and deeper in color than the evening before.

Together we planned how to turn these delicious fresh vegetables into exotic dishes that would best release the unique flavors of our garden. Marta proposed a Cretan bean stew with spinach. We made it together, following the recipe from the saveur.com website, then delighting in how the flavors of the large red tomato and fresh dark spinach from our garden gave depth and texture to the chickpeas, raisins, white wine, and garlic they mingled with. Crushing our fresh basil into our cherry tomatoes, with olive oil and garlic, we made pasta *all'arrabbiata*. We even made summer tomato bouillabaisse with basil rouille.

Yes, that hot summer when COVID-19 kept us locked in our homes, we gained weight. Some of us gained by eating, others by drinking, and most of us—including me—by both eating and drinking too much. Marta and I enjoyed the pleasure of long evenings full of card games and cocktails outdoors in our gazebo. We would sniff to discern the exotic perfume of our gardenias over the scent of our mosquito spray. We experimented with different cocktails. We reveled in gentle breezes. Sitting there gave us ample time to gaze out over our vegetables and talk about food while sipping wine.

Yes, life was good.

Except for the dark beast who invaded our peaceful, contented idyll.

* * *

Possums are the weirdest animal alive. They're about as big as a large cat, but even a dirty, wet, stinking cat looks pretty good in comparison to a possum.

A possum's fur is sparsely distributed on a piggish body—except where the fur does not exist at all: on the long, naked tail that the animal uses to hang from a branch. Yes, a mama possum can hang and sleep like this with all of her children on her back.

The possum is the only American marsupial. She also features a bag for carrying her children. When the kids are tiny, like bees, it's no problem. But when they grow to the size of small rats, they prefer to travel on their mother's back, their sharp talons gripping her fur.

Loaded with children, a mama possum looks like the overloaded Bactrian camel of a greedy Silk Road merchant crossing the Fergana Valley. She's slow and clumsy. When scared, she may spit on you from her rat-like snout. As the camel might, to get rid of you, she can also give off a nasty smell, urinate, defecate, or hiss.

People have different pets: snakes, lizards, even roaches and crabs, but possums? No way! The possum is too ugly!

I say this, but I know the possum probably has the same opinion of my beauty that I have of hers. And yes, I admit that she has the right to live in my yard, walk around at night, and kill snakes and mice. But I don't want to see her or smell her, and especially, I do not agree to host her in my vegetable garden.

The possum is such a pest! She can take a bite out of a tomato, then go to the next one and take a bite out of that one, effectively ruining up to ten tomatoes per night. Undoubtedly, this is also the work of chipmunks, raccoons, and even squirrels. But when a scapegoat is needed, the possum is the greediest, the ugliest, and the easiest to catch.

* * *

So one summer I invested in a Safe Realese Humane Live Animal Cage—made in China, as you probably guessed from the spelling of "Release." It's a simple trap that makes one "click" sound and locks an animal inside the metal cage. No injury, no harm, just one click—that's it.

To attract an animal to enter the cage, I would put a piece of cantaloupe, honeydew melon, or sometimes pear slices inside of the trap—food that, in my opinion, would be tastier than my tomatoes.

And because possums had habitually lived in the bushes bordering our gazebo, or even under the gazebo, the best way to catch them was to put the trap near it. There were years when I was successful: two, three, sometimes even four possums per vegetable season. Almost always they were mother possums with children still on their mother's body when she was lying inside the cage.

Once the possum was caught, the next procedure—and it was tricky—was to carry her in the cage, put her into the car trunk (lined on the bottom with a piece of tarp), and drive her away to a possum-friendly area (the best definitely would have been my neighbor's garden, but it would be too close, and he is a lawyer) and … release the mother possum and her children.

It sounds easy, but it's not. It's not recommended that somebody see you releasing your possum next to his fence. Maybe he likes possums, maybe he always wanted to own one, but better not to gamble on what he thinks. In the U.S., people own guns. Consequently, the entrance to a public park, under cover of darkness, when there are no joggers is the best choice.

And this is exactly what I did. It was not too hard, especially because Wissahickon Park is close to my home. I remember the first time I did this and the first possum I caught. I was proud of my humane approach to move the possum a mile away and set it free in the forest.

I had been proud and happy for three days. That's when, unfortunately, I had caught another possum. This time it was easier. I knew how the trap worked, and I knew all the steps needed to banish the furry felons to their Australia in Wissahickon Park.

But my good mood was shaken when, within a week, there was possum number three in my cage. And—you would never believe this—each was female, and each had five children. It could not be an accident! As a scientist I had to verify my suspicion: Was it possible that my possum was coming back home!? All the way across town back to my vegetable garden?

After deep consideration of every option I had, I invented a way to discover the truth: When the possum was in the cage, I used a stick to delicately move her tail outside the cage. Then I sprayed it with neon paint. This mama possum left my property with a beautiful DayGlo orange tail. She returned in three days.

Eureka! She left, then she came back, again and again. A sojourner in our garden. We decided to name her Sojourner Possum.

This time Sojourner was transported to a public park on the other side of the Pennsylvania Turnpike. Crossing this river of death was the only way Sojourner could possibly make her way back.

Well, I can tell you that a possum with a fluorescent orange tail never again appeared. Did she valiantly attempt to find her favorite vegetable garden only to be splattered into eternity by a speeding truck? Or did Sojourner find a better garden on the other side, maybe a hothouse missing a low window pane, filled with Kumato tomatoes, acorn squash, Bibb lettuce, and Baby Bunch Turnips that she happily consumed, reflecting on how much better her life was? We'll never know.

Sojourner's friends and relatives, however, came in droves. Her praise of the quality of our tomatoes must have made it into the possum Facebook page. As a precaution—even if they did not return—their tails were always painted, each year in a different DayGlo color. (I am a scientist, I have already told you.)

Maybe some amateur zoologist living on the other side of the turnpike, around Plymouth Meeting, would write to the local paper about a strange phenomenon: In his neighborhood, possums with colorful tails began to appear. Or maybe children playing in the park would consider possums pretty creatures with beautiful tails? Who knows?

At the end of August that summer of 2020, the huge, almost-red Buffalo tomatoes in my garden promised paradise of the palate. I was waiting until their color was perfect. Then I would eat them with mozzarella, basil, and tasty Tuscan vinaigrette.

One, maybe two more days of waiting.

But others were waiting, too. And they came first.

They arrived at night.

One bite from this tomato. Next bite from another tomato. Twelve bites and twelve tomatoes spoiled!

I don't know about you, but I … I cannot finish a tomato started by a possum. Can you imagine its ugly, slimy snout? No way! I would probably share my tomato with a dog—if Marta did not know about it—but dogs don't steal tomatoes from a vegetable garden. Possums do! Why don't possums sate their hunger with spotted lantern flies? Red insects are not as tasty as red tomatoes? But no! My possum had to show me who was king of my garden!

OK, possum. You started it. Now is the time for my response. My "Safe-'Realese' Humane Live Animal Cage" is coming your way!

I set the trap a few yards from the gazebo along the possum highway to their favorite grocery store.

Oh, what a life it was! On another pleasant evening in the gazebo, Aperol with Prosecco filled two martini glasses. The huge cube of ice in the middle of each of them glittered, like Koh-i-Noor, with a promise of epicurean bliss.

Epicurus believed the greatest good was to seek modest, sustainable pleasure in a state of tranquility and freedom from fear. That precisely described having a drink in our gazebo in the evening.

Drinking her Aperol with Prosecco, Marta forgave me: An hour before, I had cooked pasta *cacio e pepe* that was so good—so good that she ate a lot of it. Now, she could theoretically "punish" me by refusing to drink my cocktail creation. By saying no, she could have rejected 150 calories (maybe even 300 calories). But was it humanly possible to say no to icy cold Aperol with Prosecco? Only a robot would turn it down.

We enjoyed the evening.

"Isn't the trap too close to the driveway?" she said, noticing the cage.

"No." I sipped and savored the Aperol. I felt my resistance soften.

"Maybe," I said.

After a few minutes, my wife shared her thoughts:

"I know I should not be critical when describing God's creations, but possums are ugly animals. Especially their naked tails. Uglier than a rat's tail."

Suddenly an old story I had heard clicked. "It wasn't always like this." I had to tell her the story. "Cherokee Indians knew how the possum lost its tail."

"Another of your crazy stories?"

"Not mine; it's an Indian story."

"When are you going to be serious?"

"Never. But it's a nice one. Want to hear it?"

"Why not? Go ahead."

At the time when there were no people in our Tatra Mountains, Possum was riding high. He had a long, bushy tail and was as proud of it as a politician is of his pompadour. When dancing, Possum showed off his tail to the other animals who did not have tails as beautiful as his. The most jealous among them was Rabbit, who had lost all but the stub of his tail fighting with Bear.

One day, jealous Rabbit decided to play a trick on Possum.

There was to be a dance at a great council meeting of all the animals. Rabbit's task was to send out the news to everyone. As Rabbit was passing Possum's tree, she stopped to ask him whether he would attend the event.

"Well," said Possum "only if I'm invited to dance because I want to show my beautiful tail to everybody. And one more issue: I ought to sit where everybody can see me."

Rabbit not only promised Possum he would dance; she told him she would send a tonsorial specialist to make Possum's tail even prettier than a peacock's tail.

Possum was much pleased and of course agreed to attend.

Rabbit immediately hired Cricket, who was such an expert hair cutter that other animals called him "the barber."

"Cricket, I will pay you with the best food—carrot peels, oranges, bananas. Do me a favor, and get Possum's tail ready for the dance."

"I can do it, but what do you expect me to do?"

And Rabbit told Cricket exactly what to do.

"Good story," said Marta, "but it looks like you need another half-hour, and what do you say to another drink?"

"Anything special?" I asked. I was always ready to have another drink but only if my wife considered it appropriate.

"I am not sure." Her face, her eyes confirmed her hesitation as she decided. "Do you recollect how Pat Nogar celebrated her husband's birthday on that Facebook group video chat? What were they drinking—Manhattans?"

"I think so—Manhattans."

"So, maybe it would improve your story if you bring us two glasses of David Nogar's Manhattan? Do you remember what was so special about his recipe?"

"Of course! Let me do it!"

I ran toward my bar and desperately tried to recreate what was so special in that Manhattan recipe.

"Whisky. Of course. But what kind of whisky did he recommend?

Bourbon, or rye, or Canadian? Doesn't matter, I only have Canadian. Sweet vermouth? Got it. Bitters … here they are." I measured four ounces of whisky and poured it into a shaker. Then, because it would be impossible to carry two frozen glasses, the shaker, the bottle of vermouth, the tiny bottle of bitters, and a crystal bowl with extra ice cubes, I found a Pyrex tray and arranged all of the delicate objects on top. I knew it wasn't a Marta-approved elegant tray, but it was big enough, and I hoped she wouldn't notice.

It was dark outside, and I walked carefully, assisted by the rhythmic music of the glasses clinking with each step. Without any accident, I reached the gazebo, lit by a weak bulb on the ceiling and Marta's favorite oil lamp inside.

"What are you using to carry those things?" my wife asked me. "Didn't you know that's a baking tray?"

"I know, I know, but look how much I had to carry. And when I prepare the cocktail, I can work on this tray and not spill anything. It will be handy. Look."

I poured four ounces of Martini & Rossi Rosso Sweet Vermouth (I hoped it was four ounces) from the bottle and stirred it a few times in the shaker. I intended to then add two dashes of Angostura bitters to the shaker, but the top of the tiny bottle was plugged. I shook it and shook it, but not the tiniest drop of bitters came out.

Until …

"Oh, no!" I screamed. "Too much Angostura! What can I do now? It's not going to be good!"

"Calm down. Don't worry! It'll be drinkable."

We looked into each other's eyes and toasted, and even though it wasn't a perfect Manhattan, it was sufficiently good to continue the story about the narcissistic possum.

In the morning, Cricket knocked on Possum's door.

"I will beautifully comb your tail for the dance," he said.

Possum stretched himself out and shut his eyes, imagining his upcoming glory.

Cricket began his work on Possum's tail. First, he carefully combed it so that all the hair ran in the same direction. Then, he methodically clipped Possum's tail hair close to the roots, wrapping red ribbon around the tail to hold the loose hair in place. This process took over an hour, and all this time Possum's eyes were tightly shut. Imagining the master barber creating a masterpiece of his tail, Possum had dozed off dreaming of ribbons and braids.

In the evening, Possum went to the dance hall and found that the best seat was ready for him, as Rabbit had promised. When all the animals were ready to see the most important part of the event, Possum stepped into the middle of the floor.

The drummers began to drum.

Possum began to dance and sing,

"See my beautiful tail!" he repeated with every move.

All of the animals applauded.

This pleased Possum, so he danced around the circle faster and faster, singing all the time,

"See what a fine color my tail is!"

Everyone shouted. Exuberant, Possum danced vigorously and sang,

"Look! See how my tail sweeps the ground!"

That was the proper moment for Possum to untie the ribbon. He swirled like a dervish.

"Admire the fur on my tail!"

Suddenly everybody started to laugh. They laughed so loudly that Possum stopped dancing. He looked around the circle of animals. They were laughing at him! He looked down at his tail and saw that there was not a single hair left upon it.

It was a lizard's tail!

Poor Possum was so embarrassed that he dropped to the ground, rolled over, and played dead. And to this day, Possum still plays dead when taken by surprise.

"Oh, what a sad story!" commented Marta. "Poor possum! You know, I was listening to you, and I imagined our president dancing during an official party at the White House, or—even better—having a news conference and viciously mocking his Democratic opponents, moving his head, and … whoosh! His wig is flying in the air. It would be fantastic. What a wonderful vision!"

"But his wig is glued to his bald scull with the best glue by the best barber in Washington, D.C.!" I sighed.

"Maybe we can send him a Marine Corps barber to give him buzz cut?"

"That would be good!"

"I cannot imagine! What would be better than to ridicule this pushy, vicious man?"

"Nothing!"

"And you know what?" Marta changed the subject. "This Manhattan is definitely not so good. I am not going to drink it. Sorry."

"I am not going to drink it, either," I sadly agreed. Angostura bitters had destroyed my cocktail.

We were not in the mood to collect our things and carry them back inside. We left our drinks in the tray on the floor of the gazebo. Because of our political fantasies we were in a good mood, and we liked each other—a typical old couple.

Early the next morning when I entered the gazebo, I saw a terrible picture of disaster: a broken bottle of Vermouth, one broken martini glass on the tray, glass on the floor stained with brown angostura, and next to that … a dead possum. With a DayGlo orange tail!

Sojourner had returned, and now she was dead—the result of my evening party with my wife!

I wanted Marta to see Sojourner. I walked to the house to wake her and returned with her. She was completely surprised. Completely confused. Where had Sojourner been all this time? Why had she been gone so long? How did she return?

"Is Sojourner dead?"

"I think so." She looked dead.

"What happened to her?"

"I think she broke the one martini glass, the contents spilled inside the tray, Sojourner drank it, then she drank from the other glass—the one that did not break when it fell down—and at the end she finished whatever was left inside of the bottle of vermouth."

"But not the Angostura bitters?"

"No. She tried it but did not like it."

"Smart animal!"

"Yes, Sojourner was a smart animal, but unfortunately, we killed her!"

"Are you sure she's dead?" asked my wife, who habitually questioned my every statement.

"I am sure."

"How sad!"

Poor, dead Sojourner, the Manhattan thief who wouldn't touch Angostura bitters! Like so many humans, she was attracted to alcohol. Sojourner paid for her bibulous adventure. Marta walked inside to make coffee for us. She couldn't go back to bed after this disastrous morning experience. I went to the backyard to bring a shovel and bury the corpse.

Bless the Lord! When I returned, I found Sojourner resurrected and swaying. She tumbled down the gazebo steps then unsteadily resumed the short journey from the gazebo to the bushes. From a distance I watched her stagger slowly from the site of her downfall. The last I saw of her was the fluorescent orange tip of her tail disappearing into the lilacs.

As usual, my wife was right. She questioned if Sojourner was dead, and I was glad to be wrong. Thank God! Nothing bad had happened, and the entire story ended with a happy possum reeling into the bushes.

I have never killed a man, but I have read many obituaries with great pleasure.

—Clarence Darrow

KAISER THE GERMAN SHEPHERD

When I step out of my car in the parking lot outside the Wissahickon Valley Park entrance, the first person I meet is my neighbor Julia. Although she's five or six years older than me—and I'm no spring chicken—her enthusiasm for a healthy lifestyle and her love of nature always amaze me. She's educated, intellectual, and kind, with only one tiny vice.

When she starts talking, there is no comment, no response, not even a natural phenomenon that can stop her. She talks without a break. Not eternally, but for a very long time. Measuring her talking skills in miles, on a flat, forested trail, she can talk for six miles.

"Today is just such a day that Julia will talk—who knows what about? And I won't be able to stop her stream of consciousness," I think. I'm familiar with her biography, but she considers it important to remind me that she chose Greece as the ideal country for her, left the United States at the age of twenty-something, found a Greek husband, gave birth to Greek children, lived many years on the tiny island of Paros, and taught English at a local school. A few years ago, her sons left Greece—one came to the U.S., and the other went to Japan—and then her husband passed away. Eventually, she, too, left her island to look after her mother in Philadelphia. That's why she now lives in my neighborhood.

Her ninety-four-year-old mother shows no signs of decline. She's as bright and chipper as a teenager and also can talk incessantly, but I rarely see her. Julia's mother stubbornly plans to live to a hundred, so Julia has been deprived of her former daily routine: a one-mile swim in the Aegean Sea. Now her only exercise is a daily walk in the park—usually eight miles.

We met in the parking lot, so we walk together—me with my Nordic poles, Julia with her water bottle.

She talks. And talks. She talks like hurdy-gurdy cranked by a monkey on amphetamines. She informs me that the local theater will put on *Othello* tonight, and she is going to see it.

"What about you?" she asks mid-chatter without pausing to give me a chance to answer.

"No." I answer to myself.

We walk along Forbidden Drive. Auto races were held here in the

1920s, but later, cars were forbidden entry onto this scenic road that parallels the banks of Wissahickon Creek. Beautiful autumn! As Julia chatters, I look around. Elm and aspen leaves of golden yellow compete with bronze oak leaves, maroon dogwood leaves, and bright red holly berries. I hear the distinctive "kuk-kuk-kuk" of a pileated woodpecker to my left. They're big, among the largest woodpeckers in the world, so when I look up at the trees to find the source of the whacking sound, I catch sight of its flaming red crest.

Midstream, a great blue heron smoothly lands to wade the shallows, its long neck and dagger-like bill swaying back and forth in search of a trout. The huge beeches stand out with their silver bark and golden leaves. The water has frozen near the banks, creating a grayish green sheet of ultrathin ice that thickens each hour as it expands further into the stream.

In my experience, such winter beauty exists only in Pennsylvania, in Poland's Tatra Mountains, in the Dordogne Valley, and, I suppose, thousands of places around the world unknown to me but loved by others.

Julia natters on about an article in *The New York Times* and about Tom Hanks's new movie. Do I know he has a house on Antiparos? He's a swimmer, too. She can lend me a novel she finished that's based on the myth of Achilles—it's great. Her older son has a new girlfriend. She's Japanese. Do I know that Chinese paintings have no perspective? And Japanese paintings? She finally mastered cooking risotto. Do I cook risotto? Do Poles like risotto? What do I think about risotto with octopus? And Trump. Do I think he is a madman, or a villain, or both?

Fortunately, Julia's vice makes responding unnecessary. I hardly pay attention; as all I have to do is nod my head understandingly every minute or so. It's a mildly irritating backdrop for my exquisite walk in nature. Julia knows I'm always distracted by birds, trees, turtles, and salamanders. It's OK. How could I be immersed in all this natural beauty and simultaneously carry on a conversation? Nor does Julia mind that I stop every few hundred steps to look around, admire the autumn leaves, listen to birds, search for them in the trees and bushes, pick up a stone, look at a leaf, or touch moss.

Oh, even now, how can I not stop here and there to look at the curtain of yellow leaves against the distant black spruce trees across the river? I look ahead. In the distance I see a bench commemorating someone who also certainly must have liked to walk here when they were still alive.

Julia notes I am looking toward the bench and momentarily stops her word torrent. This time she asks a question and pauses, waiting for me to answer:

"When you die, Marta and I will choose a nice place to put a bench for you. Have you thought about it?"

"Yes."

We are both silent. When will death come? How far away am I from the end of my trail?

After a while, I ask, "And what would be the inscription on it?" Perhaps I have a chance here to influence my life after death.

"Maybe something about the fact that Aldek Roman walked here with his Nordic poles and admired how the leaves turn yellow?"

"Not bad. I like it. And it's true; these leaves always delight me."

"And how about this spot, where you can see the water and the trees on the far bank?"

Spend eternity right here? Yes! This restful spot is perfect for my memorial bench.

"I think this is a wonderful spot, Julia."

* * *

A few days go by.

Walking in the park again, I pass the location where Julia and Marta will install "my" bench when I kick the bucket.

A week ago, this clearing with a view of the stream was waiting for me and, what do I see? A brand-new bench for someone else. On my spot. Shame on them!

I wonder for whom? What wretch has claimed my spot?

I near the bench. It smells of fresh paint. I read the inscription on the brass plate: "My beloved German Shepherd Kaiser. He liked to stop here."

Yes, he probably stopped, raised his leg, and … pissed.

Pissed? Was I ever pissed! My plans for eternity are all settled, and then this beast beats me to the punch and dies first. Does God have no compassion for a poor old man facing his demise? Does God favor a German Shepherd over me? This is something I definitely will bring up when I meet my Maker.

FINIS

Who teaches us more than the beasts of the earth and makes us wiser than the birds of the heavens?

—Job 35:11

Author Romuald "Aldek" Roman is a popular Polish writer whose work has never before appeared in English. He is a graduate of the Agricultural University of Cracow and Temple University in Philadelphia. He has been a naturalist in Poland's Tatra National Park, a mountain-climber, a teacher, a skier, an expert on industrial toxicity at the EPA, and a UN consultant in Poland and Romania. He has published six books in Polish, two novels and four collections of short stories, and is a member of London-based Związek Pisarzy Polskich na Obczyźnie (Association of Polish Writers Abroad). Since 1984, Aldek has resided in Philadelphia. He has been married to his wife Jolanta for 45 years, and they are parents of three grown children: Katia Roman-Trzaska, Matt Roman, and Peter Roman.

Editor James Whipple Miller managed publications in Silicon Valley before embarking on a thirty-year career in early-stage business finance. Free at last, he now invests his time in editing and writing projects that have absolutely nothing to do with finance, business, or Silicon Valley.

Illustrator George Heck, PhD, is on the Chemistry and Physics faculty at Arcadia University in Pennsylvania. He grew up in a family of artists. See his current works on Instagram: ewood1821.

FOR MORE INFORMATION AND CONTENT ON ALL
THINGS ART, LITERATURE, AND MUSIC,
CONNECT WITH US AT OUR WEBSITE AND BLOG!

www.chestnuthillpress.com

Made in the USA
Columbia, SC
22 December 2022

74764519R00176